Ludovic
Bruckstein

LUDOVIC BRUCKSTEIN

Maybe Even Happiness

Translated
from the Romanian by
Alistair Ian Blyth

istrosbooks

Ludovic Bruckstein
Maybe Even Happiness

Translated from the Romanian by Alistair Ian Blyth

First published in 2026
by Istros Books
London, United Kingdom
www.istrosbooks.com

Originally published as *Poate Chiar Fericire*,
Panopticum press, 1985.

Typesetting: pikavejica.com

Illustrations: Alfred M. Bruckstein

ISBN: 978-1912545551

The publishers would like to express their thanks to The Prodan Romanian Cultural Foundation for the financial support that made the publication of this book possible.

PRODAN ROMANIAN
CULTURAL FOUNDATION

CONTENTS

Part Three
1980–1987

Afterword

… I admire those people who think there is something to say … After all, so many things have been said without any new star appearing in the heaven and without any earthquakes being prevented.

Dogs and Cats know this very well. Dogs gnaw their bones, cats lap their milk, and they don't say anything. They bark or meow, and they don't seem to have any ambition to produce a historic woof or an earth-shattering meow.

Ludovic Bruckstein

PART ONE

1967–1969

Panoptikum

A fair in a small provincial town.

Hustle and bustle.

Among the stalls and the kiosks selling vegetables, eggs, poultry, sweets, among the motley huts and tents, where you can try to win a gaudy plaster statuette at the 'target shooting', where you can see the 'iron-bender' or the 'sword-swallower' or the 'punchbag-man', where you can test your strength against the delicate 'spider woman', among other wonders, there is also a small panoptikum.

A travelling wax museum, carted from country fair to country fair, as you can plainly see from the walls of the booth, which consist of panels made from planks joined together with all kinds of worn, rusty hinges and staples …

I hand over my copper coin and step inside.

I freeze in amazement and disappointment. Among the garishly made-up wax effigies, there is not one famous figure. No Napoleon or Marie Antoinette, no Christopher Columbus or Julius Caesar … Nothing but yellow, ordinary, dull faces, which say nothing to anybody … Glistening wax faces that laugh or weep, without their knowing the reason why, faces frightened or indifferent …

'What kind of panoptikum is this? What is the point of it? What is the need for it?' I think to myself.

But because I have handed over my copper coin at the entrance, I go to take a closer look at the wax figures lined up along the walls, and gradually I begin to recognise familiar faces ... Yes, it's as if I've seen them somewhere before ...

But when? And where?

I linger in front of one or another of the wax figures and scour my memory. And this small fairground wax museum no longer seems quite so meaningless ...

The Wunderkind

I don't avoid him like others do. I can even say that I've remained his only friend. When I see him on the street, I don't give him a brisk hello and then continue on my way out of a fear that he might detain me for a conversation. Although even I have to admit that it's very hard to have a conversation with him. For example, if the subject of Christopher Columbus comes up and I let slip, the way one does, that Columbus was the one who discovered America, he'll look at me with a superior sort of smile, even with a certain amount of scorn, and explain at length that what I claim is by no means certain, that others were there before Columbus, others who set foot on the new continent, skilled navigators, the Vikings, and so on and so forth ... Another time, if, having learned my lesson, I say that Christopher Columbus didn't discover America, that others were there before Columbus, and so on and so forth, he will look at me for a long moment, in a lofty sort of way, smiling an indulgent smile, and pointedly declare, 'It's by no means proven that Columbus wasn't the first ...'

But even in less controversial matters, things play out in exactly the same fashion. If I claim, purely by the by, that, let's say, 'It's a nice day today,' he'll come back with, 'What are you talking about, Grig? Can't you see that the air is too warm, that it's too dry? Ultimately, it's very unhealthy weather!' But if I say that it's too hot, his instant, indignant retort will be: 'What do you expect in July!'

He knows everything better than everybody else: the climate, geography, history, literature, arts and crafts, physics, including the atomic variety, the Earth, the planets, the galaxies and what lies between them, the microcosm and the macrocosm—he knows all of them better than his interlocutor and talks about all of them at great length and with the greatest confidence. Which is why everybody avoids him. When one of his acquaintances notices him in the distance, either he dodges down a side-street or he quickens his steps and starts breathing heavily, so that he can quickly shake his hand and apologise for being in a rush, for having to dash because he's expecting a guest at home or because his wife is waiting for him outside the cinema ... The excuse naturally depends on what time of day the undesired encounter occurs, on the particular person's presence of mind, and on the direction in which he is headed.

But not I, I don't avoid him or quicken my pace when we bump into each other. As a matter of fact, since we both retired, even though I still do a few odd jobs, take on a few projects, we see each other more often, on the street in the evening or in the park, sitting on a bench, when we both go out to take a little air, and then we stop to chat. Which is to say, he does most of the talking and I remain silent. But I've grown used to it. After all, I've known him since we were little. I often used to go to their house and I know almost everything about him. We grew up around the same courtyard, a large cobbled courtyard that gave onto the street, in front of a tall, splendid house with seven steps, and, on either side, lower, rented houses. He was Marcus-Augustine—his mother, an ambitious woman, had insisted on giving him three names:

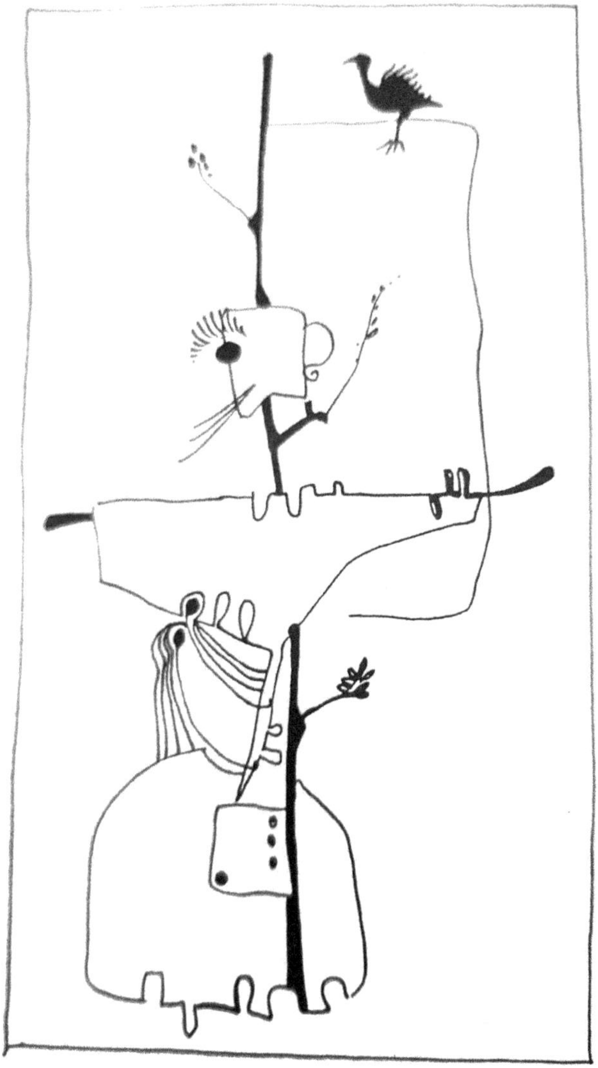

Marcus-Augustine-Anghel, as she'd seen was the case in the best families, but people called him by only two of them—and he lived with his parents in the tall house, whose windows looked out onto the street, while my mother and I lived in a little room in the corner of the yard. My mother sometimes took in their laundry, in lieu of rent, and on days when there was a large amount of washing to do, I would eat with my mother in their kitchen. His parents were nice people. His mother, a tall, thin woman with unruly, curly hair poking out from under her headscarf, would work side by side with my mother on the laundry. Other than that, she was always busy with something whenever I saw her: tidying up around the house, cooking, washing the dishes, darning socks. His father, a strong, jovial man with a round face and a ginger moustache, was an upholsterer, a good craftsman who used to make armchairs so comfy you'd never want to get back up once you sat down in them, and in time he opened his own upholstery workshop in the centre of town, which did good business.

I would often go to their house or he and I would play together in the cobbled yard. Even though I was about five years older than Marcus-Augustine, I took great delight in his toys: all kinds of cars, a red fire engine, which even had tin firemen inside, and a train that went round and round on a track: a locomotive, goods wagons and carriages for the people. He would quickly grow bored of them and leave me to play by myself, watching me with a rather scornful smile, the same smile that he smiles even today. His smile has remained unchanged.

He was an only child, and when he first uttered the word 'ma-ma', just like that, splitting the two syllables, his parents, and his mother in particular, were in seventh heaven. And when a few weeks later, he also said 'da-da', their happiness knew no bounds. They kissed him, cuddled him, gave him chocolate, and adored seeing it smeared all over his chubby cheeks. After which, with increasing frequency, almost like clockwork, the baby started uttering the words: 'ma-ma, da-da … ma-ma, da-da …'

Later, once he started going to school, his satchel filled with textbooks, exercise books and sandwiches, he would come home and say things like, 'It is cold all year long at the North Pole,' or else he would utter just a single word, for example, 'Guatemala,' and his parents would nudge each other on the sly: Did you hear that? Guatemala … Gua-te-ma-la … Ah, how much geography he knows! He knows all the countries in the world, even the really small ones, the ones so tiny you can barely see them on the map, but he knows them by heart. San Marino, or Andorra, whose capital is … what is it? Who's ever heard of them all? Who could remember them? But Marcus-Augustin, Mummy's little Marky, knows them all. And physics too, and the climate, where it's hot, where it's cold …

Sometimes, when his parents nudged each other and made signs and exchanged glances, it wouldn't be sufficiently on the sly and the boy would think to himself in satisfaction: 'How charming they are. And how naïve … Like children … Grown-up children …'

Later, however, when he was in the upper forms of lycée, his parents began to annoy him. 'How uncultured they are, the poor things!' he would think to himself. After which, he stopped limiting himself to just thinking it and even told them aloud: 'My God, how uncultured you are!' And for good measure he would fling in their faces a quotation from Horace: *Odi profanum vulgus* … the rest of which he forgot. His parents were left petrified with fear and admiration.

On hearing the words of his son, the father lowered his brawny arms in helplessness. 'What can you do with him? I didn't have the chance to receive so much schooling, my father was a carter, with a single horse, my mother raised seven children … And as an apprentice I spent three years learning how to sweep the master's kitchen and doing his shopping before I had a chance to pick up the trade of upholsterer, and even then mostly on the sly …' But his mother, sorely affrighted by Horace, started choosing her words carefully. She no longer dared to say: 'How hot it is today!' Rather, she would say: 'What a high temperature there is today!' She wouldn't say, 'Open the window to let in a little air!' but rather, 'Open the window to let in a little climate!' She would doggedly read novels and gazettes—the literary and arts gazettes that her son bought, she would read them from cover to cover, including the reviews, even though she didn't understand a jot of it all, but she would find some choice, awfully nice words there—she would read them during the day, as she stirred the onion sauce, and she would read them at night in bed. Her husband would toss and turn in the next bed, unable to sleep because of the lamp, which sometimes burned until after midnight. But Marcus-Augustine's mother tried hard to be up to the mark and not to give herself away in front of her son's friends when they came to visit him. Marcus-Augustine only laughed at her. He laughed in irritation. His mother annoyed more and more often and the poor woman couldn't understand why …

As you can see, time was passing and Marcus-Augustine didn't stand still. He kept on cultivating himself. He studied music, and even learnt to play the violin, as his parents bought him an expensive violin with a beautiful pig-skin case, a real rarity. He took private lessons with the best teacher in town, who charged a hefty sum per hour. Nevertheless, being an honest man, after a time the teacher started telling the parents that although the boy was diligent, no complaints on that score, he didn't really have an ear … And there was also the fact that he couldn't bend one of the fingers of his right hand. A good thing that it was his right hand, he could still hold the bow come what may, but if it had been his left hand, then that was a completely different matter ... All the same, the fact that he didn't have an ear ... And then there was his sense of rhythm ... The father listened to what the teacher had to say, nodding in understanding and resignation. 'What can I do with him? If that's what you're saying ...' But his mother was enraged. She immediately withdrew her son from lessons with the hapless teacher and inquired left and right: 'Does anybody know a good teacher? That one is the worst ... Doesn't know a thing! He charges a huge amount of money but isn't worth tuppence ...' And so on and so forth.

Marcus-Augustine also painted. But it soon transpired that he was colour blind. He couldn't tell red from green or yellow from orange. Anyway, the shapes he painted were correct, the house was a house, with rectangular walls and a sloping roof like any self-respecting roof, but the colours ... The sky was yellow, the roof was green ... Some found it unique, something new, which had never been done before ... But *de gustibus non discutandum*, as Marcus-Augustine furiously told his critics, to the delight and terror of his mother, who, since the Horace incident, had developed a real fear of Latin.

When they cobbled together an amateur theatre company in that small provincial town, the Dramatic Society of the County Seat, as it was officially known, Marcus-Augustine was one of the first to join. At Marcus-Augustine's insistence, the director, who was a literature teacher, gave him the leading rôle in a historical play. The script was decent enough, he'd learned his lines well, and he could reel them off flawlessly. The difficulty was the pauses between lines. The director couldn't make him keep quiet where and when he was meant to ... Marcus-Augustine worried lest the audience somehow think that he had forgotten his lines and that was why he had paused ... But when it came to him moving around on stage, he was completely wooden. Hardwood. It was as if he had put down roots through the boards of the stage. The director would explain it to him, shout, lose his temper, mop his sweating brow with a huge blue handkerchief, and finally he had to transfer him to another, lesser rôle, after which he placed him in yet another rôle, in which he had only to enter, stand in a doorway, and say, 'Dinner is served!' He could do that, and even did it very well. But a few days before the première, in high dudgeon, he ditched the theatre and the whole 'Dramatic Society etc.' And after the première, he panned the director—the hapless literature teacher delivered a *mea culpa* and acknowledged his mistakes—he panned the author of the play, dead for a century and a half, he panned the performance, the sets, the actors. The whole thing couldn't have come off worse. Particularly the lead part, he said, which had been acted abominably: no stage diction, no pauses for effect, no stage business … And besides, he'd missed out some of the words, no, worse than that, he'd missed out whole passages, in the first act, and in the second act, and in the third and the fifth … After all, he knew the whole script by heart, nobody could fool him …

He even went to university to study for a degree in law, or it may have been economics, but during his first year, far away from the parental home, he had come down with a head cold and as quick as a flash his mother had boarded the first express train and brought him home wrapped in shawls. After which, I think he carried on studying something part time, but to this day I don't know whether he ever completed the course. Today, he is an old man, but I've never dared to ask him whether he ever graduated or what his degree was in, lest he think I'm judging people without degrees. And besides, he himself has a highly categorical saying, which he often pronounces: 'The number of dunces that the universities churn out …' The fact is that his mother, whenever she saw him beating his brains out over a book, used to tell him: 'If it's too hard for you, son, pick a different degree ...'

Eventually, enough was enough, he couldn't take living at home with his parents any more:. The old folk grated on his nerves, particularly his mother, so he moved out and rented a flat in a villa in the swanky part of town. He used to return home only three times a day, for his meals, and he instructed his parents to visit him only once a week, on Sunday mornings, when he didn't have guests. His parents couldn't understand why he had moved out of their house. His father would have liked to slap him around the chops, but he realised he had left it a bit too late, while his mother was grief-stricken, but nevertheless regularly paid the rent on the flat in that swanky street lined with villas.

I don't know whether Marcus-Augustine managed to complete any degree, but I do know that he managed to make a gentleman of himself, which is to say, a petty official in the town hall, which was not such a petty achievement as it might seem. First of all he worked in the clerks' office, a place most suited to one like him, who knew everything, who could do everything, because that was where all kinds of documents arrived concerning matters of trade and industry, of agriculture and commerce, of taxation, education, culture, sanitation, septic tank drainage, etc., etc., applications and complaints—even though there was not much need for his expertise, since all he had to do was register the documents and pass them on. In time, they transferred him to the archives, which again was a place most suited to someone like him, who knew everything and was able to put everybody and everything in their place.

When I went to university—first having worked for five years in the forest felling timber and then as a bookkeeper, so that I could save up the money—he was by then a petty official in our town, and when I returned many years later, I found him where I had left him. To tell the truth, it was some seven or eight years before I returned to our town. I was a student in the capital, I didn't go home in the holidays, because there was nothing for me there, my mother having died in the meantime, so I used to work on building sites to earn extra money. A good few years therefore passed before I completed my architecture degree and I returned to find Marcus-Augustine at his desk in the clerks' office. Or was he in the archives by then? I can't remember. When he spotted me, he placed a friendly arm around my shoulder and gave me a broad smile, that famous smile of his.

'I read about it in the papers. Congratulations on the award, Grig!'

'Oh, it's no big deal,' I said, as modest as could be, and really it wasn't.

'The designs for a mini-estate, if I'm not mistaken?'

'A mini-industrial estate … More than I am for the award, I'm happy that it's going to be built in our own little town …'

'That's wonderful too,' he said, patting me on the shoulder again, even though he was five years younger than me, but he had every right to do so, after all, we had played together, with his toys … 'It's wonderful, even though at your age, a Michelangelo or a Bramante …'

I don't know what a Michelangelo or a Bramante did at my age, but I felt quite clearly that he was perfectly right … But what could I do? Even if I hadn't succeeded in doing what they had done, I at least strove to do all I was capable of … But I didn't say anything to him, lest he get upset and lest he think, God forbid! that I myself had got upset.

In his youth Marcus-Augustine was handsome, with slicked-back chestnut hair glistening with brilliantine, combed in a perfect parting, with a round, rather chubby face, although it suited him well. He was dapper, well-mannered, and the girls liked him on first sight, not to mention the mothers of marriageable girls. Nonetheless, he remained a bachelor. Maybe he just didn't find the right girl, although I know that Zizi, a shrew of a girl, tall, dark-eyed, fiery, liked him a lot. Oh, how she liked him and how I suffered because of it! The girl was head over heels in love with him.

'He talks so wonderfully about literature, geography, physics, chemistry, about art, about the moon and the stars, he knows so many wonderful things ...'

This was in the beginning. Then, after a while, I noticed that their ardour cooled. And later, when the subject came up once, Zizi—somehow or other I had become her confidant, she used to tell me all her secrets, which ultimately was not without consequences—told me with a smile:

'Oh, yes, he knew so many things! And he talked so wonderfully! But I'd have liked him to be quiet sometimes ... To be quiet and kiss me ...'

I don't like talking about myself, nor is it even fitting, but since we're on the subject, let me recall in brief that after my return from university, Zizi agreed to be my wife, not with any great enthusiasm, I suspect. But we have got on well together and raised four children, two boys and two girls. All of them are now married with children. A year ago, poor Zizi passed away, leaving us eternally grief-stricken.

In the meantime, the world didn't just flow along calmly and things didn't just stand still. There were upheavals and a world war that the history books have given the Roman numeral II. Marcus-Augustine wasn't enlisted: his enlistment was first postponed and then he was exempted from service because of his not being able to bend one finger of his right hand. And also because he had weak lungs, according to his mother. He didn't go to war, but he constantly expatiated on the war and why the tactics and strategies employed by such and such a general were completely wrong and thus the outcome was predictable … In any case, he would predict everything after the fact, he would demonstrate that he had known in advance that things would turn out the way they did. When peace came, he would explain the peace too … The new geography of Europe, Africa, Asia … Atomic physics … Space flights … And no end of other things … And …

And what else might one say about him?

Nothing … that's what, there's really nothing else. The only thing was that in constantly talking like that, left and right, in constantly explaining, expatiating on things long since familiar, in discussing everything, in knowing everything better than anyone else … time passed. Now he is retired and has even more time for talk. But he doesn't really have anyone to speak to about how, for example, the recital that that famous violinist gave in the capital was abysmal, or that the theatre company that came here on tour wasn't worth tuppence, and all the other dozens of things he has to say. He is now all alone, his parents died long ago, and people avoid him. When some acquaintance spots the aged pensioner with his silver-handled black cane, he quickly turns down another street or quickens his steps to show that he has no time, that his wife is waiting for him at the cinema or that he is expecting guests at home.

But I don't avoid him. I've grown accustomed to him. After all, I've known him since he was a small child, since he first uttered with such great wisdom the words 'ma-ma … da-da …' At which his parents nudged each other on the sly: 'Did you hear that? He said ma-ma and da-da …'

1967

The Executor

She was a quiet, very unassuming woman, all until the death of that pensioner, a man she had never had anything to do with whatsoever. He was just a neighbour, that pensioner, not even a close neighbour, who lived on the same street as she did, but quite a few houses away.

Anyway, until the death of that pensioner, about whom she had no idea—after all, they barely said hello when they passed on the street, when the pensioner occasionally went out for a walk with his wife—Matilda Hanac was a decent woman, a devoted wife, an industrious housewife and, on top of that, a highly conscientious public clerk. She would get up at the crack of dawn to feed the chickens, which she raised from chicks; feed the pigs, of which she had two: fat, well-cared for porkers; feed her husband, of which she had only one, of course, and about whom she cared greatly; and feed her children, of which there were three. She would then send them all off to their proper places and about their proper business. Her husband would receive his morning coffee, his bread and butter with a slice of cheese or ham, and his sandwich for ten o'clock, wrapped in a paper napkin. He was a bank clerk. The eldest child, a son of around twenty-three, a lanky, freckled man, would set off for work at the electronics factory, where he worked as an electrician's mate. How the poor woman would have liked him to become an engineer! But the lad didn't really have the brains, so his mother had to resign herself. She did so with a feeling of regret, albeit slight. The lad was hardworking and earned a good wage at the factory, and he gave almost all his earnings towards the housekeeping.

That son, her eldest child, in whom she had secretly placed so many hopes, gave her yet another reason to be resigned to fate. He had fallen in love with a girl, a typist. Ultimately a very good girl, and beautiful too, but just as she had dreamed of him becoming an engineer, so too she had wanted her future daughter-in-law to be either a teacher, or a doctor, or at least a chemist, in any case a woman with a degree. But in the end, she had resigned herself. She had asked only that the young couple not be in a hurry to get married. Let them get to know each other better. After all, they were still so unripe, both of them, he barely having reached the age of twenty-three and she not yet having reached even twenty-one. But most of all Matilda Hanac felt she herself needed this respite, although even she was at a loss to explain why.

The other two children were a girl in the final form of lycée, studying for her baccalaureate and the university admissions exam, who wanted to be a teacher of natural sciences, and the youngest, a girl of eleven, in the fourth form. Neither of them were any particular cause for concern to their mother. Slender, blond, snub-nosed girls, both of them were diligent pupils and when they came home from school they both helped with the housework, with the cleaning and in the kitchen, wherever they were needed. They were good at everything.

Once she had packed them all off, Matilda Hanac would drink her morning tea with a slice of bread very, very thinly spread with apricot jam—she loved apricot jam, but thrifty as she was, she never overindulged herself. After which she would quickly clear the table and go to work. She was a clerk in the town's registry office, highly respected for her punctuality. The truth was that nobody could remember her ever having been late or incorrectly registering any document.

In the afternoons and evenings, the whole family would be together again. Lunch and dinner took place in silence, as if following some ancient rite, then all of them would sit in front of the television or each in their own corners, engrossed in a book. Matilda was an avid reader of romantic novels, which were melancholy at the beginning and sad in the middle, but would end happily, in the registry office. The men of the family devoured detective, adventure, sporting, and science-fiction novels, while the girls conscientiously did their compulsory school literature reading, each stretched out belly-down on a couch, propping up their heads with their hands resting on their elbows.

This is how the days passed for the Hanac family, one by one, as smoothly as a gentle brook and with no surprises of any kind. And Matilda Hanac was a contented woman, a settled woman, living a quiet life, which it seemed nothing could ever disturb. All until the death of that pensioner, a man she had never had anything to do with while he lived, as he was simply a neighbour, and quite a distant one at that, to whom she barely said hello on the rare occasions when they passed on the street.

It happened one morning, after Mrs Matilda Hanac had fed the chickens and the two pigs, after she had sent her husband off to the bank, her son off to the electronics factory, and the two girls off to school, each with their sundry sandwiches. She was just getting ready to leave for the office, when the woman who lived on the other side of the fence from the pensioner arrived at a run and all out of breath, desperately shouting:

'Come quick, Mrs Hanac, come quick! The old teacher died and his wife is out of her mind with grief, she's weeping, shouting, banging her head against the walls, I'm really scared she might … She can't be left alone a single second in a state like that …'

Matilda Hanac ran over on the instant. She entered a small hallway, where the pensioner's raincoat and black hat were quietly hanging on their peg as if nothing had happened. On the right, through a door that was ajar, she glimpsed a clean and tidy kitchen, white furniture with green trimmings, old-style but well kept, and above the gleaming nickel-plated cooker an embroidered wall hanging whose immaculate red stitching spelled out: 'Husband dear, I pray that in the pot you do not peek, Nought is there in the kitchen for you to seek.' Matilda quickly went into the room on the left, whence she could hear the widow's lamentations, she passed through a dark living room, likewise clean and tidy—black furniture, a sideboard with crockery, all of it gleaming with cleanliness—and reached the bedroom. To her surprise, here too everything was spick and span. There were embroidered coverlets spread over the beds with colourful little cushions on top. But in one corner, on a narrow couch, as if wishing not to bother anybody by taking up too much space, the pensioner lay face up. He looked as if he were asleep. His round, jovial face was relaxed and a slight smile persisted on his lips. It was also as if the wrinkles he had had while alive had been smoothed out. On the other hand, when Matilda set eyes on his wife, she barely recognised her. On the street, arm in arm with her husband, the woman had always struck her as tall and sturdy. But now, in a black dress much too large for her, which flapped around her body at every movement, in her worn felt carpet slippers, with her chalk-white, wrinkled face, pointy nose, and watery blue eyes framed by thin, tear-inflamed eyelids, she looked thin and diminished. 'How true it is that clothes maketh the man' was the thought that crossed Matilda's mind, but only for an instant, since as soon as the widow saw her, she once more burst into a fresh wave of shrill cries and lamentations, raising her thin arms and shaking them like a mast in a storm.

'Why did you leave me like this! Carol, what have you done to me! Why couldn't it have been me!' And after every exclamation she beat her head with her fists.

Matilda tried to calm her, speaking unfinished sentences about life, which has ever been thus … about death, which, whatever you might do, always comes in the end … about acceptance … She rummaged around in her memory for other maxims, but the widow went on even more vehemently than before:

'Why didn't you take me with you, Carol, my little Carol? So that at least we could have gone together … Why did you leave me all alone? Early this morning, when you first stirred, I asked you whether I should make you a nice cup of tea, with lemon, the way you like it, and you softly said: "Later … later …" And now you've gone for good …'

All of a sudden she stood stock still, wild-eyed.

'You left out of the blue, without saying anything … without telling me anything about … about what or about where you put …'

'What was it he ought to have told you?' asked Matilda Hanac.

The widow looked at her in fright, fell silent for a few moments, then erupted once more:

'Why didn't you let me go before you? Why did you leave me, my dear Carol? What is the point of life without you? "Later," you said, "later …"'

Matilda realised that she had to act and, with her sense of practicality, got down to business. She dashed out to a neighbour's to phone for a doctor so that he could issue the death certificate, she sent for a priest, she notified the undertakers.

About an hour later, a young woman who gave the impression of being a factory worker arrived with two little girls, the one five years old, the other four. The woman left the frightened little girls in the hall and quickly went into the bedroom. She said Justina, the pensioner's widow, was her aunt, her mother's sister, and that she had received news of the tragedy and had quickly come to see if she could lend a helping hand.

Matilda Hanac told her everything she had done and took her leave.

That day she was late to work for the first time ever. Her boss and her office colleagues knew that something very serious must have happened, an earthquake or some tragedy in the family. Obviously, it hadn't been an earthquake. And when she arrived, apologising and recounting what had happened, they all gave indulgent smiles.

On her way home from work she decided to stop off at the unfortunate widow's house to see if everything was in order. She found her alone. As soon as the widow saw her, she burst into bitter sobbing tears.

'Are you here alone?' asked Mrs Hanac in amazement. 'Where is your niece?'

'My niece? Is that a niece? She's worse than a stranger. She didn't come to help or to sit with me, but to rummage around the house to see what she could lay hands on … For the inheritance, that's why she came. She can barely wait for me to die too …' said the teacher's widow, dry-eyed.

That day, Matilda Hanac was late getting home too. Her husband and children were worried, frightened: she had never been late serving dinner before. Something must have happened: an earthquake or some other catastrophe, to prevent her coming home. Obviously, there hadn't been an earthquake. Some other catastrophe? The husband and son dashed to a neighbour's to telephone her office and find out whether she had been detained for some reason, and if not, to telephone the emergency ward to find out whether an ambulance had brought in any woman who had been run over by a car. Even though they knew she was very cautious. When she arrived at last and said where she had been and why, her husband was furious. Why hadn't she come home first to tell him? It was nearby. But the children gave indulgent smiles and, in their hearts, they felt proud. That was their mother: a good woman, ready to help every stranger.

But from that day forth, something strange happened: Matilda Hanac started being late regularly, late to work in the morning, and late home in the evening. She would stop off at the widow's twice a day to keep her company, to chat for a little, to ask after her health and other things. Something drew her to the teacher's wife, although she wouldn't have been able to say what. Maybe it was her quiet way of talking, maybe it was her loneliness, maybe it was her sober manner, maybe it was the fact that their ideas about life coincided: that a person should be equally as thrifty, serious, honest as her. The poor woman was so alone and had so many cares! She was ill, her chest ached, and the doctors couldn't tell what was wrong with her.

'Oh, those doctors …' At which Mrs Hanac confessed to her that her back had been aching for a long time, especially at night, after a very busy day at work—sometimes there were so many documents to register and so many things to do at home—but she never went to the doctor's, never paid any attention to it.

But just two or three weeks after her husband's death, once the two women had become good friends, the widow made her great revelation. It was a hot summer morning. They were sitting outside on the sun-drenched veranda, when, all of a sudden, the widow grasped Matilda Hanac by the arm and led her inside. They passed through the hall, through the dark living room, and went into the bedroom. A cold penumbra lingered in that room because of the lowered drapes. They sat down on the sofa in the corner. Matilda shuddered. It was the same low, narrow sofa on which the dead man had lain, with that strangely living smile lingering on his lips, the day when she had entered that house for the first time. She perched on the edge of the sofa in an uncomfortable position. Justina, the widow, moved closer, sat pressed up against her, placing her arm around her shoulders. Matilda could feel the boniness of the encircling arm. She had begun to feel cold. She would have liked to go back outside into the sun, on the veranda, but Justina started talking in a low voice, almost a whisper. The house where she lived was in her name, a dowry from her parents, who had owned a little land and had been in quite good standing in their village. She still had some jewellery, the two wedding rings, some earrings with diamonds that were small but pure, a bracelet, a gold watch, which hadn't worked for a long time, but gold never loses its value, she also had some money put aside, which she had saved from the housekeeping, but all of that was nothing compared with what her husband had saved. He had had nothing when he came to live in her house, he had been penniless, with nothing except the clothes on his back, although even those were threadbare, and that stiff piece of paper, namely his mathematics diploma, but his whole life he had saved and saved, hoarding money somewhere in secret. He had died suddenly, unexpectedly, and now she didn't know where ... That very morning, she had talked to him. She asked him whether she should make him a nice cup of tea with lemon, but he had replied: 'Later, later ...' instead of telling her where he had hidden the money. Now she kept searching the house but couldn't find it and she was tired and it was hard for her to search by herself. Her husband had been a very good teacher. Carol Grabete was a name to be reckoned with in mathematics, but he also knew physics and chemistry, in a bigger town they would probably have made him a university professor, and he wouldn't have worked until retirement as a provincial lycée teacher ... But she was the one who didn't want to leave that town, where she had the house her parents had given her for her dowry. The house was old, but sound ... And in the end, they had lived a good life in it ... Apart from his wage as a teacher, her Carol had also given private lessons, she never knew how much he earned, and his whole life he saved up money ... Who knows how much he had saved ... She didn't know, but she could more than sense that he had money. A wife can sense such things very well. But once she caught him wiring money to his stepsister. She found the receipt in a pocket, when she was brushing his best jacket ... Otherwise, he was not at all profligate, he was even very thrifty. He didn't drink, he didn't smoke, he did nothing but put money aside ... Banknotes stacked in a box ... He never admitted it, he always insisted that he gave all his money for the housekeeping, that he didn't hold anything back. But she knew very well that he had kept money hidden away ...

The secret having been shared, the two women became even closer friends. They shared all kinds of confidences with each other, they recounted to each other their small joys and misfortunes, but Matilda sensed something unpleasant hovering over the friendship, something embarrassing. Not even she herself could understand what exactly. It was a kind of embarrassment mixed with a strange feeling of vague guilt. And that feeling grew even stronger the day when she was surprised to receive at work an urgent summons to the state notary. She went to the head of her office to ask permission to leave during working hours. The head of her office muttered his consent, with visible dissatisfaction. Lately, he had become dissatisfied with her: she was now regularly late and, on top of that, she was also distracted and mixed up documents. As for Matilda, on seeing the surly manner in which her boss granted her permission to leave, she burst into tears. She arrived at the notary's office with eyes red from being repeatedly wiped dry with a handkerchief. She found her friend Justina there waiting for her. The notary told her that he had invited her to come because Mrs Justina Grabete, here present, bearer of identity card number—here he reeled off a series of six digits—had expressed her desire to appoint Mrs Matilda Hanac, here present, the executor of her will, and because this required her written consent. Surprised and embarrassed, and also, somewhere deep down, satisfied, Matilda burst into tears. She gently scolded her friend for thinking of such a thing, she protested, she cried, and finally, brought to her senses by the cold, official voice of the notary, she consented to put her signature to the document he placed before her.

The two women left the notary's office arm in arm, with warm tears streaming down their cheeks. On the street, Justina shared her plans with Matilda. She was to leave half of her estate to the church and the other half to Matilda, to do with it what she pleased. Matilda blushed, protested. Why was she talking like that? Who could know what tomorrow might bring? She ought not to think of such things. Matilda walked her home and then quickly went back to work.

A few days later, after Sunday confession, Justina told her that she had changed her mind, she wasn't going to leave anything to the church, she didn't want to say why, but she felt she had been slighted—Matilda would now be left the whole inheritance, to do with it as she saw fit. But she asked her kindly that she place a nice black marble tombstone on her husband's grave, with gold lettering if possible. A mathematics teacher the like of Carol Grabete deserved no less … And a smaller stone, of white marble, for her grave … If only she could find that money ... And the two women set about searching the bedroom, the kitchen once again. They checked the drawers and cupboards once again, they searched the chimneys, the cracks in the floorboards ...

A sense of embarrassment hovered over the whole affair, an unpleasantness, a sadness, which seeped into Matilda's soul and which she could not explain. One day, at the market, just as she was buying some vegetables, she noticed a young woman standing next to her. She realised she knew her, but at first, she couldn't remember where from. When the woman greeted her with a slight nod of the head, she remembered. It was Justina's niece, the woman she had seen on the day the teacher died. The woman with the two well-behaved, frightened little girls. On seeing her, Matilda felt both joy and a secret fear. She asked her why she didn't come to visit her aunt. The woman answered with a bitter smile:

'How could I come? Her whole life, Aunt Justina has done nothing but drive away all her relatives and everybody around her. Her whole life she has lived like that, all alone. And she kept him there like that too ... When she found out that her husband had sent a sister, an old woman of eighty, some money, she caused an unbelievable uproar and even tried to commit suicide. She went up into the attic with a clothes line to hang herself ... They say he had a child somewhere, whom he abandoned along with its mother so that he could marry my aunt. She didn't have children and couldn't abide other people's children ... If I go to see her, she thinks I've come for the inheritance ... I work hard, I'm a gilder at the furniture factory, I have two daughters, but I don't need her money, please believe me. I wish her the best of health, but I don't want anything from her ...'

Matilda was left rooted to the spot, unpleasantly surprised, but gradually, a feeling of relief took hold of her. So, the niece renounced it, she renounced it of her own free will ... Which meant she, Matilda Hanac, was in no way to blame, she hadn't gone out of her way to get it …

She often wept and grew irascible. Sometimes she had reason to weep, but sometimes she would weep out of the blue, for no reason at all. When she was late for work, and she was late more and more often, and her boss upbraided her, she would weep. At home, she neglected the housework and would weep. When her son brought up the subject of the wedding and fixing the date, she would burst into bitter tears and shout:

'There's no rush! And besides, my son deserves a different girl, not just a typist. I want you to be happy and to have the wherewithal to make your children happy. Only you should listen to me, you should do what I say …'

Her husband and the girls exchanged astonished, uneasy glances. They couldn't understand what had happened to the hardworking wife, to the understanding mother of before.

Her back pains grew worse over time. And when one day Justina told her that she had to go to hospital because her chest pains were becoming unbearable, not to mention her liver and kidneys, and who knows what other organs, and that the doctor had told her she could not put it off any longer, Matilda took sick leave and had herself admitted to the same hospital for tests. At first, both of them were admitted to the internal diseases section, and they even arranged to be in the same ward, in the next bed from each other. But soon they were forced to be parted. The widow Justine had been transferred to a different section, without being told her diagnosis. A tumour had been detected, which seemed to be malignant, while Matilda was transferred to the neurology section, where she was first of all diagnosed with asthenic neurosis, after which she was moved to the floor above, when incipient depressive mania was detected. But the two women met daily in the hospital grounds. They would sit quietly on a bench and talk in low voices. But when it was visiting day and her family came to see her, Matilda would sometimes lose control of herself and weep and shout:

'I don't want this marriage! I won't accept it! You're my son and you deserve a different girl. I'm going to make you both happy. I want you to have everything. You'll see just who your mother is!'

Her husband, son, and daughters would look at her in consternation and after the visit was over, the doctor would advise them not to contradict her any more.

So it was that her son married that girl, the typist, without telling her, the wedding was held without her, but what could they do? Life and youth demanded their dues.

The two women were placid, quiet. After the doctors had done their rounds, they would often be seen together, sitting on a bench in the hospital grounds, talking softly, sometimes whispering, as if telling secrets that nobody must overhear.

'Put a nice stone at the head of my husband's grave. Black, with gold letters: "Carol Grabete, mathematics teacher." And a smaller one on mine,' the widow would repeat for the umpteenth time, in a maudlin voice.

'Yes, yes, that's what I'll do,' Matilda would mumble sadly.

'You'll see that there'll be enough money once we find his ... Spend only as much as you can afford ...'

And after a time, she would add, with moist eyes:

'And repair the house where I lived for so many years. It's old and in bad repair, but it's a good house ... Dry, sound ... I spent so many happy days there ... maybe one of your daughters will live there ...'

'Don't talk like that ... don't talk like that ... as if you were bidding farewell,' Matilda would listlessly protest.

The doctors, the nurses, the porters would pass the two women and smile at them. They were so quiet, so well behaved that contrary to the medical indications, the chief physician allowed them to go into town on Sundays, after morning visiting hours. The two women demanded it so insistently that the doctor reckoned it could only do them good.

The weeks passed, and then months, but the money was nowhere to be found. Nonetheless, there were some surprises. One Sunday, searching the bathroom, widow Justina climbed up on the toilet bowl and right up near the ceiling, in a gap between two crumbling bricks, she found a cigarette box. In it were two cigarettes, one of them half-smoked.

'Ah, the sly dog!' exclaimed the widow Justina, angry and offended, but not without a certain tenderness. 'He sneaked in here to smoke! Like a schoolboy ... "Nothing but a ne'er-do-well," as he used to tell his pupils when he caught one of them smoking in the toilets ... You know, my dear, I forbade him to smoke, he had had chronic bronchitis ever since he was little and sometimes he used to cough in the night ... And all the while he sneaked in here to smoke. Half a cigarette at a time, the poor thing! And then he'd wait for the air to clear. He knew I'd immediately detect the smell of tobacco. That's why he used to spend so much time in the toilet. And there was I thinking there was something wrong with him! Bellyache or constipation ... The sly dog!'

In the end, almost satisfied, she put the packet in her handbag, intending to give the cigarettes to the porter. 'I haven't given him a tip in all this time,' she remembered. 'I'll give one to the man at the gate too, he always smiles so nicely when I come in and out of the hospital.'

Another day, as they feverishly searched the cellar, Matilda holding the candle, while the widow Justina scraped the dirt floor with a stick, they found a bottle buried in the sand in one corner.

'Well I'll be damned!' the widow exclaimed this time, less indulgently. In the bottle there were still a few dregs of wine. 'In other words, he sneaked down here to drink. And I categorically forbade him to drink, because he had incipient high blood pressure. I sometimes used to notice that when I sent him down to the cellar for potatoes he would come back with bright red cheeks. He would tell me it was from the exertion, because, heh, heh, he wasn't as young as he used to be, that the wooden steps were started to rot, and suchlike … The sly dog! Like a disobedient child …'

The Sundays passed one by one, all in the same way, the two old women would be seen arm in arm, one in black, the other in dark green, but with the same gleam of stubborn hope in their eyes, walking down the same street, from the hospital to the widow's house and back … Until that one particular Sunday arrived, putting an end to those walks.

It was a sunny spring day. Matilda had barely opened her eyes, she had had such a nice dream and was now trying to remember it, when Justina appeared at her bedside.

'Matilda, my dear, my darling, get dressed quickly! We're going to go and search up in the attic. We'll go through the attic again, from one end to another … I had a dream … I had a presentiment that today … today … today …'

She didn't finish the sentence lest she banish the something she sensed hovering above them.

'I had a wonderful dream too, I don't know what, but it was something really wonderful, I felt so good,' said Matilda, feverishly getting dressed. 'Yes, I feel it too, that today we'll—'

'Quiet!' said Justina, gently putting her hand over her mouth. 'Don't say anything.'

Outside, the sun smiled down warmly. The gatekeeper smiled too, politely saying hello. What nice, quiet old ladies …

He'd seen them so many times, going out like that, arm in arm. They were a fixture of the hospital by then, like the old, creaking oak gate, like the plane trees in the grounds, like the gatekeeper himself, they were a part of the same world, of that world so strange to those on the outside, but so normal to the denizens within.

Reaching the house, the two women quickly went upstairs, they climbed up to the attic with unusual nimbleness. Without a word, they began to search every corner, every chink, among the rafters. Inch by inch they tapped the fire wall, they raked the loose clay and dust on the floor. Time passed and still nothing appeared. The tension, the weariness began to show on their faces. But still they stubbornly searched.

The afternoon was waning. They were ready to abandon it all, but neither wanted to be the one to suggest such an enormity. Exhausted, silent, they searched on, when all of a sudden, beneath a sloping beam, as she raked the dust, the widow's fingernails touched something hard, which sounded like metal.

The widow quickly withdrew her hand in horror.

'It's there!'

She could say no more.

It was true: beneath the dust there peeked a box. An old tin whose enamel was chipped in places.

The two women sat down beside the tin, helpless, as if all the strength had been drained from their bodies. They looked at the tin for a long time, without touching it.

Justina was as white as a wall, and beads of sweat slowly formed on her forehead and temples, merging into ever larger drops.

Matilda was also pale, she sat trembling, as if in the grip of a fever. The candle flickered in her hand. She put it on the floor, poking it into the sand, and reached out her hand to the tin.

'No! No!' shouted the widow, lunging for the tin and grabbing it in her long, white, withered hands.

Matilda withdrew her hand, offended.

With trembling hands, Justina moved the tin closer to the candle, opened it. Inside was a bundle of letters in pink and blue envelopes, carefully tied with a red ribbon.

The widow's face turned as pink as the envelopes, and then red, a brighter red than it had been for a long time, not since she was young.

'And I forbade him to write to her or receive letters from her … The sly dog! The villain!'

She opened the bundle and they both glanced through the letters in silence:

'He's very good at arithmetic, the teacher congratulated me. Who knows? Maybe he'll become a teacher one day soon … It's obvious he inherited something from his dad …'

Justina dropped the letter and took another at random.

'I received the fifty lei, but please, my darling, don't send me any more money. I realise how hard it is for you to come by. You wrote to me that she found a receipt that you left in your pocket and had a fit of hysteria, she climbed up into the attic with a clothes line to hang herself. God forbid that anything happen to her because of me! Don't send me any more! Don't worry, our son will want for nothing. I managed to rent a sewing machine, so I can work at home too, in the afternoons, when I come home from the tailors' workshop, and late at night …'

Without her saying a word, the widow's fingers unfolded another letter.

'A lot of the time, when Nelu was little and it was hard for me and I was afraid for him, I used to think how good it would be if your lady would adopt him … It would have hurt so much not to have him by my side, but I would have suffered in silence. Only for our son to grow up in a nice house, not like mine ... Hasn't she ever talked to you about adopting a child? Now I'm not sorry that he stayed with me. I even think I wouldn't have given him away! I wouldn't have given him away for all the treasure in the world! Oh, how stupid I am! Don't you worry. He'll have everything he needs. He won't lack for anything with me ... How wonderful it would have been if we could have lived all our lives together, the three of us. But I know it wasn't possible. Don't be angry if I think of such childish things. I know that it wasn't possible. You a maths teacher, and me a stupid, uneducated seamstress. What would your family have said? What would people have said?'

The widow put the unfolded letter back in the tin and lit the bundle with the candle.

'What are you doing? cried Matilda in fright. But when she saw the widow's face, she didn't say another word.

At first the letters didn't catch fire. They blackened, they shrivelled, then suddenly they burst into flame, and, in the light they cast from below, the shadowed faces of the two women looked like skulls covered with a thin layer of yellow wax. But deep in their sockets, two pairs of eyes gleamed, staring into emptiness, without a single thought behind them.

After that Sunday, the two women never left the hospital arm in arm again.

The widow, after complaining of pains all over her body, fell into a state of lethargy. From that day forth, Matilda remained bed-ridden, in the throes of a fever. She was hallucinating.

'No! No! I won't let you take her! She's not for you! You deserve a different girl! Not a seamstress ... And you, my daughters ... I'm the one who'll bring you happiness! That tin ... Yes, I'll take it! I'm the executor of the will!'

Mrs Matilda Hanac, the executor of the will, did not live to carry out her appointed task. She died some two hours before the pensioner's widow.

The house of Justina Grabete, received as a dowry from her parents, an old house, long unlived-in, ramshackle, which had become a danger to passers-by on the street and had to be demolished. It was broken up into pieces, bricks, timbers, stones, down to its foundations.

Nothing was found.

1968

The New Hat

It was the third hat he had tried on in that clothes shop and haberdashery. A soft, dark brown, very sober hat. He made the gesture of taking it off in greeting, for, as you may well see, a hat is not a mere item of clothing like any other, an item as practical as a pair of socks, a coat, or a scarf, or an item like a necktie, which is sooner ornamental than practical, and all of which need only fit. A hat is also a means of displaying politeness and good breeding, of expressing friendship, or esteem, or respect towards your fellow man, depending on the situation. The item of clothing in question therefore also fulfils a highly important social function. And Adrian Cornel Fanea made a true religion of social greetings, which was also wholly naturally reflected in his hat. He greeted people ceremoniously and with pleasure and he took particular care in returning others' greetings, giving more than he received, smiling more warmly, with greater friendliness, greater respect, in keeping with the circumstances.

He was a knowledgeable official, an undisputed expert in financial matters, he knew and was known to a large number of people, who greeted him with particular esteem. And deservedly so, as he felt deep down inside, although without ever saying it or making any allusion to it. Indeed, Andrei Cornel Fanea knew himself to be an honest man, a principled public official, an exemplary husband, an irreproachable gentleman, who was highly courteous and considerate towards women.

'This one suits you very well,' said the saleswoman with a smile.

The hat did indeed suit him very well. It lent his face a fresh distinction and stateliness.

'Shall I wrap it up for you?'

'No, no, I shall wear it. Please wrap up the old one for me.'

He paid and left the shop in a very good mood. He set off down the street with a faint spring in his step, his black galoshes gleaming. It was a beautiful, dry autumn day, but with foresight Adrian Cornel Fanea had worn his galoshes. The weather can be so capricious, after all, and you never know when a chilly rain shower might start, so it is better to be prepared.

A few steps away, he saw Nicolae Banu, an old acquaintance, who always greeted him from afar. He made ready to make the appropriate response with his new hat, but casting him a hurried, somewhat frowning glance, Nicolae Banu quickly walked past him. 'What can be the matter with Banu? Can he be upset about something?' thought Fanea and feverishly began to rummage through his mind. 'What can I have done to him? But I haven't done anything. Nothing at all! In which case? Why did he walk past me like that, without any greeting?' All of a sudden he came to a stop, in fear and amazement. He remembered that a few weeks earlier, he had been sitting with some friends at the Zahana, over a beer, and when the subject of Nicolae Banu came up, he had said that he was a decent man, but rather too keen on playing cards. He himself had never played cards with him, but he had heard talk of it. He had accused him of being too keen on playing cards just like that, from hearsay! And now, one of the friends he had been drinking beer with must have told him …

He went on his way, angry, with less of a spring in his step, treading more heavily, as if all of a sudden feeling the pointless weight of his lacquered black galoshes on that dry autumn day. Why the hell did he have to go and say that? Was it any of his business? So what if a man plays cards among friends of a Sunday?

Absorbed in these thoughts, he realised that Stefan Albu had just walked past him. He had looked straight through him, as if he were a window, and gone on his way, without a greeting, without even sketching a greeting. Stefan Albu of all people, who usually greeted him with such warmth, with such animation, even. More often than not, he would even stop to shake his hand, to ask after his health, to talk about the weather or fishing, as he was a keen angler and took enormous pleasure in talking about trout and salmon. 'What can I have done to him?' wondered Fanea, thoroughly uneasy. And no matter how hard he wracked his feverish brains, he could come up with nothing. Absolutely nothing at all! He had never done him any harm … Nor could he have done. Stefan Albu was an official at another factory in the town, but he didn't even know which one … They had met at a do held by a society years ago, a merry New Year's Eve party. They had both attended with their wives … All of a sudden, Adrian Cornel Fanea came to a stop, horrified. Look at how something can rebound on you … And he recalled that evening, a year or two before, when he had gone to the cinema on his own. This seldom happened, but his wife was away at her parents and it was a good film. There was a crowd of people at the ticket office. He found himself standing next to Stefan Albu's wife, as chance would have it. Mrs Albu was a beautiful woman, a young woman, much younger than his own wife. He had not been able to help but make the comparison in his mind … Purely out of politeness, without any hidden intention, he asked her why she had come to the cinema on her own. It transpired that her husband was away on official business, and she loved films starring Jean Marais. They stood talking and he discovered that she lived on a distant, poorly lit street and was rather afraid to walk home alone late at night. Naturally, he offered to escort her. At the gate, he held her hand much longer than he should have, and even kissed it a number of times, making stupid hints about being invited inside. He clearly remembered that she had made elegant but determined efforts to disencumber herself … He had long since forgotten the whole episode. But what about her? Perhaps overcome by sincerity she had told her husband about it … 'Women are sometimes so capricious and unthinking!' he thought to himself in a fury, momentarily forgetting all politeness.

Deep in these thoughts, he had continued on his way when suddenly all the blood rushed to his cheeks and he turned red with resentment and fury. Gabrian had walked past him without greeting him. Gabrian the trainee, his subaltern. This was too much! And he could swear he had seen him, but Gabrian had looked him in the eye and gone on his way … What could have got into him? He treated him with kid gloves, after all. 'Gabrian, could you please do such-and-such …' 'Be so kind, my dear man …' 'My dear Gabrian, please fetch me the …' Why then such insolence? You wouldn't warrant that he was upset too! But why, pray tell! All of a sudden, he felt a pang in his heart. Yes, this time he didn't even have to belabour his much-wracked brains, which were seething like an anthill trodden by a boot. That was it! That wretched report. An urgent statement required by the ministry and covering a period of umpteen years back into the past and forward into the future, on which trainee Gabrian had worked for many days and even nights. And when Adrian Cornel Fanea had taken the report in triumph to the director, and the director had praised it, Adrian Cornel Fanea had breathed not a word about Gabrian … God alone knows, but somehow or other, he hadn't had the chance to bring it up … He had even been awarded quite a large bonus. He had intended to invite Gabrian out for a beer, but caught up in other affairs, he had forgotten all about it. Might Gabrian have found out something about it from the director's secretary? Those secretaries: they're good for everything except keeping secrets. In any case, it wasn't even a case of something secret … In the end, he was in charge of the reports, he put his signature to them, he was responsible …

He arrived home very disgruntled and in a bad mood. In the hall, he first took off his galoshes, now as heavy as lead. His wife, who as always greeted him from the doorway of the living room, remained rooted to the spot for an instant, looking at him in amazement, as if at a stranger. Fanea took off his hat and hung it on the hat stand. His wife exclaimed:

'Was that you, Adrian? I didn't recognise you in that new hat.'

So that must have been it! The hat …

And, his mind at rest, Adrian Cornel Fanea sat himself down at the dinner table.

1967

Solon, the Unknown

Alexandru Solon was a consultant. To be more exact, a grade-two consultant to an administrative department, without any great hope of ever being promoted to grade one, because the man who held that position was a highly capable official, very hardworking, who in turn had no chance of rising higher, which is to say, to the position of deputy head of department, because the deputy head of department was also a very hard-working official, highly capable, and all the rest.

But nor did Alexandru Solon have any desire to be promoted to grade one. His only ambition was to write. He wrote short stories, novellas, novels, which is to say, prose. But he had never published a single line. In the beginning he sent a short story to a magazine. He didn't receive any reply. He sent an excerpt of a novel to another literary magazine, still nothing. In a corner of a page of the magazine, below the box for the *Editorial Board*, which was made up of famous writers, it said in black and white: 'Unpublished manuscripts will not be returned.' Just once he received a reply to a submission, which went like this: 'Alexandru Nolos'—he had submitted the piece under a pseudonym—'your work displays some qualities, but it is too didactic. We advise you to read more prose and make another submission.' He didn't know what to make of

this reply. He wrote about the little people, the overlooked, even the shouldered-aside, who didn't know that they were dealing with the big people, with the chosen. The piece he sent was about an obscure grade-three consultant, who was in fact a great painter. On Sundays he would go to the woods and paint; in the morning he would get up early and paint. His boss upbraided him for sometimes arriving late at the office. His wife scolded him for throwing money down the drain on canvases and tubes of paint and for not caring about his family, his children, and so on and so forth. The message was that we should be careful about how we treat other people, because we can never know what treasures lie hidden in them. What was so bad about that?

Despite all this, Alexandru Solon had never shouldered anybody aside in his life. His boss was always satisfied with his work, and he didn't have a wife or children. He didn't have anybody. But even if he had had somebody, they wouldn't have scolded him, because paper and ink are far cheaper than canvases and tubes of paint.

He had never been rude to anybody in his life, but when he talked to a girl—the girls were usually quite indifferent to him—Alexandru Solon would think to himself in secret, almost diabolical satisfaction: 'If only you knew who you were talking to, my girl!' When he was in a good mood and went to a restaurant with his friends to drink some wine, he would think to himself: 'I finished a novel today! If only you knew ...' When he was in a bad mood, he would mutter to himself, 'If only you knew the troubles I have, how hard it is to find the right word ... how hard it is to reread a page you wrote yesterday and which you thought was a work of genius ...'

Alexandru Solon had never been rude to anybody in his life. Actually, that's not true: there was one time when he went to a restaurant with a girl he really liked, and a friend of his stole her from him. One of those slick young men with trousers pressed to a razor-sharp crease and whose heads are full of tunes from the hit parade. First, the friend asked her to dance, then he asked her again, and finally he told Solon that he and the girl were leaving together. Solon objected, the friend raised his hand to hit him, but the girl stepped between them. After which they both left together and Solon was left all by himself to finish his drink and pay the bill. After he drank his glass to the dregs, he burst out laughing. It really was a ridiculous, hackneyed episode. He hadn't even been angry at them, he thought to himself in amazement. Later, the friend married the girl, and now they have three children ... But when he infrequently bumps into her on the street and stops to chat about the weather or her health or the children, Solon smiles to himself: 'If only you knew who I am! Maybe, one fine day, when I'm gone, you'll find out ... Maybe you'll walk past the house where I lived and you'll pause in silence for a little to read the white marble plaque: Here lived and wrote etc. etc.'

Alexandru Solon was never ill. At least his landlady, an elderly and very obliging woman, a war widow, who used to tidy his room and bring him a cup of tea in the morning, had never seen him spend the day in bed or hear him complaining of any ailment, not even a headache or a toothache, or heart problems; she couldn't even remember him having a cold. In fact, he felt sorrow or joy only when one of his characters experienced sorrow or joy. But as for that, if only anybody knew, but they didn't.

One night, Solon was working on his novel about a music teacher at a school in the provinces, who was secretly a great composer. The teacher was persecuted by the head of the school, an envious non-entity, rejected by the young French teacher, whom he loved with a passion and who left him for a slick young man with pressed trousers and a head full of popular love songs. In the end, after finishing the fourth movement, 'Andante doloroso', of his fifth symphony, the teacher died suddenly, of a heart attack.

The next day, when his landlady entered the room with his cup of tea, she found him stretched out on the bed, his face as yellow as wax, slumped on top of a manuscript in a small, crabbed hand, still holding his fountain pen so tightly that it was impossible to remove it, which is why they buried him with it. It was then that it was discovered that he was forty-four years old. Everybody had always thought he was fifty, as he had a rather wrinkled face and receding chestnut hair, which revealed his skull in all its rotundity.

He didn't leave a will. All he left behind were his papers. Thick stacks of paper covered in tiny writing and methodically numbered were found in his cupboards, drawers, and even on the floor, in every corner of the room.

Three or so days later, the landlady, who had to clean his room, collected all the bundles of paper and took them up to the attic. Later, she sold them to an itinerant tinsmith, who took all the manuscripts home and with his five children made paper bags from them, which he sold at the market, making quite a nice profit for himself.

The day after Alexandru Solon's funeral, in the window of the room where he had lived for so many years there appeared a piece of card on which was written in a clumsy hand: 'Furnished room to let.'

The room didn't stay vacant for long. It was a good room, it was clean and as part of the rent, the landlady, an elderly woman, hardworking and decent, included the cleaning and a cup of tea in the morning.

1967

Symmetry

Had you asked any of the neighbours from their building what kind of life Mr and Mrs Tarna of Flat 37 on the fifth floor led, they might have answered: 'A decent life, I think,' or at best they would have said in amazement, 'I don't know'. People probably thought they got along well, and in any event, nobody would have been able to know that the couple's life had become unbearable.

How could the neighbours have known? Just like in so many other blocks of rented flats, the neighbours in that particular building knew nothing more about each other than what was inscribed on the little plaque beneath the doorbell: a name which said nothing much, an occupation, perhaps. More often than not, however, there was no room for the occupation on the little metal or wood plaque or the little slip of paper.

So it was that nobody could have known what was going on in Flat 37 on the fifth floor. The couple were seen leaving the flat, now he, now she, going about their business or to work. What were their jobs? It was known only vaguely or not at all. And on Sundays they would leave the flat together, with their little girl of six or seven or eight, it was not known how old she was, as she could have been bigger or smaller for her age, as sometimes happens with children, whose physical development can occur early or late.

So, the neighbours had no way of knowing that the marriage had become intolerable for both spouses. This despite their having married for love. It had been a very great love, with eternal vows and oaths even while they were still students. He had studied at the polytechnic, she had taken a degree in foreign languages. She translated technical manuals from German and English, he helped her organise her time, divide her hours for studying from her hours for resting, as she was quite disorganised, a daydreamer who, unlike him, did not have any precise idea of the value of time. Somewhere along the way they wedded, they barely had the time to stop off at the registry office, and after they finished university he got a job as an engineer at an electronics factory, she as a lycée teacher. They had begun to think the same, to feel the same. And, who knows how or where or when, suspicion and mistrust began to seep into their souls, symmetrically. When she was late returning from the lycée because she had a meeting or some exercises to mark, he would imagine that it was because of her colleague, the P.E. teacher. And when he came home late at night, because he was working the late shift, she would imagine that he had been with his secretary. He did indeed have a beautiful secretary, with short brown hair and large dark eyes, and likewise, the P.E. teacher was a handsome man, tall, blond, broad-shouldered, but when they each thought these things, nothing was going on with either one of them as yet. Maybe it was their mutual suspicions that caused something to develop, something ... but what exactly? Nobody knew.

Tension was building in the flat, as if in a superheated pressure cooker. When she sat with their daughter after supper, she would be thinking: 'I'm here with our daughter, while he's having fun with that woman ...' And in the weeks when he worked the late shift and stayed with the little girl in the mornings, the thought would gnaw away at him: 'I'm here with the little girl, while she's with ... with that athlete of hers!' He would utter the word 'athlete' with the scorn of one who had always regarded P.E. as a form of playing truant, a frivolous distraction rather than a serious subject.

These thoughts and worries ate away at their marriage day by day, until living together became unbearable. Well-educated and well-raised people that they were, they even decided to separate, but then something they had not anticipated got in the way: the little girl.

The child did not really know what was going on at home between her parents. The parents at least, well-educated and well-raised as they were, took pains for their daughter not to find out. Consequently, open quarrels did not erupt, voices were not raised at home, harsh, violent words were not exchanged in the daughter's presence. Mordant comments, veiled reproaches and rebukes, sarcastic remarks and digs were the order of the day. So much so that even in the absence of thunder and lightning, the atmosphere at home was never genuinely serene. The nerves that pervaded the flat gradually started to affect the little girl too, who became shut up inside herself, uncommunicative; she neither sought nor felt comfortable in the company of other children. All until one day, when she fell ill. The doctors were unable to discover what was wrong with her. She had a temperature, a fluctuating fever, her sleep was disturbed and she would wake up shouting in fright but then forgetting what she had dreamed and why she had cried out. Before she fell ill, when one of her parents, half-jokingly, half-seriously, asked her the innocuous question: 'Which do you love the most, darling, your daddy or your mummy?' the little girl would invariably answer: 'Both!' When, a little later, they asked her: 'Which would you like to live with, mummy or daddy?' she replied with a fierceness of which they hadn't thought her capable: 'With both! With both! With both!' And when one of them, her father or her mother, insisted on an answer: 'But if we did separate and you had to choose, what would you do?' the child, in utter disgust, answered in a wholly unexpected and surprisingly determined way: 'I'd jump out of the window.' Her parents were left perplexed. Their flat, number 37, was on the fifth floor, and such a reply from a little girl of seven ... So, both quickly assured the little girl they were joking and they never asked her anything of the kind again.

The child fell ill and the doctors, not knowing the whole background of the illness, were unable to make a diagnosis. They therefore treated her with sleeping pills and tranquil-lisers, with sedative syrups and injections, until she got better. Granted, she was pale and thin, but she was still able to get out of bed and return to school.

It was at this time, one night when both parents were at home, after the little girl finished her homework, after she packed her satchel for the next day and went to bed, after she kissed both parents on the forehead and nicely said, 'Good night, Mummy! Good night, Daddy!', it was at this time that Mr and Mrs Tarna held that family conference in their bedroom, at which they made that strange decision, albeit the only one that could be made under the circumstances. Talking very calmly, very quietly and reasonably, for the first time in who knows how long, husband and wife came to the conclusion that they did not get along at all and could not live together, but nor was it possible for them to separate. Would the child live either with the one or with the other, or a week with the one and a week with the other? The little girl was very sensitive and the situation would have a baleful, maybe even a fatal influence on her health, on her future. They therefore came to the conclusion, and not without astonishment, that they would have to live separately, but together. Which is to say, they would remain together, but separated. She would have the bedroom, and the living room would be his, as there was a comfortable enough couch there. They would live like that until the girl grew up and they would be able to explain the situation to her, by which time she would understand …

From that day forth, as if by miracle, the muffled rebukes, the sarcastic remarks, the reproaches ceased. The nasty digs at each other no longer furrowed the air of flat 37 on the fifth floor. They stopped suspiciously asking each other: 'Where have you been? What took you so long? Who were you with? Where are you going?' They no longer pried into each other's outfits, gestures, attitudes. The skies cleared in the flat. Everything seemed as light as a feather. Laughter and jokes began to appear again: they told each other things that had happened, but which didn't have anything to do with him or her, things that had happened to other people, stories amusing or sad, but without any home address. Just once—or was it twice?—did he receive a visit in his room, a veiled woman, who did not appear to be his secretary, the brunette with the dark eyes, but rather a woman who stayed until quite late, and the next day, his former wife and the mother of their daughter told him, as if in passing, that she did not wish to meddle in his personal affairs and did not have any objections, but nonetheless, he ought to think about what their little darling would think, what she would say if, God forbid! she found out. To which he, her former husband and the little girl's father, replied with a certain amount of embarrassment that he knew that she did not care and that for his part he had no reason to justify himself, but it was a cousin who happened to be in town and had come to visit him. Once—or was it twice?—she too received a visit in her room, from a man in an elegant black hat pulled down over his eyes, but who did not seem to be the P.E. teacher, the 'athlete'. The next day she told him, as if in passing, that it had been a relative of hers, a second cousin on her father's side, who had come to visit her—he had stayed late into the evening. After which, he, her former husband and the little girl's father, took the first opportunity to remark in passing that it would be well that she think of the child, what a shock it would be for her to find out in this way what they had both sought so carefully to conceal … All these things were said in a calm, quiet, civilised voice—in places even with a hint of friendly understanding and generosity.

'All right, Nicu, if that's what you think—'

'No, no, Anca, only if that's what you think too.'

Time passed and the girl grew up. She was now in lycée and the separated husband and wife decided that the time had come for them to have a serious talk with her, to explain the situation to her, but they kept putting it off. Neither of them knew how to go about it. They knew full well that whatever they told her, however they explained it to her, she would not understand. The girl had such blue eyes, eyes so clear, eyes that reflected her surprise and amazement so deeply.

When the girl got a place at the polytechnic, to her father's great pride, since she was good at mathematics, although she also diligently studied foreign languages and made progress in them, her parents deemed the time had come for her to know everything. There was no point in keeping it a secret any longer. But just as they were about to speak to her, they realised that things were not quite so clear and that the girl would not understand. Their Little Marietta, now Maria once more, the same as on her birth certificate, a serious, official document, looked at them both with such casual ease, with such trust and faith in her sky-blue eyes, that it was utterly certain that not even now she had grown up and was a student would she understand any of it. And in any case, how to tell her? How to begin? Which of them would speak first?

And besides, how could she comprehend that which in the interval had become utterly incomprehensible? How could she understand that after a given point their life together had become intolerable? That once upon a time there had been a beautiful secretary with short brown hair and dark eyes, or rather there hadn't been, or at least not at the time when the wife imagined there had been … Or that once upon a time there had been a P.E. teacher, a tall, blond, broad-shouldered 'athlete', who perhaps hadn't meant anything to the wife at the time when the husband thought he had … When they went over all this in their minds, using different combinations of words and phrases, it struck them as utterly commonplace … But even so, at one time there had been reasons. Reasons that weighed like lead on their souls and which stretched their nerves to breaking … What an amazing thing time is! And the distance they had placed between themselves, like a vast strip of no-man's land, while still remaining close, so close to each other.

They therefore decided to postpone their talk with their daughter, to wait another year or two, maybe even until Maria finished university and found a job, until she left home and found a place of her own. At which point their mission as parents would be complete and they would be free. As free as the birds. Free to go wherever they liked, wherever their hearts desired.

This decision was all the easier to make given that the long-awaited day did not seem so very far away. A foreign languages student—who says that history doesn't repeat itself in a way?—started paying ever more frequent visits to their daughter, a well-behaved young woman, very respectful towards her parents, he came to the flat to help her, translating for her countless pages of technical literature from French and Italian.

The long-awaited day arrived. The youngsters finished university and got married. 'What a lovely couple!' exclaimed the wedding guests on seeing them arm in arm, the groom tall and with chestnut hair, looking distinguished in his starched white shirt, the bride with blond hair and blue eyes as clear as the sky, wearing a white lace dress and holding her bouquet of lilies so awkwardly and yet with so much grace. 'What a lovely couple!' 'What a beautiful bride!' 'What a handsome young man!' 'How much they love each other!' whispered the guests at the reception as they ate and drank and made merry.

The day and the night of the wedding came and went, and the parents found themselves alone, finally alone! They had been waiting for this moment their whole lives! Now they were free once more, as free as the birds in the sky, free to go wherever they liked, as far as the eye could see, free to do whatever their hearts desired.

Late that night, sitting across from one another at the large living-room table, they held yet another family council, a council as strange as the one that had taken place all those years ago, when they decided to separate. The time had come for them to explain it all to their daughter, and she would understand. They would also have to tell her husband everything, after all he was their son-in-law, almost their own son. Both of them would understand. Understand what? What was there to understand or not understand?

They would receive postcards from them while they were on their honeymoon. 'Dear Parents, the seaside is lovely …' Or, 'Dear Parents, the mountains are wonderful … the lofty peaks …' Then the children would come to visit them from time to time, to visit their 'dear parents'. Then their grandchildren. They would in turn come to stay with their grandparents.

No, no! Their daughter would not understand it now any more than she had before, when she was in her first year at primary school... And besides, it was true that they were each free to go wherever they liked, wherever their hearts desired. But go where? What was the point now? And what did their hearts desire?

It is not known whether all this was spoken aloud over the table at the family council or whether it was merely thought. The fact is that the two were sitting face to face, looking at each other in silence, exchanging a few soft words at intervals. His hair was greying at the temples and there were deep furrows in his brow. She had white strands in her hair, which in places gathered to form slender white locks—it suits her, the husband thought to himself—and she had blueish rings around her eyes. They looked at each other for a long moment and finally they both burst out laughing. Sad, uninhibited laughter.

And so, had you asked any of the neighbours from their building how Mr and Mrs Tarna from flat number 37 on the fifth floor got along, they would have replied: 'Well, I think,' or else they would have said, 'I don't know.'

And how could they possibly have known? Here, just like in hundreds and hundreds of other blocks of rented flats, the neighbours know nothing more about each other than what is inscribed on the label beneath the doorbell: a name that says nothing...

The Acrobat

After hitting their highest notes, the trumpets abruptly stopped. The drums kept rolling, solemnly, forebodingly … Then silence. Profound, frozen silence … Up above, beneath the rather tatty canvas dome of the circus tent, in the spotlight, Micunicu took the rope in his mouth, clenched his jaws, stretched out his legs, held his arms outstretched, and remained hanging in mid-air, like a man crucified on an invisible cross … Profound silence. Nothing but hundreds of gleaming eyes gazing at him from below, in fascination. Like a field plunged in darkness, speckled with fireflies, hundreds of fireflies, or a black starry sky, with him up there, above the field, above the sky … Yes, that was how he always felt in those moments, above the people down on earth, above the stars down in the sky …

Then the drums came in again, slowly, reassuringly. He gripped the rope in his hands, the trumpets broke into a lively march, the applause burst forth. Wild applause. He always listened to it in enchantment, transported. But for the sake of that silence, for the sake of those silent, gleaming eyes, for the sake of that applause, he had discarded his real name—he had once been called simply Nicu Micu—and adopted the rather ridiculous stage name of Micunicu, which sounded foreign, exotic, particularly when it appeared in large, coloured letters on the circus poster: MICUNICU, acrobat artiste, with a red M, a yellow I, a green C, a blue U, a red N, a yellow I, a green C, and blue U ... For the sake of those silences, followed by the storm of applause, he had given up the woman he could have had all for himself, but never did, he gave up the children, the quiet, respectable job, the house he could have had, but never did, since he permanently lived in lodgings let by little old landladies in various towns, he lived in furnished rooms that smelled of mould, all of them seemingly identical, as if created especially for lonely circus artistes ...

Yes, it was worth living like that, worth living any way at all, for the sake of those extraordinary moments ... The trumpets, then the drums foreboding unsuspected danger ... Then the deep silence. The silent eyes, fixed upwards. Then the drums once more, the trumpets, the roar of the applause, happiness ... Happiness ...

But lately, the applause had grown less loud, sparser. Nor was the silence so perfect, so solemn as it used to be. Crucified, his whole body hanging from the rope he clenched between his teeth, he would hear murmurs, comments, even a soft titter of laughter ... How ill-bred! he would think. Once, he even glimpsed among the audience down below a woman unwrapping some paper and handing her child a sandwich ... He saw the white wrapper, from up above it looked no bigger than a cigarette paper, and he saw the child, as big as a doll, munching the bread ... He was horrified. Children are honest. If the child was capable of quietly eating a sandwich while he was up there, risking death, crucified, clenching the rope between his teeth, then ... then ... it meant that he was stuck in a rut, it meant that he was repeating himself, it meant that he had to do something else, something different, more spectacular ... And he feverishly began to search for new numbers. Coiling his legs together … Hugging his left arm with right foot and his right arm with his left foot … In vain.

One evening—he will never forget that evening—when he was presenting his most intricate and most dangerous number, his body hanging from the rope he was gripping between his teeth, his arms wound around his upraised legs, with his knees at his mouth, looking like a bundle of rags dangling from the ceiling, the audience, instead of watching with baited breath, inexplicably burst out laughing … A clown! I've become a clown, he said to himself in shame and fury, quickly lowering himself from the rope and making a quick bow, to scattered, pitiful applause, and withdrawing from the big top just as quickly, with a smile frozen on his face and death in his soul.

A clown! Yes, yes, yes, I've become a clown! he said to himself, walking past a circus poster, on which his name was no longer printed in large coloured letters, with a red M, a yellow I, a green C, a blue U, and so on, but in letters just as black and only a fraction larger than those advertising Kasserole the Clown, who jumped and flopped around like a deflating ball and rolled in the sawdust, cutting all sorts of capers and jabbering at the imbeciles, all in an attempt to get a laugh … The wretch! The ham!

But what about me? What have I become? A clown! A common clown, he said to himself, arriving at his furnished room, pervaded with the stale smell of mould, and flinging himself on the bed. From an acrobat artiste I have been reduced to a clown … How could such a thing happen? And what a difficult number I performed! But they laughed! What do they know? What do they know about how many nights I wracked my brains to come up with it, how many attempts I made before I pulled it off and how hard the number was to perform? You have to focus your mind, your muscles, your will on a single point … There is a measure to all things … Maybe I have exceeded it without my realising it? Where is the boundary between the grand and the ridiculous? A thread, a fine thread, on which you tread without being aware of when or how … What other number could I perform? I don't know. Nothing else is possible. No matter how much he wracked his brains, he was unable to compose something new. All of a sudden, a thought came to him with the force of a revelation: it was possible, it was possible, but not for him. Micunicu was unable to give any more. He had given as much as he was capable of, it was for only so much that he had been created, and that was all there was to it! In the end, nobody in this world is able to give more than he was created for … He felt like laughing out loud at such a madcap thought. But the more he examined it, looking at it from every conceivable angle, the more he realised that the thought was as solid as a slab of concrete. We reach our limit and we come to a stop, he thought. We come to a stop at a certain point and it is for others to go further. Every man reaches a point, after which there is no 'further' for him, he reaches a peak, his peak, whence he cannot go any higher, and then he goes downward, downward, downward, until he reaches a place whence he cannot go any lower. Oh, how horrible is the way downward! You go against your will, your legs carrying you. How do you stop your legs? There are no brakes, and the slope grows steeper and steeper … His peak had come when his name was emblazoned in vivid colours on every fence, on every wall of the towns and villages through which he passed: MICUNICU! MICUNICU! MICUNICU! in red and yellow and green and blue … And in the spotlight, high above, beneath the patched canvas roof of the circus big top, as he gripped the rope between clenched jaws, his arms outstretched, hanging like one crucified … Like the Crucified! The silence and the eyes … Hundreds of eyes aglow like stars against the dark night sky … Then the storm of applause mixed with the triumphal notes of the trumpets and the beat of the drums … Then, on one of those nights, he ought to have unclenched his jaws and fallen … He had always played honestly, showing his cards, he had worked without hidden safety harnesses, without nets stretched beneath him. He had given people nothing but honest thrills … Yes, yes, yes! Then, one of those passionate nights, he ought to have closed his eyes happily and, with a careless smile flickering on his lips, to have fallen into empty space, into eternity … He would not have had to descend from the peak slowly, painfully, constantly looking behind him …

But perhaps not even now was it too late for the public to realise just whom they had lost? He might do it, one evening when there was almost a full house, on a Saturday or Sunday … No, no! Micunicu quickly banished the thought from his mind. Now it would be a pitiful spectacle, it would be ridiculous. The other circus performers would dash to pick him up from the sawdust, the ringmaster would perhaps mutter a curse through gritted teeth, and there would be audience members who would not understand the meaning of the gesture and say: 'What a clumsy acrobat!' or people who had seen him in his heyday, who would say: 'He's past it, the poor bloke!' He would stir pity more than anything else … No, no, no! A thousand times no! If this was where he had ended up, he would have to make his departure differently … Silently, unassumingly, like an old man reaching retirement … Even here, in the silence of that furnished room, with its smell of old mould … Lying down, with a bottle of sleeping pills on the bedside table … That evening, when it was time for him to do his number, the ringmaster would step forward, discreetly wringing his large, animal-tamer's hands, and, his voice breaking, announce: 'Dear members of the audience, sad news …' And in the local paper there would be an obituary, maybe even a short piece: 'The famous Micunicu …' or maybe just the following: 'The well-known acrobat artiste, who gambled his life night after night to provide us with the purest thrills … we would all watch him with bated breath … our admiration … never will we forget him …' Maybe the reporter, taking inspiration, would add: 'As long as he walked among us, we did not know how to value him at his true worth …' But it was possible that no obituary or news item would appear in the paper and it wouldn't be any wonder if the ringmaster didn't announce the sad news but Kasserole the Clown, that ham … who would be capable, even unwittingly, the wretch, who would be capable, purely out of habit, of giving one of his grimaces as he did so …

But what did any of this matter? What did he care what would come afterward … On the bedside table sat the bottle of sleeping pills and a glass of water. He only had to stretch out his hand … It had been a long time since he had been able to get to sleep without those pills. And there were enough of them to grant him a deep, deep, dreamless sleep …

All of a sudden, as he lay there on the bed, he heard a prolonged growl. He pricked up his ears. Yes, the growl was coming from his stomach. It was suppertime. He quickly got up and went to make himself something to eat …

1968

The Two Mothers, or, No Need for the Judgement of Solomon

I

(Letters from a woman who is to become a mother without undergoing the throes of childbirth)

15 March 196-

Dear Mary,

I'm going to have a baby! At last, I'm going to have a baby!

You know how fervently I wanted it, how long I waited for it, how long I dreamed of it When I walked around the seven rooms of my house, it was as if I were walking through a desert. Among the sand dunes of the Sahara. And what hasn't my Henry done to make me happy? Two television sets, a radio, a record player, a collection of LPs, and above all else, the stereo sound system! Stereo everywhere you go: in the kitchen, in the bathroom, in the larder, everywhere the same sound quality. Not that I spend much time in the kitchen, but if I do pop in, the strains of music are there too to transport me. You know how sensitive I am. Music! Ah, Music, the greatest art! I have a cook, a maid, a chauffeur, two cars, apart from my husband's, which is solemn, like a hearse: a black Cadillac, which he uses for business. Mine are funny, one's a teal blue sports car, you know how much I love blue, most of my dresses are different shades of blue. And the other is a silver Mercury limousine, for evenings out, receptions, cocktail parties.

But to what end? My house was empty, the beach house was empty, my heart was empty. I visited so many eminent physicians, I took dozens of courses of treatment, I travelled to countless spas, but zilch! I was on the brink of losing my mind, of having a nervous breakdown, I would burst into tears out of the blue, I would make scenes in front of Henry, picking quarrels with him, torturing him when the poor man hadn't done anything at all. Life became unbearable.

I know what you're thinking, my dear Mary. Why didn't I try to adopt? I thought of that. I even visited an orphanage a few times. Oh, what darling children I saw! But I gave up the idea. The children there have been abandoned by destitute parents, or brought by people who know who the parents are, and in any event, there's a chance that one fine day they'll find out. After you've spent years raising the child and you've become attached to it, one of the parents might turn up and ask for the child back. And if they're destitute and desperate enough, they might blackmail you over it for the rest of your life. And besides, who knows what nasty traits the child might have inherited? You could find yourself raising a congenital thief or drunkard. I've read all sorts of things like that in magazines and novels. No, and again no! The thought horrifies me! I want to have a child of my own, all of my own. Nobody will ever be able to turn up and deny my rights as a mother. I wanted the child to come from a good family, to carry it inside me for the nine months, to experience labour pains, the same as any other woman, the same as the poorest and most desperate of women. And no matter what I did, it was impossible. I was losing my mind. I ended up tormenting Henry no end. I would walk around the house naked for days on end. I couldn't stand the feel of any clothes on me, it made me want to rip them up. Henry, to take my mind off it, used to bring me all kinds of things. You should see my jewellery box, my dresses, my collection of umbrellas! Once he brought me an azure dress, a dreadfully nice shade of blue. I put it on in front of him. He looked at me, happy, as I stood looking at myself in the mirror. And he asked me whether I liked it. Poor man! That was a fatal mistake. In a rage, I tore the dress to pieces. And all the underwear I was wearing. If he hadn't stopped me by force, I would have ripped my own skin too.

I was on the verge of losing my mind, I actually had lost it, but then my 'doctor' turned up. My saviour! Now I will have a child. My own child, at last!

Sorry to break off this letter, but I can hear his footsteps in the hall. He's here to give me my weekly check-up. I'll write more soon, my dear Mary.

With kisses, from your old friend,

Fanny

3 May 196-

Dear Mary,

I'm in my third month and everything is going quite well. Sometimes I have morning sickness. It's amazing, my dear, but I really do feel sickness. I have an excellent doctor. He comes regularly, once a week, and gives me these wonderful check-ups. He explains to me in detail what I'm feeling, how the pregnancy is progressing. He talks so convincingly that I really do feel morning sickness. A few times I've even had to go to the bathroom. It's utterly amazing, Mary!

By the way, I mustn't forget to tell you that my 'doctor' is actually a lawyer. An excellent lawyer. Which is why he's so good at speaking. It's a real pleasure to be examined by him. I wouldn't exchange one of his examinations for the advice of a hundred physicians. A wonderful man. He's in his sixties but doesn't look a day over fifty. Or even a day over forty-five. Tall, broad-backed, like an athlete, ruddy cheeked. Everything belies his age. Only his white hair gives him away. He's very dear to me, this 'doctor' of mine. He charges an unbelievable fee, but it's worth it. Henry doesn't stint when it comes to things like this. The dear man! For three months we've been living in peace and harmony. I love Henry. I adore him! We squabble about one thing only: he wants it to be a boy, I want it to be a girl. You know, a little girl with bows in her hair and dimples in her cheeks, a little doll. And besides, girls are more loving, they're more attached to their parents than boys, who, as soon as they grow up, leave home and go off with some girl, they forget you.

I'm contented at last. I have morning sickness, headaches. Forgive me, but I need to go to the bathroom again. I'll write to you, my dear, and keep you abreast of everything.

With kisses,

Yours,

Fanny

10 July 196-

My Dear Mary,

I felt it move! I felt it move! I'm in my fifth month and the foetus moved. It kicked its little legs. I shouldn't wonder if it will grow up to be a footballer, meaning it's a boy. Oh, you can't imagine what joy it is for a mother. I felt it move! But what am I talking about? I'm telling you, who have had three babies for real? You see how muddle-headed I am?

If you could see me in my baggy dresses! I've put on weight. I've really put on a lot of weight. Henry tells me he's afraid I might lose my mind. But no, there's no danger of that.

Apart from that, I've bought almost everything: nappies, romper suits, little blankets. The cot is waiting by my bed, and today Henry went into town to buy a pram. A modern pram with high wheels and long nickel-plated spokes.

I won't write any more for the time being. I'm burning with impatience.

With kisses from your old friend,

Fanny

21 November 196-

My Dear Mary,

I've got it! It's here, next to me, in the cot, gurgling, crying. I'm happy. I have my own baby. All mine. It has no other mother than me. It has no other father than Henry.

The stork brought it to me from over the ocean. A big stork with silver wings, a jet-powered stork, and he put it in the cot next to the bed where I'm lying confined after the birth. Believe me, I really did experience all the throes of labour. Now I have the baby. And can you imagine? It's a girl. But that's not important. If it had been a boy, I would have loved him just the same.

Forgive me, my dear Mary, but I can't write more at the moment. I'm busy. You of all people will understand when I tell you how busy and how happy I am.

With hugs and kisses, love,

Fanny

II

(and a letter from the other mother, who, after experiencing the throes of labour, has managed to stay the same nice family girl she was before ...)

21 November 196-

Dear Gaby,

Why haven't I written to you for more than four months and why did I ask you to send those letters of mine home, one every month, so that Mother wouldn't weep for worry and Father wouldn't yell in a fury, and so that both of them wouldn't go to notify the authorities that their only daughter was missing?

Now that it's all over, I can write to you: something amazing happened to me. Something unbelievable and I can't stop myself from telling you, my best friend. But shush! Not a word to anyone! You'll swear, won't you?

You know how selfish and careless Teddy is. Well, I had to go to that doctor again. As usual, he made an appointment for me. It was on a Wednesday, or a Thursday, I don't remember which, but instead of finding him in his office alone, he was there with a friend of his, a lawyer. He introduced me to him: a young blond man of about thirty-six or thirty-seven, athletic, handsome, friendly smile. After we made some small talk about the weather, the doctor left me alone with him. After looking at me, smiling, for a few seconds, the lawyer asked me no more, no less than if I was really dead set on having that ... that operation ... As for me, I didn't even let him finish, so indignant was I. How dare he? What did that lawyer take me for? How did he know about it and why was he interfering in things that were none of his business? But he just looked at me, unaffected, and when I'd finished, he calmly assured me that lawyers are as discreet as doctors. He had a warm, baritone voice, very pleasant. In which case, why was he asking me whether or not I was dead set on it? Why did he think I was there? I've no intention of being called an unmarried mother. And besides, I'm certain my parents would be none too pleased with such a grandchild. But in the end, what business was it of his? I asked, losing my temper again. Can you imagine? I was fuming. But the lawyer carried on smiling at me in the same calm way and told me he had a very interesting proposition for me. He asked me whether I might nonetheless agree to letting it go, which is to say, to giving birth for somebody else. Really? I was gobsmacked. Nobody would know anything, he assured me. Give birth for whom? Not even he knew for whom. He knew only the lady's lawyer, a lady who couldn't have children but was dying to have one. Just as the lady's lawyer would know only him, who from that moment would be glad for me to regard him as my lawyer. What could I say? I was speechless. He went on: in the fourth or fifth month, when it started to show, I would go away somewhere, to a spa at the seaside or in the mountains. Preferably in the mountains. Naturally, all expenses paid, and a 'little something' extra. Well, that 'little something' piqued my interest. Irresistibly even. There was one condition: I would have to meet him once a week to tell him in great detail how I felt, what I felt, how the pregnancy was progressing, and so on. Details that he had to pass on to the other party's lawyer.

Well, it was a deal.

Yesterday, I gave birth to the child and it was immediately taken away, by my lawyer and a wet-nurse, taken away, over the ocean. I'm now thinking about fixing myself a whole new wardrobe, I'm going to make myself some dresses that will make your jaw drop. And I'm going to get some jewellery too, really chic.

Do you know what I think? If I do this again, or better still, if I do it twice, I'm also going to get myself a car. Not a run-of-the-mill one, but something swanky. A nice Opel. Or maybe even a Mercedes. Yes, why not a Mercedes? My friend Luisa will die of envy. You know how snooty she is with that car of hers. The lawyer gave me his card, with his address and telephone number.

By the way! Now I remember: they took the baby away so quickly that I don't even know what it looks like. I don't even know if it was a boy or a girl. That's the century of speed for you, it makes your head spin, nothing less.

But shush! Not a word to anyone. You swore! God forbid you breathe a word!

Ta-ta!

Yours,

K—

(Only the initial of the signature is legible, the rest being a tangle of indecipherable letters: maybe Käthe, Kitty, Katerina? But that's of no importance …)

1969

PART TWO

1970–1979

Panoptikum

It's the day of the fair again in the little provincial town.

Hustle, bustle.

Among the stalls and the kiosks selling vegetables, eggs, sides of meat, gingerbread and old clothes, among the motley circus booths made of old planks and tent canvas, featuring acrobats who bounce like balls, the 'fire eater' and the 'iron bender' and the 'punchbag man' for you to test your strength, and the thin girl who climbs safely from the chest after being cut in two, and the 'spider woman' who smiles sadly at you from her black web, and all the other marvels to be seen, I once again spy the small panoptikum.

I once again pay over my copper coin and step inside.

I am no longer surprised. Or disappointed. After all, this time I didn't expect to see in this tatty wax museum such famous figures as Napoleon or Marie Antoinette or Julius Caesar or Christopher Columbus . . .

Instead, once more I find yellow, ordinary, dull faces, familiar to nobody . . . Garishly made-up faces that laugh or weep, for whatever reason, faces frightened or humble, proud or indifferent . . .

And beneath each of them there is a caption handwritten in black ink on white card. Beneath the bust of a man with a moustache, it says: 'A man with a moustache.' Beneath the bust of a woman with long hair, it says: 'A woman with long hair.' Beneath the bust of an old man with a white beard, it says: 'An old man with a white beard.' And so on . . .

I look at the wax figures in silence and this time I don't ask myself any questions. I'm tired of questions. And of too many answers . . .

The Tinfoil Halo

It happened exactly as predicted.

The priest, tall, thin, bony-faced, his black surplice rippling over his body from top to bottom at every movement of his arms, at every vibration of his voice, began his sermon in solemn, monotonous, measured tones:

'Dearly beloved mourners! When I heard that after great suffering and at an age that lies midway between manhood and wisdom, Stefan-Julius Manutin had passed from this life, barely having reached his fifties, I was reminded of the truthful words of Ecclesiastes, which all of you may read in chapter seven: "A good name is better than precious ointment, and the day of death than the day of one's birth." And I say unto you these words of Ecclesiastes, because it is true that the dear man to whom we today bid farewell has a name better than precious ointment and because his whole life he felt to the full the pain of the world, the pain of his brothers and sisters in faith, and ever did he seek to comfort them … He was an enlightened spirit, a great soul, a wielder of the pen whom the Lord Above bestowed with talent and grace …'

I gave a start. Exactly as he had predicted! In my ears once more there resounded the words he had spoken in a drink-slurred voice:

'Just you wait and see, at my funeral they'll go on and on about how I was a great soul, a talented writer and journalist, et cetera, et cetera … The provinces! Nobody has read a word, everybody has heard something, everybody suspects something, imagines a whole lot more, but nobody knows a thing … And it's as if your renown sticks to your skin, it even gets under your skin, like the mange …'

After which Stefan-Julius Manutin gave a soft laugh. His was a low, muffled laugh, like clods pattering onto his own coffin at the bottom of a deep grave.

This took place one night at *Let's Be Merry!*, a restaurant at the edge of town. Everybody else had gone home, I'd stood up to leave too, but when I passed the table at which he was sitting alone with a glass of cheap local white wine in front of him, he invited me to sit:

'Wouldn't you like to sit with me a little, young lady? We're in the same trade.'

I couldn't refuse. I sat down at his table. He poured me a glass of wine. We clinked glasses.

'When you hear those words, you ought to know they're not true. I was neither a "great soul" nor an "enlightened spirit", neither a great "writer" nor a "journalist" … I set out on a completely different path in life. I plied a modest, honest trade, which I held very dear, and which I'd begun to love with all my heart. It was more than a profession, it was a calling. But people have forgotten … How forgetful this world is … it wants only to remember what suits it …'

He fell silent for a long moment. In the restaurant, dimly lit at that hour by a few anaemic yellow bulbs, there was almost complete silence. The only sound was next to the counter, where the barman, a tall, skinny man with black hair glistening with brilliantine, was whispering to the fat, heavily made-up, garishly blond landlady.

Manutin sipped his yellowish wine and sourly pursed his mouth.

'Yes, everybody has forgotten … But I studied at the *école normale* for teachers and started out in life at a country schoolhouse, like my father and grandfather before me … I was appointed trainee teacher at a nearby village, Poiana Mică. Those were the happiest years of my life. I started with the primary class and taught the children till their fourth year. Three years and a bit, during which time I saw their eyes gleaming with the joy and wonder of children discovering how to read and do arithmetic … and poetry, and history, and geography … the wide, wide world, which stretches far away, beyond the village surrounded by its mountains, which many of the children's parents had never crossed … I didn't realise how happy I was until, in the middle of the school year, I bid my fourth-year pupils farewell and handed over my teaching duties to a young, frightened woman teacher … the children wept, I wept, the new teacher wept … it was as if I'd had an arm amputated, a healthy, blameless arm … I didn't realise it at the time, but I really had become an invalid, spiritually an invalid …'

He poured himself another glass and gulped it thirstily. He mopped his sweaty brow with a grubby handkerchief.

'Obviously you're curious to know why I left the village? It was a strange but yet very simple and perfectly explicable occurrence … I was young and full of love and enthusiasm for my vocation as a teacher, and that year, the fourth of my career, I wrote some notes, I don't know what to call them, a kind of composition, more or less literary in merit, titled "Our School". I described the village children's thirst for learning and the harsh conditions in which they were forced to study: a ramshackle building with peeling plaster, small classrooms into which were crammed fifty or sixty children, with three children to a desk. News so familiar around these parts as to be stale … I copied out the piece in a flimsy one-leu exercise book, using my best handwriting, and sent it to the editors of a newspaper in the capital …'

Manutin paused for a brief moment, then went on, in a studied voice of cold objectivity:

'And now please listen carefully, my young colleague! Ordinarily, one of two things can happen to such a text on landing at the offices of a large newspaper: either it will be crumpled up and thrown in the bin—"unpublished manuscripts are not kept or returned"—or at best, it will be published in the corner of a page under the heading "Letters from Readers", having been chopped up, cut with a pair of scissors, in a word, drastically edited. But a third and unheard-of thing happened to that composition of mine. Something impossible, something inconceivable! At the time, I regarded it as a miracle, and more than that, as a great opportunity! It was not until later that I was able to explain the miracle to myself completely … My piece appeared on the front page of *The National Courier*, which is published in the capital, with a headline that spanned five columns: "Country schoolteacher makes sensational disclosures." But that wasn't all. The next day, in the Sunday issue, there was a long editorial about my piece. Then other newspapers took up the subject, there were reactions, clarifications, rebuttals. I'd become famous overnight. The newspapers were full of Stefan-Julius Manutin, country schoolteacher from Poiana Mică, and his disclosures. On the third day, I received an invitation to visit the newspaper offices, and they wired me the money for the journey. They offered me the position of editor in charge of "educational and folk-cultural affairs."'

Manutin suddenly drained his half-full glass in one gulp. His face turned even redder, even more congested, his nostrils quivered, making me fearful lest he have a bad turn. But a few moments later, he continued in a calm voice:

'What would you have done, young colleague, if such a piece of luck had landed in your lap? A young schoolteacher from a village in the back of beyond, and all of a sudden you find yourself famous, summoned to cut a figure in the capital ... as a writer and journalist ... as an editor at *The National Courier*! You would have done exactly what I did. I bid my fourth-year class farewell. The children wept, the new teacher wiped away her tears and blew her nose in her handkerchief, and I myself wept. It was as if I'd had an arm amputated ... But I arrived at the newspaper offices, where I was swept off my feet, carried away into a whirlwind ... the offices, the newsprint, the ink, the proofs, the coffee, the canteens that served up vile food, the pubs and the brandy and the women ... But I didn't have to beat my brains out about writing: they were the ones who suggested the topics, told me what to write, sometimes even how to write it ... They published articles many of whose paragraphs I didn't even recognise, so thoroughly had they been edited. They even published articles which, if I think about it, I had no hand in writing at all, but which they suggested I myself had written, whose ideas I myself had come up with ... I was young at the time, a hothead, I liked the work, the commotion that went on around me. It wasn't until later, when I came to my senses, that I started to realise that in actual fact they didn't need me as a writer. They had outstanding writers there, talented, well-connected writers, cynical, hardboiled writers, who could pen anything at all, in any style at all, at the drop of a hat, whether for or against, as the circumstances required, as the political climate and the newspaper's management demanded ... There was one writer in particular, a young journalist, he can't have been more than two or three years older than me, a tall, thin fellow, with unruly red hair. Anton Borecki or Borovic was his name, I can't remember which, since everybody called him Ant, a journalist through and through, who could write anywhere at all, on the ink-stained table at the newspaper office or on the corner of a table in the insalubrious, noisy tavern across the street, or even without a table, in the lift, on the toilet, anywhere; he could write on any topic, political, cultural, economic, social, scientific, sporting, about women's affairs, about murders, any subject at all, and he could write however much was required, which is to say, the exact number of lines. He could find arguments for and against anything that were equally solid, for example he could bring to bear powerful reasons why the country had to be industrialised as quickly as possible, but also just as powerful reasons why the country should remain preponderantly agricultural. I'd only been there a few days when, probably seeing I was timid, and bewildered, and helpless, Ant took me under his wing. He grabbed me by the arm and took me to the tavern over the road from the newspaper offices, a place inappropriately called *Joie de Vivre*, and putting a dubious but steaming cup of Turkish coffee in front of me, Ant gave me the low-down: "Don't be a fool, Stef, don't go around with your head in the clouds … And above all else, don't take anything to heart. We write articles the way a cobbler makes shoes to order. What does the cobbler care if the shoe's wearer has hideous corns or his feet stink? Do you understand what I'm saying, Stef?" No, I didn't understand what he was saying at the time. I laughed. I thought he was joking.'

Manutin paused once more, staring intently at the yellowish liquid in his glass. The anaemic yellow light bulbs hanging from the ceiling had started to flicker. At the back of the restaurant the lanky, slick-haired barman was leaning even further across the counter, speaking in an even lower whisper to the fat, garishly blond landlady.

Manutin carried on in a resigned voice:

'Yes, later, by which time it was too late, by which time I was caught up in the ring dance, I realised that from the very beginning they'd needed me not as a writer, whose talent was in any case doubtful, but as a figurehead; they'd needed a young, honest, pure-hearted country schoolteacher by the name of Stefan-Julius Manutin, from Poiana Mică, to serve as a figurehead … They'd used his name as a rifle to fire off shots in various directions, unbeknownst to me; they'd used it as a battering ram to break down various locked and barred doors. You're still very young, you were a child back then, there's no way you could know about those times before the war: tottering governments, battles of inflated words between newspapers, real battles in the streets, with clubs and even guns here and there … The *National Courier* was close to the ruling party … Needless to say, the school with the two classrooms and four classes of children in Poiana Mică was plastered and whitewashed inside and out, it was given a new tiled stove, which didn't fill the room with smoke … But that was all. And presumably, the school was the only one … Yes, even now, I'm gripped by the suspicion that the school from Poiana Mică was the only one they plastered and whitewashed. Or maybe there were a handful of other schools, for the sake of show … Also, needless to say, my halo waxed large in the village, and here in my little home town, and throughout the county … They didn't build new classrooms in Poiana Mică, the children were still crammed sixty to a classroom and three to a desk. Ultimately, I didn't achieve anything, but people used to think to themselves: "We've got somebody up on high, whose words carry weight …" In the meantime, war had broken out, the *National Courier* increasingly began to take on a certain colour … The editors began to wear a certain coloured shirt … Maybe you remember the fashion in Europe at the time: brown shirts, black shirts, green shirts … For a while I pretended not to see it, I feigned colour-blindness, but one day, when the editor off-handedly asked me why I didn't wear that shirt of a particular colour like my colleagues, I answered him, partly in jest, partly in earnest, that I preferred a white shirt, the better to see the dirt on it … At least you'd know when you needed to wash it … The editor was taken aback, but he didn't say anything … It was Ant who had a word with me. When he heard about my little talk with the editor, he grabbed me by the arm, clenching it tightly with his slender fingers, almost making me yelp in pain, he quickly dragged me from the newspaper offices and took me to the tavern across the street, utterly inappropriately named *Joie de Vivre*, where, after casting a cautious look all around, he hissed at me:

'"Are you out of your mind, Stef? Don't you know what world you're living in? Come to your senses, Stef, and don't be a fool! What was he asking you in the end? To wear a shirt of a certain colour. So what? If he asked me to wear lilac long johns tomorrow, I'd do it without batting an eyelid! You don't get it: they put on a coloured shirt, they tug a few side-whiskers, and they think themselves big heroes, but as for us, we've got to make a living! Which is to say, we need to earn our daily bread …"

'"What can he do to me if it comes to that?" I blurted angrily. "He'll give me the sack and I'll go back nicely to my job as a schoolteacher in Poiana Mică …" See how naïve I was, my young colleague? At the time, I didn't know that there was no road back … that all the bridges had burned behind me … And as I said, the editor was taken aback by my reply, but he hadn't said anything. Two or three weeks later, I was called up and, with much fanfare, was sent to the eastern front along with the other soldiers in a brand-new regiment …'

Manutin took another sip of his wine. He brushed a few thin locks of hair from his forehead and went on:

'I was lucky … You know how it goes, a man falls into bad luck only then to discover that he was lucky after all, because it could have been much worse … Without luck like that in the endless series of misfortunes, a man couldn't survive. He'd be a mass of shredded nerves … Anyway, I had some good luck at the front. I was made subaltern of stores. The bakery I was in charge of behind the front line wasn't sheltered from bombs or shells, from the partisans' bullets and grenades, but at least I had fresh bread every day … Things went on like that until the winter of forty-three, when the retreat began. I found myself and the whole of my stores stuck there: forty-three heavy trucks loaded sacks of flours and bread ovens, but no petrol. To my left there was a regiment of Waffen S.S., which we were supplying with bread. I went to ask for petrol, so that I could retreat with my forty-three trucks and my men, but the Herr Sturmführer refused me. Even though I'd see with my own eyes the trucks and the tanker from which they were hastily fuelling their tanks and armoured cars. "What am I supposed to do then," I asked Herr Sturmführer, "surrender the bakery to the enemy?" At which he leapt up like he'd been scalded: "*Was? Verflucht noch einmal! Alles sprengen! Sprengen in der Luft!*" Meaning, I should blow everything up. Seeing that I just stood there, he yelled: "*Das ist Befehl!*" But he couldn't give me orders. I had different commandants. I was about to open my mouth to explain it to him, but he pulled out his pistol: "*Sprengen in der Luft!*" All right, all right, I said to humour him, but I haven't got the wherewithal. "*Sprengstoff*!" And he brings me a crate of explosives. He looks at his watch and tells me that in thirty minutes the whole "*verfluchte*", the whole "damned" bakery had to blow up. After which, sweating heavily, he went on supervising the fuelling of his vehicles from the full tankers. I didn't say anything. I ordered the two subalterns who were with me to take the crate of explosives and I went back to my bakery. And then I had a flash of inspiration. Almost a stroke of genius! Maybe the only genuine piece of inspiration I've ever had in all the years I've been a writer and journalist. Instead of giving the order for the explosives to be mounted under the trucks for "*sprengen in der Luft!*" I ordered the trucks to be drawn up in a closed circle and for the sacks of flour to be unloaded around them, thereby creating a rather original and expensive circular barricade. Sacks of flour in place of sandbags, can you imagine … I stationed my men inside the barricade. Bakers that we were, we had rather antiquated rifles, Mosin-Nagants, which were as long as a day of fasting, but if it came to it, you could shoot very well with them. The operation to prepare for battle, the only one I led during my time as a combatant, lasted exactly twenty-nine minutes. Once thirty minutes exactly had elapsed, the motorised column of the Waffen S.S. regiment passed. Herr Sturmführer jumped out of his vehicle and yelled: "*Hei, was ist los dort?* What are you doing there? Why hasn't the bakery blown up? *Sprengen! Sprengen!*" To this day I don't know where I found that magnificent calmness, but I calmly told my men that if he came anywhere near our circle of flour, we would give him a proper welcome … It seems the officer realised the situation, the rifle barrels silently poking out at him from between the sacks boded nothing good … So, he didn't come any nearer, but slaked his fury with a vulgar curse: "*Verfluchtete Schweinhunde!*" Damned pigs! Sons of bitches. And other similar things. He then quickly got back in his vehicle and the armoured column sped off. And a good job too, for him, since the artillery could be heard getting closer and closer in the rear. So, with the forty trucks intact, with the whole bakery and all the sacks of flour, I made my way back home. Then I went west, over the border, to the Tatra Mountains …'

Manutin sat motionless for a while. His round face now seemed more peaceful, his tension had eased.

'When the war was over and I came home, I had problems … Some remembered the *National Courier* and the fact that they wore a shirt of a certain colour there, but they didn't remember that I myself had never worn it ... You know, there are people who remember if you do something bad, but they always forget if you do something good, or at least the fact that you haven't done anything bad ... And then, by force of circumstance, you find yourself having to bring up the subject, which is very unpleasant ... I was forced to recall certain things, to make a speech in my own defence, *pro domo*, as it were, and that's how the fact that I saved the bakery during the war ended up saving me after the war. Things evened out for me, you might say! But I had to start all over again, and go into a new line of work. But what? What else did I know how to do? What was I in fact? In the village and here in my little home town, I was the famous writer and journalist from the capital, and in the capital, I was the country schoolteacher, the man from Poiana Mică. In reality, I had no roots anywhere, I was a failure. I couldn't go back to the village school. Imagine me, Stefan-Julius Manutin, returning to ask for a job as a village schoolteacher in Poiana Mică ... People would have laughed at such an outlandish notion, or else they would have wept ... In the capital, I was given an opportunity to write, some colleagues who'd known me asked me to contribute pieces, albeit without any great insistence, I tried to write something, my memories of the war, the episode with the bakery, but I realised it was no good ... I wasn't who they thought I was, or even who I myself thought I was ... I reread my old articles and literary compositions and I clearly saw that I'd never been who I thought I was ... But I couldn't tell anybody that. I didn't stay in the capital, nor did I return to the village where I'd been a schoolteacher, but I settled here instead, in my little home town, but I can't tell people that I'm not what they think I am ... And if I tried to tell them—the way I'm telling you now, young lady, colleague—they wouldn't believe me. They'd get upset, as if I were trying to snatch an idol away from their hearts, or in the best case, they would give an indulgent smile and say that I was modest, or bohemian, and they would admire me all the more … In the eyes of these fine upstanding provincial citizens, I am and will always remain the celebrated Stefan-Julius Manutin, an upstanding son of their town … I am esteemed and respected, and much is permitted me, and much is overlooked for my sake …'

Manutin lowered his voice and continued with a bitter smile:

'When, as quite often happens, I'm found lying in a ditch or by the side of the road, the citizens pick me up and discreetly carry me home … and nobody breathes a single word to anybody else … It's amazing, but my halo shines on, it hasn't faded in time, no matter what I might do … A tinfoil halo. It's nothing but a halo cut from tinfoil, but it shines … in their eyes, it shines like real gold, no matter what I might do … And do you know why? Because they need that halo … Do you understand what I'm saying? It was they who gave me to the Capital, the Country, the World, the Universe … And they don't want to take me back … Because they don't know what to do with me. And at my funeral, they'll say I was "a great soul, an enlightened spirit, a talented writer," and other such twaddle …'

The priest's black surplice rippled down his long thin body and his voice grew more and more solemn, more and more tremulous, as he continued his sermon:

'It is we, dearly beloved mourners, we who are called upon to interpret the words and the signs of the Lord, and in these moments of grief, let us find words of consolation to fit every occasion … If an old man dies, we rightly say that he at least knew the joys of a long life … If a young man dies, we rightly say that he did not live to know the sorrows and the sins of this earthly life. If a spotless young woman dies, we rightly say that she did not know the dreadful throes of childbirth. And if a mother of many children dies, we rightly say that she knew the throes of childbirth and leaves behind her good and worthy descendants … But what words of comfort can we find before this coffin in which lies the mortal frame of him who was Stefan-Julius Manutin? How are we to console ourselves for the loss of this dear Son of our town?'

The priest paused to take a deep breath and then raised his voice almost in triumph:

'But nonetheless, nonetheless, dearly beloved mourners, such words of comfort do exist … For truly I say unto you, if the Lord has now called him, if his mortal frame leaves us today, nonetheless his works remain among us, his thought, his wonderful writings, full of wisdom, talent, and grace …'

I gave a start.

All of a sudden, I thought I heard from inside the lacquered coffin, garnished with gold disks at the corners, the voice of the deceased, a voice slurred with drink:

'You see, you see, what did I tell you? Not even he, not even the priest has read a single word of what I wrote … Tell him I thank him kindly for his warm words, but nothing of what I wrote will remain … Because ultimately, I didn't write anything. Tell them all! Go on, tell them, as loudly as you can, if you have the courage to!'

And it seemed to me that he burst into cackling laughter.

But it was only the clods of soil tumbling into the deep grave, on top of the shiny black coffin adorned with the gold disks.

1970

The Blue Pebbles

The idea came to him when he was a child and used to play with the pebbles in the yard. The idea of collecting blue pebbles. Why blue? Not even he himself could have said why. It just came to him. Besides, what is certain is that nobody had yet thought of collecting blue pebbles.

And the idea never left him for the rest of his life. He went to school, he sat his baccalaureate, he graduated from university, he got a job as a clerk in a bank, then in a bakery, then at a barrel factory, and who knows where else, but he never forget about blue pebbles. He would walk with his head bowed—his whole life, he walked with his eyes to the ground—and wherever he spotted a pebble that showed the slightest hint of blue, he would bend down, pick it up, take it home. By the time he reached the age of sixty or so, he had amassed an impressive collection in the drawers of his old walnut sideboard. People would smile at this quirk, some would even secretly make signs to each other, as if to suggest he wasn't completely right in the head. But he didn't care. In his heart of hearts, he was sure he was doing something good, perhaps even something important. It would let people see how many hundreds and thousands of shades of blue a pebble might take. It was what he knew best, it was what he did, and it was what he would bequeath to the world. Nobody else had thought of doing such a thing. But anyway, what was it to them? What he did placed no demands on anybody else. All his life he had earned his daily bread by his own honest toil. So, why should anybody care what he did?

It went on like that until one fine day the rumour went around that a big expert on collecting was coming to town. That's what they said: a specialist, a world-renowned expert in all kinds of collections. No, he wasn't coming on an official visit—why would such a specialist come to such a small town?—he was only coming to visit a relative.

The old collector of blue pebbles gave a start on hearing the news. He didn't say anything to anybody, but in his own mind, he impatiently awaited the man's arrival. Now they would see which was right, whether he himself or those who openly laughed or secretly made signs.

And the specialist really did come. The old man invited him to his house. He opened the drawers one after the other. When he saw the collection, the expert was first astounded and then, with all the politeness of a well-bred man, he couldn't restrain his anger. A collection of 'blue pebbles'? Who had ever heard of such a thing? Stamps, yes! Napkins, matchboxes, cigarette boxes, pipes, badges ... But blue pebbles? And the renowned expert on collections became downright furious, he spoke of oddities, manias, amateurs barging in on the noble task of the collector. After which, he made hurried excuses and left.

The old man said nothing. He was left speechless, staring at the door that had closed behind the expert. But from that day forth, nobody saw him outside again, nobody spotted him picking up a pebble, wiping it and putting it in his pocket. And a few days later, the news went out. He had been found dead in his room. Nobody knew the cause of his death. Not even the doctors were able to establish it. Probably his heart.

As to the fate of the collection of blue pebbles, contradictory accounts circulated. It was said that a nephew of his inherited everything, including the sideboard with the ten drawers full of blue pebbles. That nephew happened to be a geology student and set about studying the blue pebbles and it was said that he even wrote a doctoral thesis on the subject. But according to some, the opposite happened. The young man was not a student and had nothing to do with geology or any related science. He took away the sideboard, which was an antique piece of furniture and quite valuable, threw away the pebbles, and laid out his nylon shirts in the drawers …

1970

A Funeral and its Strange Consequences

Marcu Waxman was a good man, a quiet man, a hardworking, colourless man. Nobody spoke either good or ill of him, nobody talked behind his back, nobody gossiped about him, he never quarrelled with anybody and it was utterly inconceivable that anybody else would ever have quarrelled on his account. But a man can never know what is in store for him in life, or after he dies, as will become plain from the strange events recounted in the following.

Marcu Waxman was neither tall nor short, neither thin nor fat, neither blond nor brown-haired. He had a nondescript face, somewhere between the round and the oval, of indefinite hue, and he had no distinguishing marks.

Marcu Waxman was a weaver and his whole life he worked at the same fabrics factory. He never took a day off because he was sick or for any other reason. One spring day, however, not feeling very well, he said to himself, 'I'll go to see the doctor and ask for three days off.' He couldn't really tell what was wrong with him, only that he didn't feel well. He went to the doctor. As was only natural, the doctor asked him what the trouble was, what kind of pains he had and where, but Marcu Waxman didn't really know, because when the doctor asked him, he didn't feel any actual pain. The doctor smiled, gave him a friendly pat on the shoulder, and sent him back to work. Marcu Waxman worked another three days and then died. Suddenly.

And so happened that he was dead, and they made preparations for his funeral, as they would for any other Jew. In the end, for all the sins big and small that a man commits in a lifetime, Marcu Waxman was a good Jew, a quiet, hardworking man, of whom nobody ever spoke ill or good, who never quarrelled with anybody and on whose account nobody else had ever quarrelled. The Chevra Kadisha, or funeral association, which in that little town consisted of a chairman, a secretary, and four occasional gravediggers, therefore designated a place for him in the Jewish cemetery, a plot measuring around one by two metres, the same as for any other person, be they tall or short, be they quiet or quarrelsome, be they blond or brown-haired, et cetera. The Chevra found a good spot for him, because there were few Jews left in that little town, so there were places aplenty in the cemetery, where you could lie comfortably, with all the room needed, for all eternity. They sent for the woman to wash the deceased and notified the rabbi, who in that little town, for well-grounded reasons of economy, was also the judge, the *dayan*, the *chacham*, and the cantor, all rolled into one. And it was in his capacity as cantor that the rabbi set about clearing his throat with soft-boiled eggs, to perform a nice '*kel mule rachamim*.' They also cut three planks to measure. Nor did the fabrics factory where he had worked his whole life sit idly: the management and workforce insisted on donating a few metres of the finest-quality white cloth, the kind used to wrap the body of the deceased, be he thin or fat, big or small, quiet or quarrelsome, since on the other side, nobody asks you what you did or what you were like or what you had on this side.

Everything went swimmingly until the next day, which was when the funeral was meant to take place. It was then that something strange happened. Ilonka Waxman, née Sarvari, didn't want to hand over the body of the deceased. It so happened that having been beside herself grieving for a whole day and night, Ilonka began to think of herself. Through her tears, but very determinedly, she declared that she did not want to be parted from her husband. Which is to say, she did know she would have to be parted from her husband for a time, but when her own time came, ten, twenty, thirty years later, or however long it might be, she wanted to be laid to rest beside him. In which case, why put him in the Jewish cemetery at one end of town when she would be in the Christian cemetery at the opposite end? Let her Marcu be buried in the Roman Catholic cemetery, where she herself would be laid to rest, where their children would also be buried, next to their father and mother. Ilonka Waxman was thinking of her children's future.

All the arguments brought to bear by the one side and the other, which is to say, on behalf of the Christian parish and on behalf of the Jewish community, to the effect that he wasn't a Christian, that ultimately he was a Jew; that husband and wife would be separated only in this world, not in the next; that on the other side, in heaven, they would probably meet and be able to live together, because nobody had heard of a separate Christian and Jewish heaven, and even if there were such a thing, the souls of the departed would still be able to visit each other at will, and so on and so forth. All these arguments and others similarly strong were of no avail: the wife faithful even until after death was dead set on being laid to eternal rest next to her husband and that was that! And so it came to pass that Marcu Waxman found himself buried in that little town's Christian cemetery.

Marcu Waxman's funeral was the same as his life: neither beautiful nor ugly, neither warm nor cold, neither sad nor merry, neither Jewish nor Christian. The community's rabbi, who was also at the same time its *chacham* and *dayan* and cantor, was unable to come to the Christian cemetery to intone a '*kel mule rachamim*', and the parish priest was unable to chant a 'Lord have mercy' in his own cemetery because the deceased had been born into the Mosaic faith, and his religion at the time of his death was doubtful to say the least. So, Marcu Waxman was buried amid the exhausted weeping of his wife, the sobbing of his children, the sighing of his relatives, and the tootling of the brass band from the factory where he had worked all his life, a brass band made up of seven doughty blowers, four of whom were unable to attend, however: one because that particular grey, sunless, rainless day his wife was giving birth in hospital and he was anxiously waiting in the adjoining room to see whether it would be a boy or a girl, the second because he was suffering a slight bout of flu, the third because he was a Cohenite Jew and wasn't allowed even to enter the Jewish cemetery, let alone a Roman Catholic one, and the fourth for reasons unknown to this day—he probably thought all the others would be there and that he wouldn't be missed, since he played third trumpet and only had to toot a single note every ten beats. The three that did turn up, honked a *marche funèbre* from the bottom of their lungs, which in places sounded more like a rather lively polka.

Before they lowered him into the grave, one of his fellow workers, a copyist from the personnel department, a tall, skinny, bald man, gave a short speech in a quavering voice, commencing with some general philosophical remarks, to the following effect: What is man? Man is nothing, a zero, his life is as fleeting as a butterfly's—who knows where he came up with that comparison—but despite all this, a man is a Man!

After which he passed on to matters more specific, saying that Marcu Waxman was a good man, a quiet man, a hardworking man, a conscientious worker, and that his fellow workers would never, ever forget him, that they would eternally cherish his memory, which was an exaggeration to say the least, since the next day none of them thought of him ever again.

Buried and forgotten, as the old adage goes. And, true, after the funeral there were a few days' peace. But it would seem that this time, the peace was only on the surface. Beneath it something must have been smouldering, like embers beneath the ashes. For something strange happened. Marcu Waxman, who all his life had been an honest, peaceful man, who never quarrelled with anybody and with whom it was absolutely inconceivable that anybody else should pick a quarrel, became the subject post mortem of heated discussions and fierce quarrels. A few days after the burial, it was as if people regained consciousness after a blow to the head, they recovered their wits, grew agitated, started asking in various tones of voice: What happened? How did it happen? How was such a thing possible?

'A Marcu Waxman in our strictly Christian cemetery?' some wondered.

'What business does a Marcu Waxman have in their cemetery?' others fumed.

'How could the parish priest allow it?'

'He was probably afraid lest people think him an anti-Semite …'

'How could the rabbi allow it?'

'Who said he allowed it? But does anybody listen to him? As much as they'd listen to the cat …'

This was the kind of talk heard on street corners, in the town's only bar, in its two cafés, at Saturday- and Sunday-evening card games, at home *en famille*.

Particularly worked up and depressed and preoccupied were those who somehow had a direct stake in the whole strange affair, namely those who had wives as religious and as loving as Ilonka Waxman, née Sharvari. To tell the truth, up till then they had lived peacefully in one respect, but otherwise they still fretted about what tomorrow might bring, the same as everybody else, maybe they also sometimes used to think about the inevitability of death, the same as everybody else, but they didn't think about what would become of them after they died. And now, out of the blue, they had that to worry about on top of everything else. One of them, Beeri Balmoush, a bookkeeper by profession, employed at the same fabrics factory, a mountain of a man, angrily went to the chairman of the Chevra Kadisha to take him to task and, if need be, even to pull his wispy red beard.

'How did it happen, Mr Chaim Chaimovitch?'

'You know as well as I do,' replied the chairman of the funeral association.

'But why did you allow it? What kind of association are you running here? Why did we elect you chairman? Why do you take receipt of our dues?'

The chairman was just about to answer back that Beeri Balmoush hadn't even voted in the election and that since he got married he hadn't paid a single penny in dues to the community, but seeing him scarlet with fury, he deemed it wiser to hold his tongue.

'And what have you got a mind to do with us?' yelled Beeri Balmoush, finally voicing what pained him the most.

'How should I know?' answered the Chevra chairman, evasively.

'Who the hell else should know if not you! The next thing you know, it'll be me, too ...'

'Then I think that it is something you will have to deal with yourself,' said the chairman, scratching his wispy red beard.

'Deal with it how?'

'How should I know? Maybe you ought to have a talk with your lady wife, maybe you should come to a mutual understanding …'

'A mutual understanding you say! You want me to start quarrelling about it with her already? I still have time!'

'You have time?'

'I still have time after …' Realising his mistake, he went on: 'I mean, before I pass to the other world …'

'I beg your pardon, but how do you know when you'll decide to pass … What if you leave here and get run over by a car? What if a brick falls on your head?' asked the chairman, with all the delicacy of which he was capable.

Beeri Balmoush glared at him. He wanted to make some retort, to tell him just where to go, but not finding the right word, he stormed out, slamming the door behind him.

The general agitation steadily grew, so that at the synagogue and the ritual bath, at the bar and two cafés, and on street corners, folk started to talk about making changes. The angrier ones whistled through their teeth about how the whole leadership of the Community and the Chevra Kadisha needed replacing, and why not also the leadership of the Talmud Torah Association and the Bikur Holim Society? Others said that the chairman of the Chevra Kadisha needed to be replaced, or the Community secretary at the very least. In the end, they replaced the *shamesh*, or synagogue usher, not even he knew why, since he had had nothing whatsoever to do with the whole affair.

And on the other side, they replaced the watchman of the Roman Catholic cemetery, even though his responsibility was to guard the dead, not to forbid the living to bury their dead, whoever they might be.

After which spirits gradually began to calm.

But not the spirit of Meshulem Huberman.

Meshulem was a commercial traveller who had dealt in men's braces and women's garter belts, now retired. According to his wife, her Meshulem had retired early because he used to take everything too much to heart. That fat, sweaty, jovial man, always eager to lend a hand and to help anybody solve any problem, was now more agitated than she had ever seen him. 'I'm afraid he's going to have a stroke, God forbid!' said his wife to whoever would listen. And Meshulem Huberman was agitated not because any of it affected him in the slightest, quite the contrary: his wife Reiza went to the ritual bath once a month, every Friday evening she lit the Sabbath candles, the whole Sabbath afternoon she read the *Tzeena Ureena*, and at the close of the Sabbath she would piously say, '*Got fun Avruhum.*' She was what you would call a real *chulunt jidene*, and she would never have dreamed of burying her husband in any Christian cemetery, the Lord forbid. Meshulem Huberman was unable to sleep at night because a 'problem' had arisen and he knew that it was a great *mitzva* to solve the community's problems. Our wise men, blessed be their memory, had said it many times, and it was written in many places—Meshulem didn't really know which of the wise men had said it or where it was written, but that was of no importance. The fact was that wherever and whenever a 'problem', a 'community issue,' arose, then Meshulem also put in an appearance.

And so it was that he put in an appearance at the office of the Holy Funeral Association. He sank down in the old armchair in front of the chairman's desk, breathing heavily due to his haste in coming there. He mopped the abundant perspiration from his brow and neck with a large blue handkerchief and declared to the chairman in a voice that brooked no dissent:

'We must solve the problem!'

'Solve it how?'

'I say we should post a notice in the synagogue: "All those interested in making a statement as to where they wish to be buried, a hundred years from now, God willing …"'

'But you know very well, Meshulem, that all those interested don't come to the synagogue too often,' replied Chaim Chaimovitch, the chairman of the Chevra, scratching his wispy red beard.

'You're right! Then let's post a notice in town.'

'In town? Well … It's a delicate matter, you understand, a notice posted in town, even if only on the Jewish lane, will be read by passers-by … By all kinds of people, great care would need to be taken over the wording …'

'Humph,' muttered Meshulem, mopping the sweat from his nape once more.

And from that instant, he started to work himself up, composing in his head all kinds of wordings for the notice. Twice a day, he would turn up with suggestions for the notice:

'How about this, Mr Chaimovitch, how about we say: "Notice. Those interested in reserving a good spot in the Jewish cemetery should report to the office of the Chevra Kadisha between such-and-such a time daily."'

'Again with the "those interested"? Don't you understand, it's a delicate matter …'

'Then let's say "everybody" … "Let everybody come to reserve a place in advance …"'

'Why, *plitsim*, let everybody come? What, there's not enough room? What, we should close down the cemetery?' said the chairman, getting annoyed.

'Didn't you just say that we shouldn't say "those interested"? With you, Mr Chaimovitch, a man can't do right for doing wrong ...'

So, they weren't able to agree on the notice and given the 'delicate' nature of the 'problem,' it was left for them to speak to each of 'those interested' individually. Not directly, of course, but in a roundabout, tactful way, whenever they happened to bump into them.

Meshulem Huberman was in luck. No sooner had he left the chairman's office than he bumped into Mrs Esther Arpan on the street. Her maiden name was Jacobsohn, and her husband, Andrei Arpan, was a clerk at the town hall, a man as wholesome as fresh bread.

On spotting her, Meshulem greeted her with a broad smile:

'How are you, Mrs Arpan? How is your health?'

The lady looked at him in surprise. Meshulem had never accosted her on the street before, but she politely replied:

'Well, thank you!'

This answer disappointed Meshulem. If she had started complaining about a headache, or the grippe, or anything else, it would have been easier for him to bring up the cemetery. Nevertheless, he further tactfully enquired:

'Were your grandmother, may she rest in peace, to call you to join her tomorrow or the day after, where would you wish to be buried?'

Mrs Esther Arpan, née Jacobsohn, abruptly turned pale, she looked at him in confusion for a few moments, then let out a scream and fell to the ground in a faint.

An ambulance took her to the hospital for nervous disorders. The doctor asked her the reason for the shock she had suffered, she told him that just the night before she had dreamed of her grandmother, who in the dream was waving for her to come and join her. The doctor laughed heartily and said that such coincidences were known to happen.

Mrs Arpan was released from hospital about two weeks later, completely cured, but was left with an aversion towards Meshulem Huberman: whenever she saw him, she would cross to the other side of the street.

And that was all.

In time, spirits in that little town calmed completely and today nobody talks about the occurrence any more.

And as for the 'problem', it remained unsolved. At least so thought Meshulem Huberman, because in his zeal he did not notice that only on the surface are there all kinds of fences and plots and cemeteries with all kinds of gravestones with names and symbols on them, whereas underneath the earth is one and the same.

The same earth for everybody.

1974

The Angel with the Briefcase

Jonah Puterfett was a clerk, a short man, hard-working, honest, depressed. A man who couldn't get to sleep without sleeping pills.

The depression, weariness, bitterness that had laid hold of him lately were not because of any troubles or tensions at work: at the office he was esteemed by his superiors and loved by his colleagues. Nor was it because of troubles in the family: his wife was full of understanding and his three little girls were well-behaved. Rather, he was quite simply depressed because of the 'situation'. Meaning the 'situation' in general.

Everywhere he went he came into contact with the 'situation': on the radio, on the television, among the snatches of speech he caught on the street, in the sighs and the sour remarks he overheard at the office. Everywhere, you could sense 'the situation in which we find ourselves'. He would come home from work with the firm intention of getting some rest, quickly eat his meal, place a glass of water and a sleeping pill on the bedside table: a tablet strong enough to knock out an elephant. He would fling himself on the bed and start to flick through the newspaper.

On the front page, in large letters, a sensational case of embezzlement involving a director - fifty million three thousand.

Jonah Puterfett was particularly annoyed at this three thousand: You embezzle fifty million, so what do you need with the paltry three thousand? Then, on the centre pages, the statements of ministers with and without portfolio, the comments of a general in the reserve, who sought to convince him, to convince Jonah Puterfett, that the existence of an army was absolutely imperative because we are surrounded by enemies. On page seven, a learned economist sought to assure him, to assure Jonah Puterfett, that the economic situation was precarious and that in the coming year they had better reduce the standard of living by three percentage points. Jonah Puterfett couldn't really understand how such a thing would be possible: Should they shake some of the sugar off their spoons before they stirred it in their tea? Should they put fewer tea leaves in the teapot? On the last page of the newspaper, two murders committed by juvenile delinquents, a break-in, young drug addicts, young homeless people, five traffic accidents. That's what the 'situation' looked like. And you try to go to sleep without taking sleeping pills! What was the country coming to?

'What do you expect from this country? What has it done to you? Why do you blame it for every ill?' a gentle scolding voice suddenly said.

Jonah looked up from his newspaper in surprise and saw an angel. Yes, before him stood an angel, just like in one of those naïve paintings: a translucent white apparition with wings.

'What nonsense is this?' said Puterfett to himself, rubbing his eyes and pinching his cheeks. 'It's ridiculous. There aren't any angels nowadays. And if there were, they would hardly turn up out of the blue to visit us mere mortals.'

Despite these highly logical, these highly lucid and rational arguments, the white Apparition with the wings refused to vanish. It even opened its mouth to speak, politely introducing itself, like a genuine man of the world.

'I am the angel Nachmiel. You won't know me, because I'm not one of the more famous angels, like Raphael, for example, or Michael, or Gabriel …' His voice betrayed a slight note of envy. Or maybe it just seemed that way to Jonah Puterfett, because he was in the habit of thinking in human rather than angelic terms.

Looking at him more closely, Jonah noticed to his amazement that that angel, Nachmiel by name, did not hold an olive branch, the symbol of peace, or a flaming sword, the symbol of heavenly wrath, but rather a briefcase. A briefcase like any other briefcase, stuffed to bursting point with documents.

'Heavens! You've gone all bureaucratic!' exclaimed Jonah Puterfett in his own mind, the poor man being so accustomed to thinking in purely earthly terms.

Without letting himself be bothered by his interlocutor's worldly thoughts, which, in his capacity as angelic being, he had of course overheard, even if they had remained unuttered, he sat down at the table and said:

'I'm here on behalf of the Heavenly Passive Statistics Department.' And from his briefcase he took a thick sheaf of folded pieces of paper, of the computer printout kind.

'The Passive Statistics Department?' asked Jonah in amazement.

'Yes, it's a department run by the Angel Refuel, my boss, as you would refer to him'—and here the Angel Nachmiel gave a meaningful wink—'you down here on earth, compile active statistics: How many people did a certain thing and how many times did they do it? How many break-ins, how many cases of embezzlement, how many murders, how many traffic accidents, and so on. We up on high gather statistics on how many things weren't done and how many people didn't do them … am I making myself clear?'

The angel started leafing through the pieces of paper.

'Here for example, out of the country's three million inhabitants, two million nine hundred thousand nine thousand two hundred and seventy-three people didn't commit embezzlement, or fraud, or serious tax evasion, or a break-in, the same number didn't make a stupid and inopportune political statement ...'

The angel now turned to Jonah Puterfett:

'Have you ever committed a break-in?'

'God forbid!'

'Fraud?'

'My word! How can you even ask such a thing?' he said, placing his hand over his open mouth, deeply offended.

'What about your fellow office worker Chaim Schatzman?'

'He neither!'

What about Nissim Nissim, the cashier?'

'I'd swear on my life he never has!'

'There, you see? Why don't you look around you?' said the Angel Nachmiel in annoyance. Or maybe it only appeared to Jonah that he was annoyed, accustomed as he was to such earthly concepts.

The angel continued to leaf through the pages of the printout from the heavenly computer:

'Here we have the section on children and young people. Out of three million inhabitants, one million a hundred thousand are children and young people, and of those, one million ninety-nine thousand behave respectably, they obey their parents—'

'Well, that I don't believe!' blurted Jonah Puterfett.

'Be patient and hear out the rest,' the Angel Nachmiel scolded him. 'They obey their parents to the same extent as their parents obeyed their own parents ...'

The angel turned to Jonah:

'When you were young, did you always do everything your parents told you to do? Did you follow their advice? Did you do everything they asked of you? Did they never have to scold you?'

Jonah was silent. The angel continued to leaf through the pages:

'Seven hundred and eighty thousand children and young people do not drop out of school or university ... Seven hundred and seventy thousand do not receive bad marks ... Six hundred and ninety thousand do not fight in the breaks between lessons ... One million ninety-nine thousand do not play truant or break their neighbours' windows ... One million ninety-nine thousand nine hundred do not commit crimes or take drugs ... One million nine hundred and ninety thousand nine hundred and ninety-nine ...'

The figures filled the air with their warm, soporific, monotonous drone. Jonah Puterfett fell softly asleep, with a serene smile on his face.

On the bedside table the glass of water and sleeping tablets remained untouched.

1976

The King's Fool

The king's fool was floating in Heaven, among the angels and the pure souls, and he felt at peace. After all, there was neither justice nor injustice there, neither good nor evil, neither delicacy nor crassness, and as a result he didn't have to play the fool, there was no need for him to conjure up all kinds of spirits and perform all kinds of somersaults.

The jester was floating there, nothing but a soul, in the company of other spotless souls and white angels, in heaven's expanse, which was without beginning or end, and he felt happy. Happy in a manner of speaking, since as is well known, there is neither happiness nor unhappiness there. Be that as it may, he felt in his element. A long time passed in this way, a timeless time, until one fine moment—it wouldn't be possible to say one fine day, since as is well known, there is neither day nor night there—the fool felt something alien insidiously enter his soul. Something strange, wholly worldly, and resembling desire. Yes, it was as if he became nostalgic for the Earth. Whence such a sensation in a place where there was neither feeling or non-feeling? How did it find its way into his pure, translucent soul? Nobody knows and nobody would be able to explain it. After all, there are so many inexplicable things in the other world.

The fact is, he felt an insane longing to see once more the world in which he had lived. And above all else, he was burning with curiosity to meet the king's jesters who had succeeded him, to see how the profession had progressed, to hear what madcap, meaningful speeches they reeled off, what acrobatics they performed.

When he told the angel of the fools, who looked after him in heaven, that he longed to see the Earth again, the angel was not at all surprised—presumably surprise doesn't exist in Heaven, either—but rather he gave him a little push and the king's fool started to float downwards or upwards—since it would seem that neither up nor down exist in those endless outer spaces—and thus did the fool set off towards the earthly globe.

As he approached the Earth, he began to coagulate, as it were, he developed a skeleton of white bones, filled with all kinds of organs, over which were stretched thin layers of flesh, crisscrossed by veins, capillaries and nerve filaments, all of which was wrapped in skin. By the time he reached the Earth he had once more become the little man he was hundreds of years before, with his puny, child-like body, his wrinkled face, like an old man's, and his beady eyes, glittering with intelligence.

And the jester set off in his bright motley garb, half red, half green, shod in slippers whose points curled upwards like chili peppers. He went merrily on his way, hopping and singing, along the dusty country road, and he walked and he walked until he came to an inn by the wayside.

He went inside to regale himself. He sat down at the corner of a long table in the dining room and asked the innkeeper for a roast chicken and a glass of wine. It had been hundreds of years since he last ate chicken or drank wine. And he was eager to taste them again. The innkeeper, like every other innkeeper in the world, with his shirtsleeves rolled up and wearing an apron of dubious cleanliness, brought him his order. The fool smacked his lips in delight. 'Mm, nothing has changed, the taste of the roast chicken and the wine is the same as before,' he said to himself, wiping his mouth in satisfaction at the world being as well-organised as he had left it.

At the same long table in the inn's dining room there sat another man with a bowl of potato soup in front of him. He was neither short nor tall, neither fat nor thin, and had a nondescript face, with two inexpressive eyes, a nose, two ears, a mouth, and so on, in short, a citizen like any other citizen.

Impelled by curiosity, the fool struck up a conversation:

'What is new in these parts?'

'Nothing new, thank you for asking,' replied the nondescript citizen in a colourless, indifferent voice, without looking up from his potato soup.

'And how does His Majesty the King comport himself?' the fool further enquired.

The man gave a start. He looked up and regarded him for a long, suspicious moment. But on seeing what he looked like, with his puny, child-like body, his face as wrinkled as an old man's, got up in his bright red and green outfit, looking as if he were from a different world, the citizen burst out laughing and answered:

'We haven't had a king for a long time!'

'Then what do you have instead?' asked the fool in amazement.

'We have a president.'

'Then how is His Majesty your President? Good? Bad?'

'Good or bad? He's the same as every other president …' Then, after casting a suspicious glance all around and assuring himself that nobody could overhear, he added, 'And his lordship thinks that if he eats his fill, then the whole nation is full …'

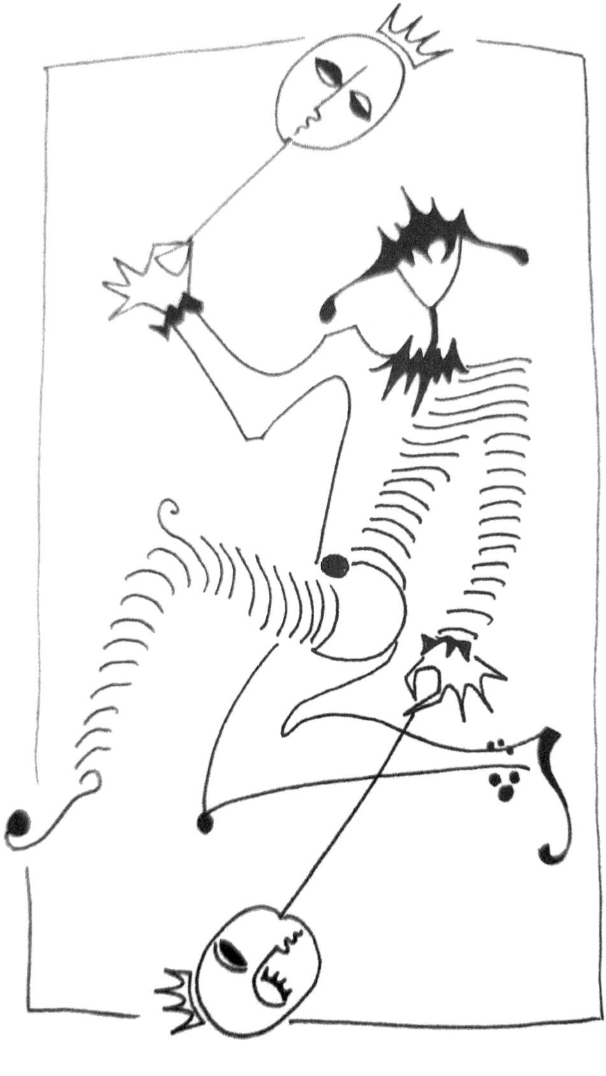

'But what does his fool tell him?' asked the fool, intrigued.

'His fool? What are you talking about?' asked the citizen, in astonishment at the question.

'What do you mean? The president's fool, his jester ...'

The citizen laughed at this in great amusement:

'Our president doesn't have a fool!'

The king's fool stared at him, wide-eyed in fright:

'What, he doesn't have a fool? But that's terrible ... How can he govern without a fool? Who is there to tell him the truth, honestly and without fear or bias? Look, I myself, as you see me here, once told the king: "Majesty, you think you're God Almighty because your ministers and courtiers have stuffed your head about how you're divinely appointed, about how you're the greatest, about how you're the wisest, about how every syllable that your mouth utters is the purest wisdom ... Whatever nonsense you come out with, they gasp with admiration and say: 'How great is our sovereign!' And you, Majesty, have started believing it all, because you're all puffed up with pride and you've lost your wits ... You think yourself divinely appointed, when in actual fact you're just like anybody else. You eat the same as all those who have something to eat and you're oblivious to those who don't have anything to eat ... And when you go to that place where even a king must needs sit at squat, you smell just the same as the lowliest peasant in your kingdom ..." I told him all that and I laughed in his face. I split my sides. And my laughter couldn't have been more genuine. You should have seen the poses he struck, as if he were master of the universe, no less! He'd become insufferable ...'

The citizen's hair stood on end at that:

'And what did the king do?'

'Oho-ho! He flew into a rage and gave me a hard kick up the backside. What else could he do? After all, I was the fool, I was his fool ... His Majesty's Fool! And the next day, the king ordered the barns to be thrown open and for bread to be distributed among the people … And as for me, he gave me a brand-new pair of green silk trousers, with yellow stripes, trousers so beautiful they took your breath away … But wait for the surprise: inside the trousers, in the seat, was sewn a small cushion …'

And in his reedy, strident voice, the fool chortled at the memory. But the citizen saw nothing funny:

'In our country, nobody would be so foolish as to be a fool like that … If a fool were to talk like that to our president, he wouldn't get a pair of silk trousers with a cushion in the rump, but in the best case he would be thrown in the madhouse…'

'What? A fool in the madhouse?' exclaimed the jester in astonishment. 'What a waste! What stupidity! Doesn't your president have a sense of humour?'

'No, he doesn't. He has less humour even than the dirt under his nails … Around here, humour is pure madness …'

The citizen, as nondescript as every other citizen, paused before continuing darkly:

'In the best case, the president would put him in the madhouse … Because in the worst case, he would put him in prison and never let him see the light of day again.'

Hearing this, the king's fool looked around in fright, quickly paid the innkeeper for his meal, and went on his way.

And the fool, with his puny child-like body, his wise face as wrinkled as an old man's, got up in his brightly coloured outfit, half red, half green, with his pointy slippers that curled like chili peppers, went on his way down the dusty country road, and he walked and he walked for who knows how long, until he reached another inn, at the edge of a large town.

The inn resembled the first. And the innkeeper resembled the first: the same apron of dubious cleanliness, the same shirt with the rolled-up sleeves, the same obliging expression. At a table sat a citizen who resembled the first as closely as two drops of water: the same nondescript face, the same inexpressive eyes, a face consisting of a nose, a mouth, two ears, and so on, in short, a nondescript citizen the same as every other citizen, and before him a bowl of potato soup or perhaps bean soup.

'What a small world!' the king's fool said to himself, who had experienced the boundlessness of heaven, 'how small is this world of men!' And again, he ordered a roast chicken and a glass of wine, his favourite meal there on Earth.

Gnawing a bone and sipping his wine, he again felt a yearning to meet a living fool of the present day, in the flesh and bone, to see him, hear him, to find out how he lived, what jokes he told, what meaningful antics he performed.

In a roundabout way, he tried to engage the citizen in conversation:

'What is new around these parts?'

'Nothing new, thanks for asking,' replied the citizen in a colourless way, without looking up from his bowl.

'What is His Majesty the King like? Good, bad?'

The man looked up from his bowl and on seeing the jester, as small and puny as a child, with his large head furrowed with wrinkles like an old man's, dressed in his bright red and green motley, he burst out laughing.

'Our king? We don't have a king, we have a president.'

'And how does your president treat you?'

'The same as every other president,' replied the citizen, shrugging his shoulders. 'He thinks everything he does is good … And that what is good for him is necessarily good for everybody else.'

'But what does his fool do? What does he tell him?'

'His fool?' laughed the nondescript citizen. 'I've never heard of such a position. The president has ministers, he has advisers big and small, but he doesn't have a fool.'

The jester looked at him in commiseration:

'Then who is there to tell him the honest truth? Who is there to tell him everything he thinks about him?'

'For that we need no fool … Here, anyone can tell the president anything,' said the citizen, his chest swelling with pride.

'And do they tell him?'

'Oho-ho! You should hear how they tell him!' laughed the citizen. 'You see, here we have an opposition. They tell him if he does anything bad. They're never remiss!'

'And if he does something good?'

'Then the opposition still tell him he did something bad, or else that he ought to have done it better …'

'Interesting!' said the king's fool. 'But who pays this opposition? The president, of course!'

The citizen burst out laughing:

'What? The president should pay the opposition? It's the opposition who want to take his place, to make their head the president, understand?'

'Then why should he believe them if they want to replace him?' asked the fool in angry disappointment. 'You see, the king used to pay me generously to tell him the truth, I would eat at his table, he would have clothes made for me from the same silk as his robes, I lived in his palace. He knew that I would never take his place and he believed what I said. When I told him something unpleasant, he could be furious, but he believed me … He had no reason to doubt me … He doubted his flattering courtiers, his servile ministers. He could never know what lurked inside them … He even doubted his closest relatives … Who would have told him the truth about him? The honest truth? If his father told him, it might have been out of senility, if his brother told him, it might have been out of envy, if his wife, the queen, told him, it might have been out of jealousy, if his son told him, it might have been out of impertinence ... But he never had reason to doubt his fool, whom he himself paid.'

The fool called the innkeeper. He paid for his meal and once again set off down the road. All of a sudden, he stopped. Where should he go? What should he seek there on earth? He was sick of it all.

Before he could even express the desire in his mind, he felt a nudge, which obviously came from the angel of the fools, and found himself floating upwards or downwards in the boundless immensity.

As he floated, he shed his bright motley, half red, half green, his pointy slippers that curled like chili peppers, and his uncomfortable integument of flesh and skin, the bones of his skeleton dissolved, and he remained nothing but spirit.

And once again, he floated in the boundlessness of heaven among the angels and the pure souls and he felt happy, which is to say, in his element.

And he never felt a yearning for earth again.

1976

The No-Deadline Suicide

It was a beautiful day, one of those days so painstakingly described in novels, a day caressed by a warm sun, a day of white clouds as fluffy as sheep gambolling across the azure sky, a day of green meadows and paths of yellow sand, a day of flowers and leaves and songbirds and so on and so forth, and that fine day, Adam Adami, a middle-aged man, stooped, red-headed, pale-blue eyes, otherwise a very quiet man, a very mild, unassuming man, who in all his life had never joined a political party, be it left, right or centre, or even any association for or against anything, such as a society for the protection of animals or an association to ban smoking, although that's neither here nor there, so anyway, that fine day, Adam Adami sat down on a park bench in the centre of town and was all of a sudden struck by the irrevocable fact that his entire life theretofore, amounting to a total of forty-seven years, had not been worth living. And having come to this conclusion, albeit only in his own mind, a decision followed hard on its heels, as logically as A follows B:

'I'm going to commit suicide!'

Truth to tell, nothing was going well for Adam Adami. He'd never won the lottery, he didn't have any success with women, he didn't find any pleasure in hard liquor, smoking, or playing cards, he didn't take hashish, he wasn't climbing the ladder at work, and to top it all, everybody kept annoying him with all kinds of stupid questions he couldn't answer.

At the office of the import-export company where he worked, the boss would niggle him: 'Why did you put this document in file 7787 and not file 8878?' At home, his wife would exasperate him: 'Why did you come home so late?' or 'Why did you come home so early? They haven't given you the sack, have they?' It didn't matter what time he came home, it was never the right time. Or 'Why did you buy apples?' Or 'Why didn't you buy apples?' Whatever he did, it was never the right thing. And his only son, who had just turned seventeen, whenever Adam Adami pointed something out to him or imparted precious advice, his only son would invariably reply with the same irritated question: 'Why don't you leave me be, Dad?'

Worse still was that in his moments of respite when other people weren't asking him questions, Adam Adami would ask himself questions: 'Why can't people get along? Why do they lie to each other, deceive each other, hold each other in contempt, envy each other? When they can get away with it, why do some act all high and mighty, why do they lord it over others, whom they deem beneath them, and trample them underfoot like worms rather than treat them like human beings supposedly created in the image and likeness of the Lord Above? And why do people make war and kill each other? And he would carry on in that vein, asking banal, clichéd, childish, unanswerable questions, but which tortured and pained him personally. Sometimes he would even be filled with fury. War, what idiocy! What stupidity! How can grown men take up arms and make war? What blind force drives them to it? And here Adam Adami would set about making naïve calculations: one of those huge, clever fighter planes, the ones with the electronic brains, which sow so much death on a single bombing run, costs let's say so many millions, and using that money they could manufacture this many extra motorcars. Now, by making a simple calculation, on paper, in black and white, of how many warplanes there were in the world and how many cars could be manufactured instead of them, and then totting up the population of the world, including all the Papuans and Patagonians and subtracting the old people who didn't want a car and the children who couldn't have one yet, you came to the astonishing result that all the people in the world, including him, Adam Adami, could have their own car parked outside the entrance to their building. Or even their own building ... Because if you extended the calculation and added all the other money spent on tanks, warships, submarines, uniforms, epaulettes, officers, cooks, maintenance and so on, the black-and-white result was that every family in the world could have their own house and garden ... The dream of every humble clerk: a house with a garden around it, a few fruit trees in front, a few beds of onions, radishes, tomatoes at the back ...

But in addition to the gigantic, apocalyptic pains of the world, which he felt personally, as if they were his own, Adam Adami was also secretly tortured by a number of difficult, personal 'philosophical' questions, not only impossible to answer, but also impossible to endure. Or else the answers to them were so simple as to be unbelievable ... And so, his inner tension swelled to bursting point ... 'What purpose do I have in this world?' he would ask himself. 'Why was I born? Just so I could shuffle pieces of paper back and forth in an import-export company? Was it worth being born just for that? Was it worth my consuming so many slices of bread and so many cups of black coffee, which the peasants of Europe and South America and the devil knows where else toil and sweat to produce, just so I could shuffle stupid bits of paper back and forth?'

Adam Adami felt that he was capable of something else in life, capable of much more … But he didn't know what …

But what happened that beautiful day, a day straight out of a novel, with its warm sun and fluffy white clouds in an azure sky and all the rest, came as the last straw. Like any other man of flesh and blood, endowed with thought and sensation, Adam Adami too had an ambition, a powerful, natural, and innocent desire: to get ahead at work, in other words, to be promoted to deputy head of department. In any case, it must be wonderful to be deputy head. For a start, you had a good salary and you could eat better and dress better … And then there was the respect! The respect above all else … The honour! The unwashed rabble no longer walked past you without so much as a second glance. On the contrary, even the washed raised their hats to you then, and neglecting the 'deputy head' part they greeted you with a 'Morning, boss!' or 'My respects, boss!' and so on. And at work you no longer sat in a room crammed with seven desks all but pressed up against each other, you no longer had to listen to the insipid stories and off-colour wisecracks of your colleagues, but had a desk of your own in your own little room separated by a glass partition from the lowlier clerks. And once you got a deputy head of department's desk, the secretary also discreetly handed you the key to that locked toilet … For at the import-export company where Adam Adami worked, the same as at any other self-respecting establishment, there were two lavatories, one for the lowly clerks, and another, secured with a Yale lock, for the bosses. In the depths of his soul, Adami burned with a desire to be able to use that toilet cubicle, which he pictured as immaculately white, a place where if need be you could sit quietly, leafing through the newspaper, where you could let your thoughts roam free … But there you have it, you can't stop people nurturing all kinds of wishes, of both the open and the secret variety …

Adam Adami therefore burned with the desire to become a deputy head and according to his own objective, honest, and humble reckoning, now that he had worked for twenty years in the import-export department, he was more than entitled to the position. Even though in his heart of hearts he was convinced that he could also handle very well the position of head of department, or even deputy director, or maybe even director; but each man to his own fate … Well, the deputy head of department was retiring and Adami was expecting to be called to the boss's office … In fact, no, he deserved to be invited to the deputy director's office. Or why not the office of the director himself? How many times had he daydreamed about it? The director, a formidable man with a neatly clipped, greying moustache, invites him to take a seat in front of his formidable ebony desk, he hands him a box of the finest imported cigars, which Adami timidly declines:

'My apologies, sir, but I'm an inveterate non-smoker …'

Smiling at this witticism, the director says: 'Is that so? An inveterate non-smoker … Bravo!' and touched by the modesty of this faithful clerk, he clears his throat and searching for the words, continues: 'So, how to put it, my dear Mr Adami …'

Or maybe he continues in a warm, friendly manner:

'My dear Adami, we're aware of your diligence, your dedication, your merits, which is to say, your devotion to our import-export company, and this is why we have decided to appoint you to the important position of—' and so on.

But recently the deputy head had retired, he'd received the requisite gifts, a box of imported cigars from the department and a box of export chocolates from his colleagues, but still nobody summoned Adami, neither the director, nor the deputy director, nor the head of his department … The word was going around that they were going to bring in a deputy head from outside, who didn't have a clue about importing and exporting, but who happened to be a second cousin of the director's secretary. A cousin, in a manner of speaking …

The situation had become unbearable. Colleagues had started exchanging pitying glances on the sly, and to his face they addressed him in affectedly gentle tone, the way you would talk to a sick man at death's door or one of life's terminal failures …

So, it was no wonder that that beautiful sunny day, with its fluffy white clouds against the azure sky and all the rest, Adam Adami, on sitting down on a park bench in the centre of town, came to the conclusion: 'Life's not worth living!' and decided: 'I'm going to commit suicide!'

That moment, Adam Adami didn't realise what an amazing thing had happened to him. A true miracle …

Sitting on that park bench and making so private a decision, what Adam Adami didn't realise was that thenceforth he was no longer alone. On the contrary, he had joined a gigantic society, a kind of party whose anonymous members were in the thousands and tens of thousands, scattered all over the world, a party which, had it had a name, would undoubtedly have been called the International Party of Suicides, or I.P.S. for short.

But that party didn't have a name or an acronym or a symbol or a flag or funds or statutes or membership cards; it didn't convene general assemblies or meetings, it didn't organise demonstrations or tea dances, it didn't stand in elections, it didn't have a leadership or ambitious leaders, it didn't have slogans such as 'Long Live Such-and-such a Day' or 'Long Live Such-and-such a Person' or 'Let us Fight for Such-and-such a Grand Cause', or anything else for that matter. It was a large, a huge party, but a modest one, which existed in consummate secrecy and clandestinity. And how could it have been otherwise? What country in the world, what self-respecting public authority would have legally registered a party whose aim was the eventual suicide of its members? So, it was a kind of secret organisation, but whose members had no knowledge of each other, which is perfectly understandable, since who would have gone and divulged to his peers, 'Well, there you go, I've decided to take my own life'? Everybody would have laughed at him, wouldn't they?

In short, this party had one thing alone, but an important thing, let us admit: a completely new way of looking at life and the world, shared by all its members, wherever they might be. It wasn't some new concept or ground-breaking ideology, it wasn't some new truth or other, backed up by reams of research, but quite simply a new outlook on life and the world, which its members had arrived at in the most natural way possible.

So, Adam Adami, on that beautiful day straight out of a novel, with its sun, its fluffy clouds, its azure sky, its meadow, and so on and so forth, after making that desperate decision, began to view the world with different eyes. He even became a different man. Having been short, stooped, a red-headed man with pale-blue eyes, he all of a sudden seemed to grow taller, straighter, and his eyes turned a clearer blue. He all of a sudden felt a head taller than other mortals, than all those destined to die natural deaths or in ordinary traffic accidents. Adami began to view the world from on high, not with pride, not with smugness, God forbid! What would have been the point in being proud when tomorrow or the next day you wouldn't even exist? With understanding, tolerance and generosity, Adami now gazed down from above on other people's petty worries, the way you would gaze down at a seething anthill.

And sitting alone on his park bench, Adam Adami all of a sudden burst out laughing … Ambitions … Chasing after money, when you need so little to be able to live. Chasing after aggrandisement, when tomorrow or the next day you can be bobbing in the water as limp as a rag or hanging from a tree with your tongue protruding … And then what will it matter if you were once large or small, rich or poor, chief or deputy? What will it matter if you are given a state funeral with a plethora of speeches or if just two or three friends and a couple of gawpers follow your coffin in silence …

He just needed to take a look at himself, who for the better part of his life had been consumed with the ambition to be deputy head of department. So, what if he did become deputy head? They would call him 'Mr Deputy Head' or maybe dispense with the title and call him 'boss!' and he would have access to the toilet they kept locked … He would have a better salary, he would be able to eat better and dress more presentably … What did any of that matter? Hermits eat roots and dress in rags, nobody calls them 'Mr Hermit!' or 'hermit-in-chief', but even so, they're no less happy than other mortals …

Adam Adami felt as if a great weight had been lifted off his heart, and now he floated as light as a feather 'mid heaven and earth.

Adami stood up from that park bench where he had come to the decision to put an end to his life and he went home.

His wife greeted him as usual with the clichéd, irritating question, 'Why are you home so late?' But he didn't get annoyed. What did it matter? After all, tomorrow or the next day he wouldn't exist …

'Why don't you just leave me be, Dad?' replied his son in reply to some piece of parental advice on Adam Adami's part.

But he didn't get annoyed. What did it matter, if tomorrow or the next day …

And all the questions that he kept asking himself ceased to torment him. Why can't people get along? Why do they lie, deceive, despise each other, why do they trample each other underfoot? Adami had found an answer to all these questions, an answer so simple that it seemed a stroke of genius. Because they are human … Nothing but human … Not wood, not iron, not gold … And not angels or any other variety of seraphic being …

And the answer to the hardest question of all, his personal 'philosophical question', was now so easy that he was amazed at how it could have tormented him for so bitterly long a time. Namely, the question of his purpose in this world. Had Adam Adami been born solely to move pieces of paper back and forth in an import-export company? The answer was simple: Yes, that was what for! In any event, anybody could ask himself a stupid question like that. Did the head of his department have a purpose in the world? Wasn't it to draft boring letters? What about the director, the lofty director of the import-export enterprise, what was his purpose in this world? What were all of them in the face of the world's immensity? Nothing. Each was a speck of dust, maybe some were bigger specks, but specks they were. The dust of the earth …

But it seemed that every speck of dust was necessary. Otherwise, why would dust exist?

The next morning, as he entered the office as usual, Adam Adami was in for a surprise. No sooner had he sat down at his desk in the corner of the room with the seven desks than the boss came up to him with a big smile on his face and breathless with excitement announced that the director was waiting to see him in his office.

The director, a formidable man with a neatly clipped greying moustache invited him to take a seat in front of his formidable ebony desk, proffered the box of the finest imported cigars, which Adam Adami declined:

'My apologies, but I'm an inveterate non-smoker, sir …'

The director smiled at this choice witticism:

'Is that so? A non-smoker … and an inveterate one at that … Bravo!'

Then he continued in a friendly voice: 'My dear Adami! We are aware of your dedication, diligence, aptitude, in short, your merits at our import-export enterprise, which is why we have decided to promote you to deputy head of department.'

Any other time Adam Adami would have been filled with insane joy, a joy he would barely have been able to control; he would have made a deep bow and stammered in gratitude:

'I, I, I thank you, director, sir!'

But now he made a deep bow and murmured:

'I thank you, director, sir.'

And in his own mind, he asked himself what was the point. If tomorrow or the next day he was going to be neither deputy head, nor clerk, but nothing …

Adami felt proud and self-confident, like a mediaeval knight in heavy chainmail that was impervious to life's poisoned arrows; neither praise, nor insult, nor humiliation, nor reassurance nor anything else could wound his heart.

Any ambition to climb the company ladder, any desire for aggrandisement, had vanished within him. A year later he was promoted to head of department.

In his own mind, he smiled. What did it matter?

Two years after that, he was promoted to deputy director.

In his own mind, he chuckled. What did it matter if tomorrow or the next day …

Some five years later he was made full director. He made an elegant bow to the chairman of the import-export enterprise when he informed him of the appointment—by now he had acquired elegant manners—and in his own mind he burst out laughing. What did it matter if tomorrow or the next day he would no longer be a part of this world of shadows gay and sad …

Adami had no more ambitions, no more desires of any kind. Strangely enough, one desire did actually remain: the desire to do good. He did his job honestly and conscientiously, he looked out for his colleagues, he helped the weaker ones, he tried to lift up the humble, he respected the toil of the lowly clerks, he even went so far as to speak words of praise when his subalterns did their job well, which is something extremely rare in a boss; in a word, he was good to everybody, maybe because it was in his nature or maybe because in his heart of hearts he felt that even if there was nothing else in this world that he needed, he would need people's good opinion when he departed for the other world. In any case, it's nicer to say, 'He was a decent man' than for them to say in a certain tone of voice, 'Best not to speak ill of the dead.'

But ultimately, it was of no importance. Ever since that beautiful day straight out of a novel, with its warm sun and fluffy white clouds gambolling against the azure sky, with its green meadow and sandy yellow paths and so on and so forth, when he decided once and for all to put an end of his life, Adam Adami had noticed to his amazement how few things are genuinely important. In fact, what he noticed, again to his amazement, was that the only important thing in life was life itself, lived as best it can be, for its own sake, as each sees fit.

As can be seen from the whole progression of this story hitherto, Adam Adami's firm decision to put an end to his life had no deadline. All the members of the huge party of suicides scattered throughout the world proceeded likewise. And it's true, once the decision has been taken, what does it matter whether the suicide takes place tomorrow or the day after or the day after that?

Our modern, civilised world is addicted to statistics. Statistics have planted both feet in our lives, they poke around in everything we hold private, showing us for example, in figures and percentages, how much chicken we eat on average or how much toilet paper we use, and so on and so forth.

Well, a recent statistic, which wasn't made public, revealed some interesting data about members of the I.P.S., which is to say, the International Party of Suicides. It was ascertained that the members of this party, hovering constantly between life and death, end up living a perfectly balanced everyday life, without excess or vices. 99.99 per cent don't try to drown their sorrows in alcohol because they have nothing to drown; 98.07 don't gamble because they have nothing to win; 97.33 per cent don't chain-smoke because they have no reason to be anxious; the average age of these suicides is 88, and not one case of suicide has been recorded among them.

1977

The Diamond Ring

The marriage of Albert Osterman to Clara-Giselle, née Barabancik, could be regarded as just as good as other marriages of its kind, given that despite stumbling-blocks, known and not so well known, they had reached the threshold of their silver wedding anniversary.

During these twenty-five years of marriage, Albert had grown accustomed to loving his wife for the way she was, with her sometimes annoying dresses, her sometimes burnt meals, and the nagging stereotypical of the semi-neglected wife, while Clara-Giselle, née Barabancik, had grown accustomed to loving her husband for the way he was, with his going out on business in the morning and returning home for lunch, and then going out again and returning in the evening, wiping his dusty feet on the doorstep and then assuming his classic lolling pose in his deep, soft armchair, with his reading his newspaper and falling asleep in front of the television set, no matter what was on, except on Saturday evenings, when they broadcast national and international football matches.

They didn't have children, so they lavished their attention, tenderness, nagging, and gifts on each other.

Throughout the years of this marriage, just as good as every other marriage of its kind, Clara-Giselle never told her husband what wedding anniversary gift she would like to receive, she wanted it to be a genuine surprise, she loved gifts and she loved nice surprises, and her husband always managed to surprise her by buying her exactly what she needed the least or not at all. If he bought her a red handbag, it would be absolutely certain that she needed a white one, if the gift was violet-scented perfume, you could be sure that rose was the scent being worn right then, and so on. He never managed to hit on exactly what she needed, maybe because not even she herself was very sure as to what she needed. But her husband never knew that he didn't hit on what she needed, because she, a blond, delicate, well-bred lady, never told him that she had no use for his wedding anniversary gift, but quite simply she didn't use it: if it was a hat, she wouldn't wear it, if it was a handbag, she wouldn't carry it, if it was a perfume, she wouldn't put it on.

This time, however, months before their twenty-fifth wedding anniversary, she expressed a wish.

'Alby,' she said, 'Alby, my dear, up to now I've never asked you for anything, but now I know you can afford it, which is why I'd like …' and here she fell silent. And the silence had an effect.

'What would you like, my dear? Tell me!' he encouraged her, almost touched by her hesitation.

'Don't think me too extravagant, but I'd dearly like a … a diamond ring. Like my friend Dora's.'

Albert smiled to himself. Dora Feinstock was the wife of a diamond polisher, which is to say, he owned a small factory for polishing diamonds, and his wife's ring, the same as all her other jewels, was in fact part of the business's inventory. But what do women know? They see only the glitter of the precious stones and have no idea what is behind them. And Albert then kissed her on the corner of the mouth and magnanimously replied:

'A diamond ring you shall have, Clara-Giselle.'

Albert Osterman felt satisfied at being able to promise her this gift, firstly because she fully deserved it, being a good wife with whom he had made a good marriage, like every other marriage that succeeds in reaching its twenty-fifth anniversary without earthquakes or other serious shocks. Secondly, it wasn't the first time he had bought her jewellery, and practical man that Albert was, he knew that ultimately such a ring is not only a gift but also an investment: when you went out with a wife thus bejewelled, your prestige and your credit definitely rose. And thirdly, Albert Osterman was happy that he was in a position to afford to buy his wife such an expensive gift.

How could he have suspected that in so short a time the situation would change and everything would be turned on its head?

Yes, everything would be turned on its head. Three months earlier, when Albert Osterman made his promise to his wife, he had done so with an easy heart, even with a feeling of pride, and certainly the feeling of a man who had the means and knew that he could keep his promise without any great effort.

But now, in the space of the last two months before the wedding anniversary, his confidence began to teeter. His businesses, only yesterday so prosperous, today abruptly came to a standstill, what is more, they even began to go in reverse without the driver intending it. The pace of construction work abruptly slowed, sales of building materials in his shops and warehouses began to drop vertiginously, his stocks of unsold goods became a burden that weighed heavily in both the retail outlets and the accounting ledgers, as well as on the bald round head and stocky shoulders of Albert Osterman. The stacks of planks, the sacks of cement and plaster, the sheets of metal, the iron bars were stuck there in the desolate yards and warehouses, where no customer set foot for days on end. You might think that building materials sitting nicely in warehouses are a fortune that doesn't need feeding, but you would be wrong. They had started to gobble up sums of money, to incur expenses: rent on the warehouses, interest on loans from the bank, even higher rates of interest that verged on usury for loans from private persons, upkeep of the goods, the inevitable deterioration of a part of materials left unused, payment of loans due by means of fresh loans taken out as a last resort and therefore at even higher rates of interest; such financial juggling ends up drastically eroding a businessman's wealth.

Such was the situation in May, when Albert Osterman was due to buy the diamond ring as a wedding anniversary gift. And Albert was exhausted and depressed.

The simplest thing would have been for the two of them to sit down in their armchairs one evening, to turn off the television set, and for the husband to explain the situation to his wife. She would have understood. During quarter of a century of marriage, Clara-Giselle had been able to understand so many things that she would undoubtedly have understood this one too.

She would have understood and she would have been frightened to death. She would have panicked. The spectre of poverty would have loomed in the doorway and would have hastened the bankruptcy, the collapse that could otherwise have been avoided. 'When poverty comes through the door, love flies out of the window': Albert knew the saying well, he had experienced it for himself. A long time ago, when they were still young newlyweds and head over heels in love with each other, he had had some business problems, things had gone badly, and ... No, it's not true that poverty brings husbands and wives closer together, that need unites them, that lack makes them help and encourage each other. Such things are fairy stories invented by sickly romantics, by masochists, by authors of sentimental schlock. Poverty is cruel, merciless, ugly, dismal, dirty, it's poverty and nothing but … It strikes without mercy in all things; it gnaws away, destroys even the noblest souls … Once it enters the house, poverty little by little brings irritability, bickering, darkness (both figuratively and literally, because it demands that electricity be skimped on), cold (both figuratively and literally, because it demands that heating be skimped on), and hunger (literally, because it demands that food be skimped on), amongst others.

No, and no again! Albert was determined not to let poverty enter the house. Anywhere but his home! Let it enter his business, if he couldn't stop it, his bank accounts, his tangible and intangible assets, if it couldn't be turned back, but not his home! He would barricade the doors and windows, but poverty would not enter! Not a hint of poverty! At home, there would be no knowledge of it, no inkling. His wife was not allowed to discover anything of the shocks and earthquakes going on outside; she would therefore have to receive the ring for their silver wedding anniversary.

'She has to receive the ring, understand me!' he explained to his childhood friend Jakil Senderovitch, a goldsmith, jeweller, engraver and watchmaker, to whom he had gone to pour out his grief. 'Tell me what to do? I have a policy whose payment is due … but on the evening of 7 May, year in progress, I have to appear with that blasted ring at our celebratory dinner for two at home.' And here Albert quickly clapped his hand across his mouth, lest his involuntary cursing of the ring somehow bring down misfortune, God forbid!

Jakil lifted his head from the gold seal he was engraving. He removed the black loupe from his right eye and blinked both his small, green, cunning eyes. He was a small man, short,

with a humped left shoulder, grey shaggy hair, as spiky as a hedgehog, and eyebrows and a moustache that had remained as black as a raven's feather. Next to the tall, broad-backed Albert, with his big, round, bald head, shaved cheeks and upper lip, and bushy russet eyebrows, a well-dressed, confident man, the jeweller seemed a ragged, comical dwarf from some second-rate fairy story. The big, strong Albert and the virtually hunchbacked Jakil had been friends since childhood, they had grown up on the same street in an outlying district of the city, they had attended a few classes at lycée together, when even the boldest bullies dared not lay a finger on the feeble Jakil, even though they would have loved to with all their heart, since they knew they would have had to deal with Albert; after which their paths separated. Albert went into the building materials trade, having inherited the business from his father, and Jakil became the apprentice to a watchmaker and jeweller, where for three years he swept the workshop and carried the basket for his master's wife when she went shopping, all the while seeking to purloin the secrets of the craft for which he had a passion. Later he became a journeyman, then saving up the money to buy a tool today, another tomorrow, he was finally able to open his own workshop specialising in watchmaking, jewellery, and engraving in gold and precious stones.

On hearing Albert's words, he pondered for a long moment, then, as if struck by an idea, he determinedly said:

'A ring you shall have, Albert!'

The jeweller's green eyes took on a strange glint, his white hair and black moustache seemed spikier than ever, and an evil smile flickered across his thin lips.

'How shall I have one and how much will it cost?' asked Albert.

'It won't cost you anything. I'll make you it out of revenge ...' said Jakil, and here his voice sounded sardonic.

'Out of revenge? I don't understand,' said Albert in fright.

'It will be my revenge, our revenge, Albert! Don't you think the time has come? Haven't you started to experience certain things for yourself?'

'Who are we going to take our revenge on, in the name of God, Jakil? Have you gone mad?'

'On this world of fools and snobs. Anyway, you'll see! Come back on the 7th of May, in the morning, and you'll get the ring.'

And Jakil Senderovitch would not say another word.

Jakil refused to say another word and Albert left, like a sleepwalker, his head reeling. How was he going to make her a diamond-studded ring of platinum without it costing him anything? Maybe Jakil thought Albert was going to pay in instalments? But why had he been talking about revenge?

For two weeks, Albert Osterman went around in trepidation, waiting for the 7th of May, which, like every other day, whether awaited or not, inevitably arrived. In the morning, as soon as the hour came for the shops to open, he appeared in Jakil's workshop. With solemn mien, his diminutive, hunch-shouldered friend opened a small strongbox, produced a box of black leather, and snapped open the catch. The freed lid merrily flew open.

'Do you like it?' asked the jeweller.

Albert was transfixed, unable to utter a single word. On the sky-blue silk lining of the little box, there peacefully, majestically, lay a ring studded with glittering stones. The workmanship was superb, the white metal masterfully engraved, the stones set in it with needles that entwined like the petals of tiny tulips. The ring had a calm brilliance, an elegance and dignity hard to put into words. A jewel such as Albert had never seen, although he had seen quite a few in his life.

'Take it!' said Jakil solemnly. 'It's yours!'

'You're mad!' Albert replied harshly.

'No, I'm not mad!'

'The price! Tell me its price!'

'This ring has no price. It cannot be paid for. You wouldn't have been able to pay for it even in your best of times ...' and here Jakil gave a sardonic smile that was full of mystery.

'Then you found a buried treasure, you came into an inheritance and you don't know what to do with it ...'

'Neither of those ... I have no platinum and I have no diamonds. I've never had any, all my life I've crafted them for others. It was the workmanship that was mine ... you understand? The *workmanship*!'

The dwarfish, hunchbacked jeweller found himself yelling the last word in a fury.

A frightened silence descended between the two friends. Jakil then continued in a gentle voice:

'The ring is made of a white, stainless metal, which resembles platinum, and the stones are paste, polished glass ...'

Making an involuntary gesture, Albert placed the box with the ring on the table.

'There, you see? You're just like the others,' said Jakil with a sour smile. 'When they see a jewel, they admire the precious metal, the gold, the platinum, its weight in grams, how many carats the precious stones have ... And they forget the workmanship, without which all those grams and carats would be meaningless. Now you have a ring whose grams and carats are worthless, but whose workmanship is priceless ... Nobody will know apart from the two of us ... And the two of us will laugh at them, in secret ... But if you don't want it, Albert ...'

And Jakil, the little hump-shouldered jeweller took the box, looked at the glittering ring resting in its sky-blue silk lining, and was about to put it back in the strongbox when Albert quickly stretched out his hand for it.

Albert stretched out his hand and took the ring. That evening, before the celebratory dinner for just husband and wife, complete with a white damask tablecloth, silver cutlery gleaming in the light of the crystal chandelier, whose every bulb was lit, and the frail yellow light of the two long slender candles in their silver sticks on the table, before that dinner, with a feeling of bashfulness that was even wonderfully in keeping with the occasion, Albert opened the black leather box lined with sky-blue silk, took out the ring with its glittering stones, and placed it on his wife's left ring finger.

Clara-Giselle was in seventh heaven. The ring really was beautiful, more beautiful than she could ever have imagined, more beautiful than all her friends' rings.

The next day, a number of friends and their wives were invited to dinner.

'Oh, what a wonderful ring!' exclaimed Clara-Giselle's friends, their cheeks red with admiration, their voices green with envy. 'What an expensive ring! It must have cost a hundred thousand at least …'

A ring that cost more than a hundred thousand was the rumour that spread through the town. But at the same time, there was news that travelled in the opposite direction. No matter how tightly Albert Osterman sealed his house against rumours and worries from the outside, Clara-Giselle, a good wife the same as every other wife like her, found out, and one day, tenderly kissing her husband, she said:

'Albert, my dear, I know that you didn't want me to find out, but there it is, I've found out. You have difficulties, you have debts to pay … We could pawn the diamond ring or …'—here her voice trembled with slight hesitation—'or we could even sell it … Yes, why not? If you think it would help, I can't go on seeing you worried like this …'

'No, no, my dear! How could you think such a thing?' he protested, genuinely terrified at the thought. 'Promise me, Clara-Giselle, that you will never attempt to sell or pawn this ring!'

'I promise, Albert.'

'Swear!'

'I swear, Albert, my dear!' And she thought to herself: 'How much he loves me!'

And so it was that the ring strengthened the marriage of Albert Osterman and Clara-Giselle, née Barabancik, who for all the stumbling blocks known and unknown had reached the other side of their silver wedding.

A ring worth over a hundred thousand was the rumour that spread through the town and people were filled with admiration. And that was Albert Osterman's unexpected good fortune.

The pressure from his creditors abruptly slackened. They were no longer so agitated, they were no longer so vehement in their demands that their loans be repaid. If Albert Osterman, they said to themselves, the proprietor of so many building-materials warehouses, a skilled and honest merchant, saw fit and was able to buy his wife a diamond-encrusted platinum ring in such hard times, it means that he isn't so badly off as is rumoured … it even means he's not badly off at all. Consequently, their money was in a safe place, they said to themselves, their minds at rest and breathing sighs of relief. And many of them even went to offer him further loans at reasonable rates of interest.

If, through some unfortunate accident, the town had found out that the ring was made from imitation platinum and set with imitation diamonds, they would instantly have pounced on the unfortunate debtor and devoured him. Which would have had catastrophic consequences, because Osterman would never have been able to pay off all of his debts at once, and his creditors, assailed in their turn, would not have been able to pay off their debts, and so on, until the whole pyramid of loans and debts collapsed. Which is why, had anybody gone and told them that the ring was not genuine, the townsfolk would have been capable of lynching him, or tearing him to pieces. People believed in that ring; they needed to believe in it, as if in an idol. Without ever having seen it, the townsfolk thought about that Idol-Ring, with respect and veneration, as if it were a powerful, protective deity, which gave them a feeling of confidence that everything was in order, that they could sleep easy.

A ring worth a hundred thousand, or more, made of platinum, diamond-studded. The rumour spread through the town and reached even the ears of Jakil Senderovitch.

The jeweller, a small man with a humped shoulder, with a bristly head of hair and moustache, blinked his greenish eyes in satisfaction and chortled with laughter inside.

1978

Hotel * * * * *

Dolly and Matty lie on the wide plush-covered bed and look up at the ceiling. The ceiling is modern, stuccoed with asymmetrically arranged geometric figures. Very interesting. You could just lie there looking at it. And not understand anything of it. And not think about anything.

The room is a marvel. Never have they stayed in such a room. Never have they relaxed in such a room. The geometric, modern furniture, made of wood laminated with matte blue Formica. A rectangular table, two armchairs upholstered in lime-green plush. And the bed! Yes, the bed is a marvel in itself. Wide, square, all covered in a plush that shimmers with hints of greenish-grey. Dolly's slender, coyly rounded outline is lost in the expanse of the bed. And Matty's lanky, bony body, which is bent slightly forward, tentative, like a question mark, is also lost in the greenish waters of that wide bed. Two motionless outlines, frozen in admiration.

But even so, there are so many other things they might do. They could go down the white marble stairs, sit down in the lobby and watch the foreign guests coming and going, the few foreign guests, now that it's late in the season, the women in long elegant dresses with dazzling jewellery, the men in perfectly tailored suits, speaking all kinds of languages, laughing in multifarious voices.

They could walk the labyrinth of corridors on the ground floor and gawp at the windows of the little shops and boutiques, where they sell expensive cigarettes and lighters, glossy illustrated books and postcards, paintings and dresses stitched with gold and silver thread, and all kinds of souvenirs made from wood and shiny metal.

Without leaving their room, they could press the button of a bell and the maid would come to tidy up. But everything is tidy. They could press another button and the waiter would come, and then they could order some tea and biscuits, a chocolate cake, or even a copious meal.

They could leave the hotel and go for a walk around the little town of that spa resort, do some shopping, visit the park, have a sandwich at a café.

There are so many other things they might do.

But they don't feel like leaving the hotel. They don't feel like leaving the room. They don't feel like leaving the bed.

An expensive room, which they got cheap, at a reduced rate, for that weekend at the tail end of the tourist season. And with payment in monthly instalments. The Anonymous Shareholding Company where Dolly worked as a secretary had given her an excursion with accommodation at this five-star hotel. At a reduced rate and with payment in instalments. Six monthly instalments, in fact. And Dolly came here with her husband Matty, who is a machine operator at a print works; young newlyweds, they haven't a home of their own yet and they live now at her mother's, now at his parents'. They have bought a colour television set in instalments and it is hard and rather ridiculous to lug it from one place to another. Possessions, clothes, crockery you can leave in one place and another, you don't need them all at once, but you need the television set every evening. And besides, at his parents' it's noisy, there are three young children in the house, and they don't have any peace or quiet at her mother's either, because she talks to them all the time: 'Who shall I talk to if not my own daughter?'

But here there's both peace and quiet. Dolly and Matty lie on the bed, motionless, and look up at the ceiling, which is stuccoed in a modern, asymmetrically geometric style.

Tomorrow morning, as soon as she arrives at the office, the telephone will ring, and it will be Mimi, her best friend, a secretary at another Anonymous Shareholding Company, who, eaten away with curiosity, will ask:

'What was it like, Dolly? What did you do?'

And she will answer:

'What did we do? What did we do? Oh, Lord, what a nice time we had ... We had such a nice time ...'

1978

Dryness

Dr Filip Onda was happy to have received such a position. At a famous clinic. And as for him, he was young, capable, and eager to heal the sick. When he entered the office of Professor Hammerfest, the director of the institution, he greeted him in a strong, warm voice that rang with barely restrained enthusiasm:

'Hello, professor, I'm happy to—'

'Hello,' muttered the professor, drily, curtly.

Dr Onda regarded him in slight consternation. Professor Hammerfest, the director of the clinic, had a dry, solemn face. He gave him a few general instructions in a dry, impersonal voice:

'In the clinic can be found all the necessary instruments and apparatus. No outside instruments or apparatus are to be brought into or taken away from the clinic. No outside medicaments are to be brought into the clinic and no medicaments are to be taken off the premises of the institution! We have our own suppliers and our own patients!'

Professor Hammerfest pressed one of the buttons on his desk. A tall woman in a white medical gown entered. Her hair was black with russet highlights and she had a beautiful oval face.

'Dr Ancona will show you the wards.'

Dr Ancona was beautiful. Her black hair had hints of russet at the roots, as if from dryness. And seen from close up, the skin of her face was rough and dry. Her voice too was dry, as she gave curt, colourless explanations, without a smile, without a sigh, without making any reaction to Dr Onda's remarks, which were intended to be jocular.

'The air is excessively dry here … don't you think so, doctor?'

'Yes, it's dry,' she replied curtly. Had she understood the allusion? Dr Onda couldn't tell. He couldn't pierce the soul of anybody in that building. It was as if their souls were bounded in a nutshell of dryness.

Even the patients on the wards, lying in their immaculate white beds, were dry. Rough faces, dry voices. Dr Onda looked outside at the square garden enclosed within the white walls of the clinic, and the grass was withered, the leaves were dry, the rough trees were parched, even though they were tended by three skilled gardeners, who were also patients of the clinic. The gardeners too had yellow, wrinkled skin, like the leaves in the garden. And the square of sky that was visible above the inner courtyard of the clinic also looked yellow and dry, without a single hint of rain or even so much as a fluffy white cloud.

Whence all that dryness in a clinic that was otherwise clean, beautifully organised, expensive, equipped with all it could possibly need? Dr Filip Onda wracked his brains day and night trying to find an explanation.

Days passed, months passed, and Dr Onda felt the dryness settling on his soul too. He found himself talking to people coldly and drily, his smiling face had become grave, and wrinkles had appeared on his forehead. What was going on in that clinic? He found no answer to the question.

He was about to resign himself to it when the answer unexpectedly arrived, thanks to an occurrence. One evening, when he came home from the clinic, he found his wife stretched out on the couch. She wasn't feeling well. The doctor took her blood pressure and was left astonished. And frightened. The dial showed extremely high blood pressure. High blood pressure in his wife, who her whole life had suffered from low blood pressure, and as a result was always tired, sleepy, and kept herself awake by drinking strong coffee? It was then that Dr Onda noticed that the blood pressure gauge with which he had taken his wife's reading wasn't his. By mistake, he had put a gauge from the clinic in his medical bag. He measured his own blood pressure and it was likewise high. The next day, early in the morning, he went to work and tried out some other blood-pressure gauges. They all showed he had high blood pressure. In horror, he realised that everybody in the clinic was being treated for high blood pressure using dehydrators, medicine to drain the water from them, leaving them dry, withered, muted.

He went to the director and reported his finding. They had to replace the apparatus, change the courses of treatment, everything had to change, he urged.

Professor Hammerfest, the director of the clinic, looked not at all surprised. He regarded him coldly, mutely, before answering in curt, dry, biting sentences:

'I told you from the very beginning, Dr Onda, that we have our own suppliers of apparatus and medicaments. And we have our own patients! Go to the suppliers and demand they change their production process! Go to the patients and tell them their treatment is no good, when they have become accustomed to their condition and feel well. It seems you did not understand, Dr Onda! We cannot change anything! And ultimately, why would we wish for any changes? Are you so sure as to what a normal blood-pressure reading is? Do you know so perfectly what is normal and what is abnormal?'

Dr Onda left the director's office in bewilderment. He didn't know what to do.

What happened next is rather foggy …

According to some, Dr Filip Onda publicly exposed what was going on. He wrote moving, thunderous pieces in the newspapers, real speeches for the prosecution, with titles such as 'Stop drying people up!' and 'To dry people up is barbarism!' The newspapers sold like hotcakes. Passages from these cries of alarm were broadcast on radio and television. The uproar lasted three weeks and Dr Onda was sacked from the clinic.

According to others, Dr Filip Onda, after a brief but fierce struggle with his conscience, admitted the truth and the usefulness of Professor Hammerfest's ideas, and carried on working at the clinic, assiduously prescribing dehydrator medication.

The years passed and he became a professor and director of the clinic, and welcoming a young enthusiastic new doctor, he said in a dry voice:

'We have our own suppliers and our own patients …'

1979

PART THREE

1980–1987

Panoptikum

The day of the fair once more in the little provincial town. The Circus is here!

Hustle and bustle. Sounds.

The wonted sounds of bargaining and haggling at the stalls selling fruit and vegetables, eggs and poultry, fish and bleeding hunks of meat, Turkish delight and gingerbread, old clothes and motley haberdashery. The wonted sounds of the Circus: the raucous laughter of the clowns, the straining of the iron-bender, the wet smacking of the fire-eater, the soft moaning of the spider-woman, the rat-a-tatting of the tin target, where you can win a rosy-cheeked doll or a white-plaster swan. And the hoarse cries of the barkers: 'Step this way! Step this way! The eighth wonder of the world! The ninth wonder! The tenth!' The Circus is full of wonders, after all.

To the side, I recognise the old hut on whose peeling walls is painted in gaudy, crooked letters: PANOPTIKUM.

For the umpteenth time I pay over my copper coin and step inside. Here, within the broken-down walls of this travelling museum, the sounds of the fair fade away, and it is pleasant, it is cool. And I feel a closeness to these silent wax faces, which laugh or weep, for reasons unknown, and each of which resembles someone, precisely who is unknown, as if they were moulded by some clumsy, hapless artist, who has never been able to get it right, never been able to make them the way he wanted.

And before you know it, the questions come flooding once more: Who were these figures? What lives did they live? Where did they lead those lives? If they ever lived at all ...

Utterly pointless questions.

But we like to torture ourselves, to make things complicated for ourselves, to distract ourselves with questions and reassure ourselves with answers. When ultimately, all things have their own meaning, when all things simply are the way they are. And never have they not been either one way or another. In which case, what is the point of the question?

And I find myself shrugging my shoulders and laughing at the thought, which is so terribly banal as to appear downright bizarre ...

A Failed Love Story

Yes, people are right! They're perfectly right, Nick Trauler said to himself.

'My dear sir,' had said a pretty young brunette at the reception laid on by Éditions Micro et Macro in honour of his latest novel, *Stellar Catastrophe*, which had become a bestseller within days, 'my dear sir, why do you write novels that treat only of big subjects, cosmic, atomic, electronic subjects, novels of international, intercontinental, interstellar espionage? Why don't you write a simple, a touching love story, at least once? People are so desperate for love.' Having said which, the young brown-haired lady had given him a discreet, elegant wink.

'Yes, why don't you write a novel of love,' asked his publisher, Mr Karmandel of Éditions Micro et Macro, 'after all, the short love scenes in your superb novels are very well done.'

Yes, people are right, Nick Trauler said to himself and that very night, taking inspiration, he began to write.

Julietta descended in the lift from the thirty-third floor and entered the bar on the ground floor. Camillo, who was sitting on a high stool at the bar, leisurely sipping a scotch and soda with ice, felt a pair of eyes looking at his back. He turned around. On seeing Julietta, he was electrified … Maybe it would be more up to date if I wrote:

Camillo was electronised … I'll think about it some more, Nick Trauler said to himself.

There was no doubt about it, nowadays you didn't have to try to persuade people that there was such a thing as love at first sight. And if you thought about it, every love began with seeing someone for the first time, just as every long march began with taking the first step. Who was it who said that?

Anyway, the two young people met. She, Juliet (look how the name just popped from his fountain pen without him thinking about it—a good job the young man in love wasn't called Romeo … that would have been too much!), Juliet Hampersilk, was secretary to the director of a large insurance company, Fortuna Ltd., whose offices were on the thirty-third floor of a skyscraper, and he, Camillo Spadillo (an interesting, unusual Italian name, which delighted Nick Trauler as it spontaneously emerged from his fountain pen), was a computer programmer who worked in the same building, the same skyscraper, but on the third floor.

And their love developed smoothly, beautifully, swelling like a foam rising from the depths of the soul. They were always together: at the cinema, the circus, the theatre, even at the Luna Park, where they rode the swing and flew on the rocket and drove the dodgem cars and tossed white hoops without landing any of them around the necks of the bottles, laughing like children all the while, never suspecting the looming catastrophe.

One sunny day … that's not right, how could it be a beautiful day like today? One cloudy day, with a grey sky as heavy as lead, as they came out of the cinema after watching a thrilling spy film, not that they had paid much attention to it, Juliet suddenly felt dizzy, her vision clouded, and she fell down on the pavement unconscious. People crowded around. Frightened cries. The shrill, piercing siren of the ambulance. In hospital, blood tests, examinations, diagnoses … The need for an urgent operation … The operation is a perfect success, but the disease is incurable. The swift X-ray. She only has so many months to live …

Wait, stop, Nick Trauler! the writer shouted at himself in his mind. What are you doing? This has been written before. A great love. She gets cancer … There was even a syrupy, tear-jerking film adaptation of it, a box-office hit.

He paced up and down his room in irritation before coming to an abrupt halt. An idea! Why did it have to be her, the frail, blond girl? (Juliet couldn't be anything but frail and blond.) Why not him? Young, handsome, Italian, raven-black hair, healthy, athletic: he would be the one who fell ill … The contrast is far too glaring … And he oughtn't even to beat his brains out about it. The only thing for it was to rewrite the whole episode … He dashed to the wastepaper basket, fished out the crumpled page, smoothed it on his desk, set about copying it …

One cloudy day, with a grey sky as heavy as lead, as they came out of the cinema after watching a thrilling spy film, not that they had paid much attention to it, Camillo suddenly felt dizzy, his vision clouded, and he fell down on the pavement unconscious. People crowded around. Frightened cries. The shrill, piercing siren of the ambulance. In hospital, blood tests, examinations, diagnoses. An incurable disease. He only has so many months to live …

No, no, no! author Nic Trauler yelled at himself in disgust. That's been done to death too! Only the other day, he saw a film, rather a mediocre one, to tell the truth: he was an athlete, a runner, she a bank clerk. After training at the track, he starts panting, collapses on the ground … And so on and so forth …

Nick Trauler paced up and down his office in a fury, like a caged lion … What was he to do with these two likeable young people after they meet and kiss and fall madly in love? How about this for a solution, a highly original one: both of them are ill. With an incurable disease. Which of them will be the first to go? One beautiful spring day, they decide not to wait any longer. Arm in arm, they go to the thirty-third floor of the skyscraper, where she works as a secretary to the director of the Fortuna Insurance Company … What a drop! From up there, the cars look like children's toys, brightly coloured, red, blue, green, silver …

Nick Trauler burst out laughing. What a tragedy, Good God, what a harrowing tragedy … How many lacy lady's handkerchiefs will be soaked in tears … Maybe it will lead to a contagious outbreak of suicides among despairing lovers, as had happened when the respectable Johann Wolfgang von Goethe had published his novel *The Sufferings of Young Werther*? And then there was the press. He could almost picture the strident headlines and the reviews: 'Tawdry tearjerker,' 'What a cheap sob story,' 'Unbelievable schlock from an author previously capable of writing novels of the calibre of *Men and Titans* and *The Giants and the Green Grass*,' and similar write-ups. He came to an abrupt halt and clapped his palm across his forehead. A bolt from the blue. How had he not thought of it from the very start? An idea that was as simple as it was a stroke of genius. Like Columbus's egg! Neither of the two lovers is ill. Both of them, both Juliet and Camillo, are the picture of health, he athletic, with raven-black hair, she blond, frail, but sturdy, ruddy-cheeked, and beautiful, and the young couple are in love and finally they marry …

Henceforward writing it was a breeze, and it was as if his fountain pen flew across page after page. Their love overcomes every obstacle, burning like a flame, brighter and brighter. She, Juliet, with great tact and finesse, rebuffs the advances of her director, and the director, filled with admiration at his secretary, gives her a raise. He, Camillo, elegantly and amicably ends a prior relationship, with a girl whom he had never promised anything and who therefore knew theirs would be a passing affair … He stands up to his parents, decent folk, in the salami trade, who had hoped their son would marry a wealthy girl … She overcomes her mother's objections—her deceased father had been a reserve fireman—and above all the fierce opposition of five maiden aunts, who in unison claimed that a girl like Juliet could snag a big company director: how many directors, even directors general, hadn't fallen for their secretaries or typists? She could even snag a husband who was a textiles manufacturer, or a prince in exile, the possessor of who knows what fortune in gold and diamonds … But Juliet wouldn't hear of princes or manufacturers or big directors, she wanted none but Camillo, the computer programmer, and Camillo wanted none but her … Nick Trauler's fountain pen flew across the page, racing to capture the ideas and episodes that crowded headlong through his mind … And in less than three months the romantic novel *Juliet and Camillo* was ready.

Radiant, exhausted, he delivered it to the director of the Micro et Macro publishing house, Mr Karmandel. Three days later, he received a telephone call. In a tone that was both extremely polite and embarrassed, the director apologised for not being able to publish the novel. The risk was too great … To publish in today's market a romantic novel in which neither of the lovers fell ill with one of those modern, incurable diseases … A novel about two healthy, normal young people, who love each other and marry, and who, it may be supposed, will have chubby, healthy babies … It would be ridiculous …

1980

No Hurry

What I say is that in this life one of two things can happen to us: either we live or we don't live. But there's no choosing which. There are those who would like to live and it doesn't happen, and vice versa, those who would like to die but live.

Who would like to die only in a manner of speaking, of course! They say: 'Oh, how I wish I were dead!' or more elegantly, 'Oh, if only I didn't exist!' or 'Oh, if only I could lie down in bed, never to rise again!' 'Oh, oh, oh!' But if somebody came and said: 'All right then, I'll fix it for you,' they would change their minds. They would put it off, saying, 'Let me wait and see, let me think about it some more, there's no hurry ...'

I even think the dead would like to come back to life. If we told a dead man, 'Look here, my good man'—if we put it to him delicately and politely like that—'we could solve your predicament, bring you back to life, let you pick up from where you left off: work, playing the lottery, attacks of the gout, quarrels, going to balls and *thés dansants*, outbursts of jealousy, and all the rest,' I don't think he would turn us down flatly. Maybe he would fall to thinking and say, 'I can't give you an answer straight away, let me have some time to think about it, after all, there's time here aplenty ...'

He's a decent chap, our medical orderly. And strong, too. He can lift you up with just one hand, grasping you by the collar, as if you were as light as a snowflake. Or he can clamp you in his arms so that you can't move a single internal organ or external limb … complete repose! 'Mr Karstenthal,' the orderly gently tells me, 'Mr Karstenthal, the doctor wants to see you!' Apparently, I've been behaving well lately, I've been calm and quiet, I haven't shown any signs of madness, I've been thinking rationally, like any other sensible person with his two feet on the ground, and consequently the doctor would like to discharge me.

The doctor beams at me with the whole of his round, rosy face, smiling like a new-born baby. But there's no hurry, doctor, that's what I say! Let me think about it, give me some time. There's plenty of time, isn't there? Time is boundless, whichever direction you go, there's no limit to it. In which case, what's the hurry?

And where am I supposed to go? The outside! What does the outside mean? Aren't we people here on the inside not the same as those on the outside? We're pent between four walls, but aren't the people on the outside also on the inside, pent between all kinds of walls, which have been erected around them whether they like it or not?

And let's suppose I leave here and I'm on the outside: what am I going to tell the people on the outside? Have you been in 'there', some of them will ask me sympathetically, others with concealed sarcasm, have you been in 'there' and you haven't told us? What will I tell them, doctor? As for me, I admire those people who think that there's something to say … After all, so many things have been said without any new star appearing in the heavens and without any earthquakes being prevented. Dogs and cats know this very well. Dogs gnaw their bones, cats lap their milk, and they don't say anything. They bark or meow, and they don't seem to have any ambition to produce a historic woof or an earth-shattering meow ... I was just talking to Dr Ickson, Maverick Ickson, who is Chairman of the World Movement and handles huge Funds via the biggest banks in the world—he's in my ward, the third bed on the left from me—and Dr Ickson says that the Movement is highly important ... Although viewed from another angle, it's utterly devoid of significance, as movement is the opposite of repose, and repose is nothing other than remaining still, it's motionlessness, non-being, which is to say, nothing! And the opposite of nothing, or the anti-nothing, is still nothing ... Dr Ickson, the Chairman of the World Movement, explained it to me clearly, as he was writing out checks for astronomical sums drawn from the Swiss Federal Bank, the Chase Manhattan in New York, the Dresdner Bank, and others, without the slightest tremor of the hand, without the slightest twitch of a muscle on his long pale face, without even a blink of his darkly glowing coal-like eyes.

The Chairman of the World Movement has a thick chequebook, whose leaves were drawn for him by Mr Leonard Hermelin, the drawing and calligraphy teacher, seventh bed on the right in our ward. Every cheque is identical, traced in Indian ink, so that you'd swear it was actually printed, and I saw with my own eyes how Dr Ickson gave Director General Pincovsky a cheque for One Hundred and Fifty Million ... That's how he wrote it out: One Hundred and Fifty Million, in capital letters ... Mr Arthur Pincovsky is the director general of the Primal Impulse Anonymous Shareholding Company. He's an engineer and inventor. He invented the primal impulse—what am I talking about? He didn't invent it, properly speaking, that would be ridiculous, I mean he received the primal impulse, as he explained to me in simple terms, telling me about the primordial foot that kicked Repose in the backside, as a result of which the world, the universe were set in motion, the planets started orbiting, the waters parted, and the waters from above and the waters from below gathered together, the plants and animals commenced their cyclical transformations, and so on; it's as if it broke the banknote of the Impulse into smaller change, it tore the Impulse into smaller pieces and assigned the appropriate pieces to a motorcar, to a steamer, to various pieces of factory machinery, so that they could all move without needing fuel. Just as the universe, the sun, the moon, the planets, and so on move without petrol or diesel ... He even gave a public demonstration of it. He went on a voyage in a steamer driven by a piece of the primordial Impulse. The liner sailed away nicely, but when it was far out to sea, it sank. Mr Pincovsky barely escaped death by drowning. As you can imagine, they wanted to kill him and to destroy his invention, so that no trace of the primordial Impulse would be left. It was the powerful oil companies, they couldn't sit with their arms folded and watch the experiment turn out to be a success. Think what would have happened if oil had become useless overnight, nothing but a dirty, worthless liquid. The derricks stop drilling, the oil wells stop pumping, the refineries stop refining, the oil tankers rust in their docks, the petrol stations stop filling cars, oil company employees, from doormen to directors general, find themselves out of work, pieces of paper stop circulating in those huge gleaming glass and steel office blocks that scrape the sky. They want to destroy his invention, but Mr Pincovsky continues the fight from here. And he's financed by Dr Ickson, Chairman of the World Movement. Yesterday he gave him a cheque for One Hundred and Fifty Million ... Here, in the main ward, second bed on the right, Mr Pincovsky is safe. The whole world thinks he's insane ... And in the meantime, he can work in peace, developing his 'Primordial Impulse' project. Just the other day, he said to me: 'Mr Karstenthal, you're an engineer: don't you want to work for me? We need you ...'

You want to release me, doctor? But there's no hurry, that's what I say. There's time aplenty … True, I speak logically, rationally, like any other person with his two feet on the ground. But ever since I arrived here, I've spoken just the same way, except that there was nobody to listen … And besides, what will I tell the people on the outside? Those people, they want nothing but words to tickle their eardrums, or failing that, words that will pass their ears by … And whatever I tell them, they'll just nod in agreement, lest they provoke me, and they'll pity me in secret. Among themselves they'll say 'he talks quite normally' and 'did you hear the way he talks?' They think they're sound of mind, but actually they're the same as us, except that there's nobody to keep them under observation …

And, really, why should you release me, doctor, when I don't want to be released, rather than releasing Mr Leonard Hermelin, the drawing and calligraphy teacher on our ward, seventh bed on the right? He so desperately wants to get out, so he can see the virgin forests of the Solomon Isles. The jungles of the Solomon Islands … That's his dream! Call it an *idée fixe* or whatever you like, but who does it harm? And he has his passport ready and waiting. He made it himself, the whole design, the calligraphic script, all the signatures and stamps. As well as all the entry and transit visas for all the countries on the way. The only thing missing is his exit visa. Why won't you issue it to him?

Oh, how this life of ours is organised! When you want something, you don't get it, when you don't want it, you get it. Or else we only think we want it because we can't get it, and vice versa, we think we get it because we don't want it … Ugh! It's enough to drive you insane, nothing short!

Take me, for example, my whole life I wanted to be someone, to get somewhere, and now I no longer know what it was I wanted to be or where I wanted to end up. I know only that I could have been the President of the Honduras, the Emperor of Japan, the Governor of the Solomon Islands; I could have been anybody at all. And anybody could have been me. In which case, what's the problem? Yes, tell me what's the problem, doctor?

1980

The Young Diplomat

He changed his surname to Rafaeli. Which sounds nice. In Italy, it would have been Rafaello, with two l's, and in France, it would have had two l's, but a y at the end. His real surname was actually Refuelson, and his first name, Samuel, which could easily have been shortened to Sam. He was tall, with chestnut hair thinning above his brow, a tanned face, and a delicate, diplomatic smile that played around his lips.

The young man had a good career ahead of him, so said everyone who knew him. An uncle of his, Chaim Refuelson, the elder brother of his father, who was a doorman at the Foreign Ministry, wangled him a job at the ministry. In the morning, when he entered the ministry with his colleagues, he would give his uncle a wink on the sly… But his uncle retired, after which he didn't have to wink any more. He could enter and leave the ministry with the same solemn, important mien as all the others.

Atalia he met at a garden party, at Mirella's, the daughter of the director general from the ministry. Atalia had been a friend of Mirella's at university. They'd both studied English.

As soon as he set eyes on her, Samuel Rafaeli exclaimed to himself: 'She's the one!' Or something similar. Without his face giving away the slightest hint, naturally. Atalia, was tall, about an inch smaller than he was, she was blond, and she spoke five languages. He could picture her as the ambassador's wife at a diplomatic reception, receiving the guests, smiling—she had a charming smile, and eyes that were as blue as can be—and saying a few words to each diplomat in his own language.

They met again at parties, at soirées, at picnics, at balls. The young man began to make diplomatic allusions, ultimately quite transparent ones, which Atalia did not rebuff. Sam Rafaeli was tall, an inch taller than she was, he had chestnut hair and a bright future ahead of him.

One night, after a very successful ball, after dancing, champagne, high spirits, and a raffle, he asked her whether she had come by car. Atalia burst out laughing:

'By car? Well, the thing is that I forgot to ask Daddy to buy me a car ...'

How extraordinary, a girl like her, and she's modest too, thought Rafaeli to himself. Yet another of her qualities. A rarity. Her friend Mirella had pestered her father and hadn't let up until he bought her no fewer than two: One was a red sports car, the other an elegant old black car for soirées and banquets.

'If such is the case, then please permit me, Miss Atalia, to offer you a lift home in my motorcar,' said Samuel Rafaeli in a ceremonious manner.

'I permit you, Mr Sam Rafaelly, I permit you!' replied the girl with equal ceremony.

They both burst out laughing.

In the car, Sam grasped her shoulder:

'Atalia ... tomorrow, which is to say, today, since I forgot it's past midnight, so, this evening, at seven o'clock, I shall telephone you ... I should like us to go out together, just the two of us. I shall come to pick you up at home ...'

'Very well,' said the girl softly.

Sam started the engine.

'And now, please be my guide, Atalia!' said Sam, with a hidden meaning. 'Show me the way ...'

'I hope it won't seem too long,' laughed the girl.

'That now depends on you!'

'Only on me?'

The young man fell awkwardly silent. The girl went on in a blank voice:

'Very well, then, start the engine for now! Turn right … right again … now turn left and join the coast highway …'

The sound of the car's engine was an even, muffled rumble. A warm, pleasant languor filled Sam. He was silent, relaxed. He didn't feel the need to talk; it was pleasant just to sense her next to him.

'Now, at the intersection turn left … just a little farther … we're here!'

Sam Rafaeli stopped the car. He looked around him, blinking as if he had just woken up.

'This is where you live?'

The horizon was glimmering in the dawn light, the air was milky, damp. A housing estate to the south of town. Grey, mouldy blocks of flats. Laundry hanging from lines strung up between windows.

'This is where you live?'

Samuel Rafaeli's voice was as if muffled by a veil.

'Yes,' she said. 'This is where I live, in that building, with my parents.'

And she pointed at one of the blocks of flats, which was in no way distinct from any of the others.

That evening, at seven o'clock on the dot, the telephone rang. Atalia picked up the receiver. It was Sam Rafaeli. He apologised for not being able to come. An unscheduled meeting at the ministry …

1980

Somebody

Eleven months of the year, Bercu Borsht was nothing, he was a zero, and only for one month of the year was he a somebody. You might even go so far as to say that for that one month he was an important person.

Bercu Borsht was a tailor. Eleven months of the year, from June to April, he worked in the room he rented in a basement, he tailored suits, he patched, he removed stains, he ironed trousers, he did whatever was asked of him, he didn't work fixed hours, he worked in the day, he worked at night if he had an urgent order to meet, and he saved up money to make the journey to his home town, where he would stay for a month. The whole of May.

In that little town, which he had left many years before, he was still a tailor, but now, returning as a visitor, for one month a year, he was somebody, an important person, even. Once a tailor's apprentice, then a journeyman, he played for F.C. Perseverance, albeit mostly in the reserve, but that is neither here nor there, given that his name was known, for when somebody asked who was in the reserve, they would say, 'so-and-so, and so-and-so, and so-and-so, and Bercu Borsht.' He regularly attended the training sessions and the balls the sports club held, he regularly paid his dues, and when he was older, nearing thirty, he stopped playing football altogether; he was no longer even in the reserve, but the F.C. Perseverance management committee co-opted him and he regularly paid all the club's taxes, and he recruited new members, and he raised benevolent funds for the football team. To save the club money, he even went so far as to sew and patch the footballers' blue shorts and yellow-and-red-striped jerseys.

But that was a long time ago. In the new town where he lived among new people, strange, distant people, Bercu Borsht was nothing, he was a zero, and only for one month of the year was he a somebody. In the town where he lived there was a football team, too, but it had no need of him as a dues-paying member, it had no need for him to pay its taxes or raise benevolent funds, since it was the team of a large stuffed-fish cannery: the back of the footballers' blue jerseys was even emblazoned with the factory's emblem, a plump, round carp and the inscription, in letters large enough for all the stadium to see, 'The Stuffed Carp'. Here, for eleven months a year, he was nothing, he sat bent over his sewing machine and his sewing table, tailoring and patching, and he sewed coats and jackets and trousers, almost without lifting his eyes from his work. He saved up money. Here he was nothing, but there, in his little home town, he was really somebody.

The hovel on Maize Street, which was the name of that narrow, dusty lane that led to maize fields at the edge of town, the hovel where he had once lived, no longer existed; it had been demolished to make way for some large, drab blocks of flats; his parents and three younger brothers and sisters were no longer there, since they had not come home after the war, and so now every year he stayed for a month at the Palace Hotel, the most elegant hotel in the centre of town—that's what they called it, 'The Palace'—and he would order a copious, festive dinner, with flowers and candles, with slivovitz and champagne, and meatball soup, and roast lamb, and compote, for his friends and local officials. Yes, local officials too, since to the meal he invited the chairman of the General Sporting Association, and the chairman of the Boxing Club, and the chairman of the Athletics Club, and the chairman of the Winter Sports Society, and other chairmen and their wives. And the little town's deputy mayor, who had once also been a footballer for the erstwhile F.C. Perseverance—the town's club was now called Progress—would raise his glass of champagne and make a toast in a vibrant voice: 'Here in our midst we salute—' that's what he said every year—'Here in our midst we salute our friend …' and everybody at the long table would drink slivovitz and champagne, and they would loudly slurp meatball soup, and munch well-browned roast lamb, and smack their lips.

And as round as a full moon, crowned with slicked-back hair as yellow as straw, the face of Bercu Borsht would turn red, radiating light and happiness.

Year after year it was the same, except that his hair faded in colour as time passed, as did his fellow diners', it faded more and more, and his face, like those of his fellow diners', grew more and more wrinkled, but the toast rang out just as vibrantly as before: 'Here in our midst we salute our friend …' 'We warmly salute him!' the chairman of the Boxing Club, an erstwhile bruiser with a face now as wrinkled as a fig, would sometimes interpose, before the deputy mayor resumed: 'Yes, yes, here in our midst we warmly salute our friend …'And the meal would be as tasty as ever and the drinks as strong as ever.

This was how it had always been until this year. For eleven months, from June to April, Bercu Borsht was nothing, almost never lifting his head from his sewing table and his sewing machine, but on the morning of the first of May, when he was due to go to the airport, having packed his suitcases the night before, he found to his amazement that he could not get out of bed. He almost felt like laughing at this strange turn of events. A neighbour, an elderly widow, went to call a doctor. There was nothing much more that could be done .

The Chevra Kadisha—the Holy Funeral Association—settled on a place for him in the new cemetery, which was as large as a whole town, with lots of districts, which is to say, different sections, each with row upon row of white grave markers. Two gravediggers trundled the trolley on which was laid his body, covered with a black cloth, the property of the Chevra Kadisha, to which was affixed with a pin a note that read, 'Bercu Borsht, section 26, row 17, grave 22.' After the trolley came an usher from the Chevra Kadisha, limping and murmuring psalms, and after him came Bercu Borsht's neighbour, the elderly woman, who had brought a friend, also an elderly woman, since she was afraid to go to the cemetery alone. And that was all.

Two men coming from the opposite direction stopped at the edge of the path to allow this surprisingly small funeral procession to pass.

'Who could it be?' asked one of the men.

'Certainly somebody ...' murmured the other man, for the sake of something to say, not knowing how much truth there was in his words.

After the trolley and its attendants passed by, the two men lingered for a few moments and then went on their way, in the direction of the cemetery gates.

1981

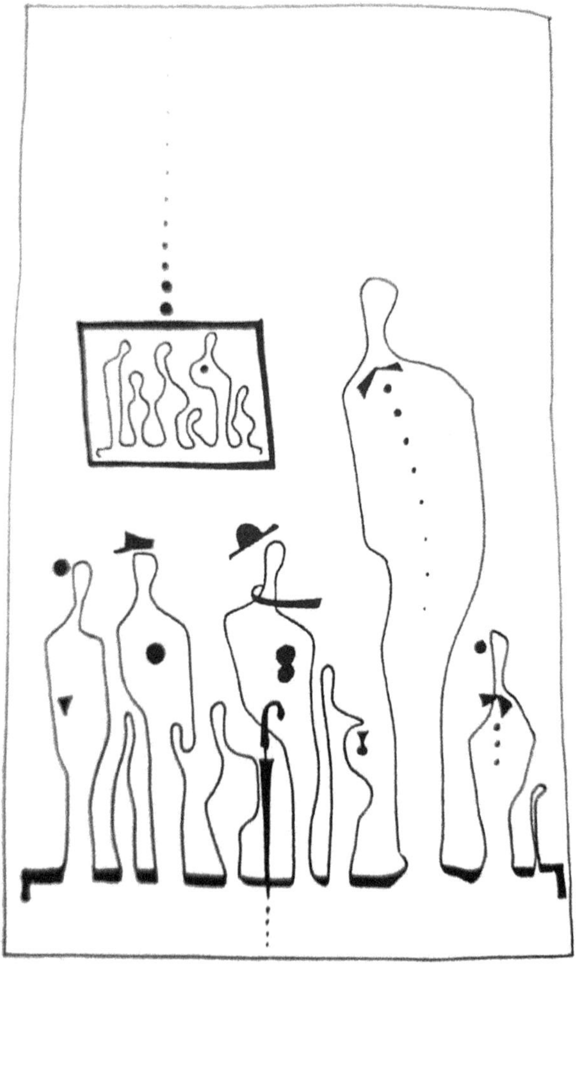

Watchman at Seven Stores

'Toll 1 dime,' read the brightly coloured letters on the sign at the right of the road. Holding the steering wheel with one hand, Martin Lebensohn rummaged in his trouser pocket with the other.

'I've got a ten-cent coin,' I told him.

The young man took the nickel coin from my hand and, slowing down at the barrier, tossed the toll in the net of the machine.

'Are you a vegetarian?' I asked after a while. At a lavish meal with the family he hadn't touched the boiled and the roast meat of every variety, eating only a large bowl of salad dressed with salt and soy sauce.

'I love animals and don't like to eat them!' he said, a slight smile fluttering around his thin bluish-red lips like a warm breeze.

It was after midnight on the highway from New Jersey to New York and we were on our way to Queens. After dinner with the family, Martin had offered to give a few of the guests a ride home in his car. He lived in Queens too, not far from the house where I was staying. I sat in the comfortable passenger seat next to him and looked at his smooth, delicate profile as he calmly drove the large sky-blue Cadillac, an old model that he had bought second-hand for a few hundred dollars. He had chestnut hair, cut short and swept back, without a parting, a high, smooth forehead, without wrinkles, a slender nose, thin bluish-red lips, and a regular chin, although his jawbone was a little too prominent, jutting out beneath his earlobes. And he had very clear blue eyes, set beneath thin, nicely arched eyebrows.

'Toll 5 cents' I read on another sign at the side of the highway.

'You have to pay all kinds of tolls here,' said Martin, with an apologetic smile.

'No problem! I've got change,' I said.

Martin slowed down, took the five-cent coin from my hand and tossed it in the net of the machine. Like a spider's web, the net caught the coin, after which it rattled down into the square belly of the machine.

'They say you do meditation.'

'Kind of . . .'

I pressed the point: 'And there's some kind of secret keyword?'

'Not at all! There are no keywords, and no secrets of any kind,' Martin said, with a soft laugh.

'Are you part of a sect?'

'A sect? I don't know. Everything in this life has to be categorised, and labelled, and numbered, and catalogued . . .' he said, and a shadow seemed to pass across his face.

After a time, Martin Lebensohn went on: 'There are about four hundred of us all over the world. We meet once a year, we stay together and think.'

'About what?'

'There is no "about what". We ponder anything at all, in a relaxed way, without any tension.'

It sounded so simple, but even so, I still didn't understand. After a time, I ventured to ask:

'And each of you tells the others what you've been doing, what you've achieved?'

Martin laughed out loud at that: 'What we've achieved? What does that matter? In any case, each of us is content ...'

'Toll 1 quarter' exclaimed a sign in big yellow letters. Martin began to rummage in his pockets.

'It's all right, I have a quarter-dollar coin,' I said. 'For the last few weeks, ever since I've been roaming this big America of yours, from one coast to the other, I've broken quite a few dollar bills and collected a whole load of nickel and copper coins in my pockets.'

The monotonous, muffled rumble of the old Cadillac's engine. The yellow beams of the headlights on the asphalt of the highway ahead.

'At your uncle's, Professor Sandberg from Wellington, in the living room, above the piano, I saw a sepia portrait. Actually, a self-portrait ...'

'You recognised it?' asked Martin in surprise.

'It wasn't so hard ...'

The portrait really had been exceptionally interesting. And strange. A self-portrait in profile, showing the young man's well-proportioned naked torso, with the harmonious muscles in a state of rest, but with the head turned away from the viewer so that only a part of the prominent jawbone and left ear were visible. It was as if the artist had turned away his head at the last moment, in embarrassment, not wishing to reveal his face, not even in profile; not wishing to show himself to others, as if saying: 'Look at me, this is who I am!'

'Why did you give up painting? You had a career as an artist ahead of you.'

'I was suffering from stress, from anxiety, other people's envy up ahead of me ... Critics, galleries, manipulation, publicity ... And for what?'

'What do you mean, for what?'

'Exactly that: for what? What would have been the point of it, if I'm contented otherwise? Ask yourself the same question and try to answer it!'

I was a little thrown off balance by such a direct answer:

'Yes, well, you can't just answer like that ...'

'Oh, can't I?' said Martin Lebensohn and gave a soft laugh, without any hint of triumph.

'But at least you should have completed your art degree at Cornell University! How could you throw it all away like that, out of the blue, after two and a half years of study?'

'Yes, I should have completed it and received that piece of parchment with a big red wax seal, I should have stiffly, solemnly taken my place in an upholstered museum chair, or played the pompous expert in the offices of an art review, or dealt with matters pertaining to art in an office at Hillsboro Town Hall, or maybe opened a painting school for grandmas in Shadow Village ... As you can see, the possibilities were endless ...'

An iron bridge loomed out of the night.

'Toll $1.50.'

'Quite a heavy toll!' remarked Martin.

'It's all right, I have the money.'

Martin stopped the car. This time, a man wearing a peaked cap took the toll and handed him a receipt.

'But in the end, what are you going to do? What job are you going to take? At dinner, somebody from the family asked you about how your shops were doing? You don't much look like a shopkeeper ...'

'You're right, I don't look like one, and I'm not one, either ... But I'm the watchman at seven shops ... In quite a bad neighbourhood of New York ... A grocery, a fruit and vegetable store, a butcher's, a barber's, a hamburger joint, a store that sells buttons, and another one that sells children's toys.'

'A night watchman?'

'No, during the day. At night, there's nothing inside the stores for burglars to steal, but during the day, they can pull a hold-up ... "Hands up! Give me the money in the till!"'

'Do you carry a gun?'

'I don't think there's any need. Anyway, the robbers don't come. They know the seven stores are guarded. And the owners, hardworking, decent folk, know their stores are guarded. So, everybody's happy.'

'What about you?'

'I'm happy too!'

I couldn't control my annoyance:

'You're the watchman at seven stores and you're happy, but ... but ...'

I stopped myself. But not soon enough, it would seem.

'But what about the future? That's what you were going to ask, isn't it?' exclaimed the young Martin Lebensohn, almost triumphally, as if he had known from the very start which way the conversation was heading. 'Yes, yes, the future ... The future ... The future ...'

Martin's voice became more and more colourless. And the word was drained of meaning, like a deflating balloon.

'The ... fu ... ture ... the ... fu ... ture ... the ... fu ... ture ...'

The word disintegrated into syllables that grew ever more isolated and meaningless.

'The ... fu ... ture ... the ... fu ... ture ... the ... fu ...'

In the denseness of the night, after a bend, the white, glimmering lights of Queens suddenly loomed ahead.

1981

Apocalypse

He was a clerk at the B.S.P.P., the Bureau for Solving People's Problems, and his name was Leon O. Grubich.

This Grubich was an outstanding clerk. He stapled documents all day long. He used thin metal clips to join together the separate sheets of paper, the reports and annexes, and the annexes to the annexes, so that they would be held together in the right order, each page in its proper place, so that they wouldn't be mislaid, so that they wouldn't fly off where they shouldn't.

He had a stapler, an excellent device. A good brand from the Far East. It was engraved 'Made in Taiwan.' Or 'Made in Hong Kong.' And from the managing director he would receive little boxes of staples. He would load the stapler with them and staple sheets of paper. He would staple them together to keep them nicely in order. And he was contented. He felt safe. He could feel the Earth, solid under his feet, as it orbited the sun and rotated on its axis; it was a matter of physical geography that really had nothing to do with him.

Leon O. Grubich was contented and felt completely safe.

All until one fine day, when something happened. There were no more staples left in his box and as usual he went to the managing director of the B.S.P.P., the Bureau for Solving

People's Problems, to ask for a fresh box. The director was not in his office. And the secretary did not have the key to the metal filing cabinet. Nobody had the key to the filing cabinet. Leon O. Grubich fell to thinking: What if the managing director was ill and nobody could open the filing cabinet to give him the box of staples. Or what if something happened in the world, what if connections with the Far East were severed and no more staples arrived. What if there were no more staples! Good God! He could picture the enormity of it. He could sense the scope of the catastrophe. Pieces of paper flying everywhere, reports fluttering over the office desk in disarray, sliding onto the chairs, down the hallways, blown on the wind out of the office windows into the street, into the park opposite, into the trees, onto the grass, onto the glinting surface of the lake, hundreds and thousands and millions of pieces of paper, reports, official documents, annexes thereto, and annexes to the annexes thereto ... No more complaints would be able to be solved, no more resolutions could be passed, no more rubber stamps would be able to be applied, no more postage stamps would be able to be affixed. Not one piece of paper would be able to be found. Nothing would be in the proper place. People's problems wouldn't be able to be solved ... Everything was teetering, toppling, there was no solid ground underfoot ... Furious people were taking to the streets with banners and placards. The police formed a line, but they couldn't withstand the weight of the crowd, tyres were burning, there was smoke, teargas. Angry mobs were besieging the office, rising like liquid in communicating vessels, up the main stairs, in the lifts, up the service stairs, to the thirty-seventh floor, they were overturning the desks, the shelves of files, throwing chairs out of the windows. They were entering his office, they were knocking him to the floor, he could feel the soles of boots and spikes of high-heel shoes trampling his chest. The weight was unbearable. He was suffocating. He was about to breathe his last …

'Here!' he heard, all of a sudden. It was the curt voice of the managing director of the B.S.P.P., the Bureau for Solving People's Problems, who was holding out a box of staples. 'But whatever is the matter with you, Mr Grubich? You look as if you've just witnessed the end of the world …'

1983

Visiting Day

I was sitting by myself on the wooden bench at the bus stop, waiting for the last bus to take me from that godforsaken hill down to the train station in the valley, where I was going to catch the evening train home.

I was the last to leave that day. The guard walked up and down the corridor a few times, shouting in a voice made hoarse by drink: 'Visiting day is over. Go home!' But I didn't feel like getting up to leave. And I don't understand why not. She was lying in bed, on her back, her eyes closed, her lids clenched tight, breathing with difficulty, noisily, like a cracked bellows. And I was sitting on a chair next to her bed, my head drained of thoughts. But how much can a man think, when it comes to it? And about what? And why?

Outside, the air was warm, stagnant. An anaemic lemon-yellow sun had sunk behind the hill atop which sat the main building, surrounded by pine trees, and the shadows of those trees were lengthening over the grey tarmac. The well-mown lawn in front of the building was grey too. And the sky was grey, with bluish-grey clouds hanging here and there, pointlessly. Would another bus come at that hour? Or had the last bus left already? I was alone at the bus stop, or so I thought.

All of a sudden, I heard a muffled voice next to me:

'Who is it you have up here?'

It was an elderly man, puny, with a withered, bony face in which two small eyes blinked behind narrow steel-framed glasses. He had unusually thick white hair, which he wore swept back in a tousled mass like tongues of cold flame. I hadn't heard him creep up and sit down on the other end of the wooden bench at the bus stop.

'Who is it you have here?' he asked, pointing his head at the building among the pines.

'My wife.'

'Which section?'

'Six.'

'Hmm …' he said before falling silent.

But I soon sensed him fidgeting, leaning forward, then to one side, as if unable to find a comfortable position on the bench. There was none but the two of us and the tall pines and the grey light of the all-enveloping dusk. It was obvious that he was unable to remain silent, that he felt an imperious need to talk to somebody.

'And what do the doctors say?'

I made no reply. What were the doctors from section six supposed to say?

'I understand,' said the man with the tousled white hair and the steel-framed spectacles. 'Maybe it's better this way …'

He looked to one side. How could anybody say, 'it's better this way'? He probably sensed my questioning look because he quickly added, as if in apology:

'Mine has been here for twelve years … Section three … Stationary. Neither progress, nor regress. Twelve years … For twelve years I've been coming here every week, on visiting day. She greets me with her dark eyes wide open, with her face motionless. Sometimes I even think to see the flicker of a smile … But maybe it's not true. I only think to see it … I tell her about everything that's happening in our little town, about relatives, friends, acquaintances, weddings, divorces, all kinds of things. I don't know whether she understands, or how much she understands of what I tell her. I don't know anything … Sometimes she looks at me and from her large dark eyes I see that she wants to respond, to tell me something. And Good God, how I would like her to be able to talk! To be able to tell me that there was nothing between them … That I only thought there was … Or that it was something insignificant. A game, innocent fun … I don't ask her about it any more, but maybe that's what she wants to tell me. Before, I used to ask her countless times and she would laugh at me, and I would be reassured. Her laughter was so serene. And she would tell me that I had an over-active imagination, that I imagined all kinds of things. And I would believe her. But then the thoughts, the doubts would well up inside me again, and she would reassure me again. I needed her voice. I couldn't cope without her speaking … All until one day, when I found her on the floor in the kitchen, unconscious, face down. A brain haemorrhage … Now she's grown fat, always lying in bed or sitting in the wheelchair, her face is round and she looks at me with her large round eyes, and I'd like her to laugh at me and tell me that there was nothing, nothing, nothing …'

I heard what sounded like a hiccough. Then he was silent for a while.

'Mine keeps her eyes closed.' These were the words that went through my mind again. 'She keeps her eyelids tightly, stubbornly shut. And she breathes noisily, difficultly, like a pair of broken bellows … Section six … What are the doctors from section six supposed to say?'

'She looks at me with her dark eyes, wide open … What joy if she were to regain her speech, even if for only a few seconds, long enough to tell me: "Nothing … it was nothing …".'

He fell silent once more. The lenses of his narrow spectacles were steamed up, opaque. His unusually thick hair seemed to blaze in a mass of cold white flames.

Finally, he resumed in a faint voice, almost a whisper:

'I think I must have gone insane. For twelve years, it's the only thing I think about. I banish the thought only for it to return. I banish it again and it creeps back inside, here inside my head. You understand? I'm a placid madman. Nobody knows anything. I work, I do everything at the office, I come home and clean the house, I go to the cinema, the theatre, I read the newspapers, I watch television, I walk in the park, I politely say hello to my neighbours, but I'm insane. And nobody knows ...'

There came the rumbling sound of an engine, nearer and nearer, and two headlights furrowed the greyness of dusk.

The bus had arrived.

1984

Shoes: A Light Summer Story

The tour guide spoke into the bus's microphone:

'Ladies and gentlemen! We'll be making a thirty-minute stop. You'll find here a restaurant, where you can have tea, coffee, or soft drinks and eat authentic pizza, a sandwich, or a dish of macaroni. Please don't wander off! It's now ten o'clock, and everybody must be on the bus in thirty minutes.'

The holidaymakers got off the bus. They were at the edge of a picturesque little town: narrow streets, old one-storey houses whose fronts were decorated with stucco flowers and whose windowsills had living flowers in plant pots.

On the lane behind the restaurant, where they served espresso coffee, soft drinks, slippery macaroni, and pizzas with chilli peppers, there were a few shops: a small grocer's, a barber's with gilded scales above the entrance, the old emblem of the guild, a shop with large, handsome windows on which were inscribed the words 'Funeral Director' in white letters on a black background and behind which were displayed all kinds of coffins: solid wood, lacquered black or dark brown, with gilded, silver or bronze studs, or more modest affairs, painted white or in plain varnished wood, and next to the funeral director's was a small shoe shop.

Well, it was to this little shoe shop that Melania Hammerstamm dragged her husband.

'But I want to have some coffee!' her husband complained.

'You'll have some after.'

'There won't be enough time!' essayed the downcast husband.

'You'll have some! You'll have as much coffee as you can drink, Jean!' Melania barked angrily. 'We didn't spend so much money on this foreign holiday to waste our time drinking coffee! And besides, in these little towns, you sometimes find very good things to buy very cheap, real bargains.'

The husband knew full well that there was no argument he could bring to bear and so he followed her inside the shop.

The shopkeeper, a short, jovial, solemn-looking Italian in a black suit, white shirt, and black tie, seemed somewhat taken aback by their arrival.

Melania asked to see a pair of white shoes. The shopkeeper obliged her, looking at her with a certain amount of commiseration: 'Maybe someone asked her to buy them …'

But Melania sat down to try on the shoes. She walked a few steps up and down the shop, which was as narrow as a passageway. The shopkeeper looked at her in increasing puzzlement. 'She must have something … something that doesn't give her long,' he thought. Melania asked for another pair, this time light blue. 'Impossible! How can the lady smile so serenely? Such a thing you do not buy with a smile on your face,' thought the shopkeeper.

'That puts paid to my coffee!' said the husband to himself angrily, looking at his wristwatch.

Finally, trying on the ninth pair of shoes, Melania said in a determined voice: 'Yes, these are the ones!' A pair of pale pink shoes with a black ribbon. 'I'll take these!' she told her husband. She thought the shoes went very well with the muslin headscarf she was wearing.

The time was also up. The bus blew its horn. The husband paid for the shoes. Hastily, angrily. Everybody else was already aboard the bus. Only one couple was missing: the Hammerstamms.

As she boarded the bus, Melania felt the ribbon of her right shoe snap. The shoe almost fell off her foot. On the bus, she discovered that the stitching of the other shoe had come undone. She nudged her husband in the ribs:

'Tell the guide to wait, I want to go back and change them. Better still, I'll return them and have a few words with that elegant shopkeeper whose face looked like a funeral, in his black suit and his black tie …'

'Can you believe this?' muttered the husband through clenched teeth.

The guide took up his microphone and spoke:

'Ladies and gentlemen! We'll now be continuing our journey. Before I forget, I should tell you that every place has its own customs, its own quirks. You may have noticed a small shoe shop next to the Funeral Director's. In this region it's a custom for the dead to be buried newly shod, which is why they sell cheap shoes there. Not for wearing in this world, but to wear while at rest in the next world … And now, ladies and gentlemen, coming up on your left you will see a castle on top of a hill … The castle was the residence of the Count of Vilalonga … the original structure is mediaeval …'

1984

Escape

The huge aeroplane gently landed on the runway. Bernard Rochberg quickly unfastened his seatbelt and hastened to be among the first to disembark. 'Thank you! It was a pleasant journey,' he said, smiling politely at the pilot and stewardesses who, standing in a line at the door of the aeroplane, were saying goodbye to the passengers.

How annoying the passport and customs formalities were! He had nothing to declare! A present: a silver bracelet engraved with African motifs. Something very authentic, but which would be of no interest to customs.

Rochberg couldn't remember ever having been so impatient to get home as he was now. And he had been away only two weeks. And how far away Nairobi had seemed to him this time, even though he had been there nine times before now, sent by his construction firm to check the progress of work being carried out in Kenya. Engineer Rochberg had reviewed progress on the construction of new housing blocks in the Kenyan capital and then hurried back home. The chief engineer, who ran the building site in Nairobi, asked him to stay another week, until they poured the foundations of the shopping centre that was to house shops, a bank, a post office, and a food market, but Rochberg didn't want to stay another day. He missed home and the few hours' flight to Lod airport seemed an eternity to him.

Bernard Rochberg felt that his life had reached a major turning point. The only turning point that could occur in the life of a bachelor. Marietta was just right for him, 'tailored to fit,' Rochberg said to himself with a smile. She was half an inch shorter than he was, and seven years younger. He had just reached the age of forty-seven, and before his departure to Africa, the two of them had drunk a bottle of champagne to celebrate her birthday. Her fortieth. The roundness of the number seemed to infuriate her, it sent her into a panic, but after a few glasses of sparkling, crystalline champagne, she had grown exuberant and merry. And she smiled, showing every one of her small pearly white teeth.

Yes, Marietta was just right for him, created just for him. Up until now, nothing had ever been just right for him. It was as if it were fated. None of the encounters arranged by his friends, nor happening spontaneously, had worked out. Rochberg had vague memories of faces, figures. These last few years, he had read the small ads in the newspapers, under the headings 'acquaintances', 'marriages', and had laughed to himself. There was always something that wasn't quite right for him. 'Intellectual 5'7" seeks man right for serious relationship.' And he was five feet five, two inches shorter than her, which would obviously be catastrophic … Or else he would read: 'Cultivated blonde, 35, seeks partner between 35 and 45.' And he was now forty-seven … And so on and so forth … Naturally, he could have tried, he could have ignored the inches and the years, but he had a dread of such 'first dates', which more often than not turned out to be depressingly disappointing.

No two ways about it, Marietta Contini was just what he needed to find, without having looked. For he had long since tired of looking. Marietta was just what he lacked. Both of them needed to escape: he from his loneliness hitherto, she from a constraint that had lasted too long. And they escaped together.

When he left, he gave her the keys to his apartment on North Street and the keys to his car, a smart steel-blue BMW, and sent her a telegram from Nairobi to tell her he would be arriving at two in the morning. They agreed that she would pick him up in the airport in his car.

No, he had nothing to declare, Rochberg irritably told the customs officer, and went outside the airport building. The lights of the city winked merrily in the night. All along the iron railing, friends and relatives were waiting for the new arrivals. Shouts, whoops of joy, embraces. Bernard Rochberg stood watching for a few minutes. He couldn't see the blond head and svelte figure of Marietta. With his briefcase resting on top of his large suitcase, he slowly pushed his trolley along the line of people waiting behind the railing, closely examining them. He couldn't see her. He was waiting for a shout: 'Bernard!' The shout did not come. Maybe she was late and would arrive any second, out of breath having run. The fact was that he didn't know whether she was a punctual person or always late. But maybe she hadn't received the telegram?

The people waiting for the new arrivals had thinned out. They had gone home. And all of a sudden, Bernard found himself alone. A porter, a policeman, a sleepy desk clerk passed from time to time, entering or leaving the airport building.

Rochberg headed for the taxi rank. Five drivers rushed at him all at once to grab his suitcase, but from his booth the dispatcher shouted over the microphone: 'Leave this fare for Joshua!'

A young man, tall and thin, nothing but skin and bones in fact, appeared from behind the booth. 'Take my car,' one of the drivers called to him.

‘I have good friends. They won’t let me fall down,’ said Joshua, the young driver, with a bitter smile. His hair was cropped short, like a bristle brush, and the yellow skin of his face was stretched taut like parchment over his protruding cheekbones.

‘Yes, well, it’s good to have friends,’ said Rochberg, vaguely.

In his mind he asked himself why Marietta hadn’t come to the airport. She can’t have received the telegram. There was no other explanation. Or maybe she was ill, he suddenly said to himself. Why hadn’t he thought of that?

She had been pale, frightened, as if pursued, the day he met her. He had gone to the architect’s office to collect some plans and she was working there as a draughtsman. She was blond, pale, serious. She had rings around her eyes, which suited her well. She was slightly plump, the round number of her age having rounded her figure, making her round breasts stand out in aggressive relief beneath her demure white blouse, buttoned to the neck.

Rochberg invited her out for coffee. The little Lutz Café was deserted at that time of morning. Yes, she had managed to escape, but she felt pursued, as she confessed to him. But once three months had passed, she would be free to live her life as she saw fit … Rochberg didn’t understand why it had to be three months precisely, rather than two and a half or three months and one week … After which, they met a few more times and, on the day when the three months were up, Marietta told him, radiantly: ‘I’ve escaped! I’ve escaped the grip! Now I’m free! As free as a bird!’ After which, he gave her a set of keys to his house on North Street and the key to his BMW. And he felt a change approaching in his life of bachelordom … His escape from loneliness …

The engine of the taxi rumbled monotonously, the lights of the city winked palely, coldly in the night.

‘I had my own car, my own house, a wife and children … Two years ago, I still had everything,’ muttered Joshua, the driver.

‘What happened?’ asked Rochberg.

‘It all began with an operation on my appendix. A minor operation … But it was unsuccessful. Pus collected. Then I had another operation. Then another. Up to now I’ve gone under the knife five times … Unbelievable … And in the meantime, everything has gone: the car and the house, my wife and two children. She shacked up with the grocer from the corner. An older man, a decent sort, a childless widower, who gave us food on credit for almost a whole year …’

‘What about love? Where did the love go?’ asked Rochberg, all of a sudden filled with a dull fury.

‘The love? When there are two children you need to feed, when you have to buy them shoes and school books …’ The driver’s yellow face contorted in a bitter smile. ‘And what a wedding we had! Five hundred guests. They danced until dawn. I paid the band to play another five hours after midnight … Oh my, how they danced! Lord God, how they danced!’ said Joshua, whistling between his teeth.

Bernard Rochberg all of a sudden felt an emptiness in the pit of his stomach. She had lived with a friend for fifteen years. A well-known lawyer. He had a family, a respectable wife, and four daughters. The eldest daughter had got married just the other day. He danced at the wedding and she smoked cigarette after cigarette in bed … And it couldn’t go on … Until when? Until all the daughters got married? And after that? She reached the age of forty and that number, so round a number, had irritated her, sent her into a panic. And after a few glasses of champagne, she had grown exuberant and merry, as if overflowing every dyke. And she laughed, liberated, laughed with every one of her pearly white teeth … She could have a daughter as well, or two daughters ... And marry her off in eighteen years' time ... Enough, she said to herself! It can't go on like this, ad infinitum! It's over, he no longer exists! She had tried six times to escape and six times she went back to him. A telephone call, a fleeting glance, a light touch on her arm, and all her resistance broke down ... Now was her seventh attempt to escape ... And she had the keys to a different apartment. And the three months had passed ...

Bernard Rochberg paid the driver.

'Oh, that wasn't why I told you the story ... But if you talk about it, it's as if it hurts less ...' said Joshua, the young driver, who was just skin and bones, smiling in embarrassment.

The house was empty, completely dark. The key was in the letterbox. In the living room, on the table, next to the car key, was a note. Bernard Rochberg was in no hurry to read it. Probably banalities: 'Forgive me ... I had no choice ...' or something of the sort. Bernard sank into a deep armchair, all of a sudden filled with absolute tranquillity. And he smiled to himself. Everything was perfectly clear, after all ...

1984

Maybe Even Happiness

She was beautiful. He was as ugly as a monkey. All of a sudden, he embraced her, he hugged her tightly to his chest and furiously said:

'What are you waiting for, woman? A fairy-tale prince? Well, know that I am the fairy-tale prince!'

She struggled in his grip. But he did not loosen it:

'I am your fairy-tale prince, dressed up as a monkey. But in time the enchantment will fall away and you'll see me as handsome and strong and as wholesome as fresh bread ...'

He felt her resistance weaken.

They had met at a sanatorium in the Arsa, where she had gone to rest with a childhood friend. She fully deserved a rest. She had worked long and hard and under pressure on the summer collection. She was a creator of dress designs and despite fierce competition the factory had agreed to take three of her summer dress designs and a design for a bathing suit. The bathing suit in particular filled her with pride and satisfaction. It was a highly ingenious design that managed to expose the greatest amount of female flesh to the sun and men's gazes, while still managing to cover the minimum that needed to be covered. A real success! She was happy and exhausted and went to the sanatorium in Arsa, where, in the dining room, the man opposite her had vaguely said, 'the salt cellar, please!' without addressing her, and she passed him the salt cellar, which had been to hand. And her friend, a cheery girl who laughed at everything and anything, whispered to her, giggling: 'Ugh, he looks like a monkey!' And she then quickly clapped her hand across her mouth lest the man notice her giggling at him.

A few times the man asked permission to join the two women on their walks through the woods. And the women thus found out that his name was Samuil Drathve and that he was an inspection engineer with the telephone company. 'The trouble I've had with one of your telephones!' she exclaimed. 'It stops working twice a week.' The engineer told her he was genuinely embarrassed to hear it and promised to take care of her line personally. With professional seriousness, he made a note of the complainant's telephone number and name: Anita Enghel. And once she was back home, Anita found herself receiving telephone calls: 'Hello! Samuil Drathve here, from telephone inspection, do you have any complaints?' And they would both burst out laughing. Sometimes she would be irritated and laugh because of her irritation. And when they met and she sensed him looking at her in a certain way, she would tell him she felt nothing for him and that that look of his annoyed her, it annoyed her badly ... And that he should stop looking at her like that ... And he would say to himself that he ought to stop once and for all, that he wouldn't inspect her telephone ever again. In the end, what did he care about her telephone ... She was beautiful, with chestnut hair, arched eyebrows above her green eyes, a delicate nose, thin lips, healthy teeth, while he was ugly, with beady, darting eyes set deep in their sockets, a splayed nose above protuberant lips, and looked like a monkey. She felt nothing for him and he ought to have left her and her telephone alone. If she had no feelings for him whatsoever ... But then why was she prepared to meet him? Why didn't she refuse to go out with him to the cinema or the theatre? It depended on her mood. The other day he asked her whether she would like to go out that evening to see a good film. She told him it was a Thursday, and she couldn't go to the cinema with him on Thursday. He didn't pick up on the right emphasis: she hadn't placed it on the 'him' but on the 'Thursday' … And he felt offended. Nevertheless, maybe she meant to say that she couldn't go with him on Thursday, but on Friday she could, or on Saturday or Sunday, on Monday or Tuesday, on Wednesday, yes, she could go with him … But ultimately what was he meant to understand by it?

After a year of marriage, Anita Enghel divorced her husband, who had lived all his life with his mother. His mother had carried on living in the same house after they got married. And she couldn't get on with her mother-in-law. The classic situation. And an ordinary one. Her husband was a well-bred, elegant professor of the history of civilisation, and they had parted in a very civilised manner. After which her friends and relatives looked out for her. 'You're thirty-eight years old and you can't stay single.' And they set up dates for her. A lawyer, a widower with two children, who cracked off-colour jokes; a taciturn district physician; a stylish official in the foreign office. Once, they introduced her to a very rich businessman who was in construction and had tractors and cranes and trucks and blocks of flats, a well-built man with slicked-back black hair and a strong, square jaw, with which he noisily crunched biscuits, who was always talking proudly about his tractors and trucks and cranes, about how he had started out with nothing, as a taxi driver, and look how far he had come … Then she met the director of a large bank, a nice blond-haired man with the beginnings of a bald patch, who lived with his mother and an elder brother who refused to marry. He, on the other hand, wanted to marry and get away from that house and from under his mother's thumb. He dreamed of moving into a house of his own at long last. He visited her a few times. Then his visits abruptly ceased. From relatives she found out that he had died suddenly. A heart attack. And so, Anite Enghel was irritated, and she categorically told the telephone engineer that she had met at the sanatorium in Arsa that she felt nothing for him. And he told her that he understood her perfectly. And dozens of times he told himself that he ought to leave her in peace, that he ought to stop checking her telephone line, which ultimately was a line like any other line. And what was the good of bandaging his head if he hadn't banged it. He'd had enough of a headache when after five years of marriage his wife had left him. She was a nurse at the hospital and she'd gone off with a rich, elderly orthopaedist. After carrying on with him for who knows how long. He had felt humiliated, as if he'd been dragged through the mud. He had thought of committing suicide. But now he could no longer understand why he had.

He felt that she was giving in. He held her in a tight embrace and moved his broad, flat, monkey-like nose closer to her fine, delicate nose. 'Yes, yes! I'm the fairy-tale prince! And you'll see, Anita, in time the enchantment will fade away and maybe you'll see me as handsome and strong and good … And we'll live happily ever after. My God, what am I saying? Yes, yes, maybe even happily. Who knows?'

1984

Uncle Sammy from America

'Don't write me any more such letters, don't ask me for anything else! Because you're not going to see a single cent from me, not a penny will you see from me as long as I live ...'

David Turkeltaub read in bewilderment the letter from his Uncle Samuil, or Sammy as he was now known: Sammy Turkeltaub of Cleveland, Ohio, the United States of America.

'Why is he so angry?' he wondered. 'What did I do?'

About three weeks earlier, he had been on the regular TAROM flight when it landed at Lod Airport, he had been given accommodation in a hostel for new arrivals in Ashdod, and he had written a letter to his uncle, in the following terms, as he recalled:

'Dear Uncle Sammy,

I've arrived in Israel from Vișeul de Jos in our country with my wife and our three children: Iancu, who's finished lycée, Sarale, who's in her fifth year, and Miriam, who's in the second year of primary school. We have been given accommodation in a building for new arrivals in Ashdod. We didn't bring many belongings with us, some clothes, a few dishes, a radio, we didn't have enough money to bring anything else ...'

Why was Uncle Sammy so angry, wondered David Turkeltaub. You'd have thought he'd been hit over that head of his with a club, that head of his with the greying temples.

'... you'll not see a cent from me for as long as I live. When I arrived in America, I went around faint from hunger and I slept under bridges and on the sidewalk. And nobody asked after my health. But now twelve nephews from my father's and my mother's side write letters to me. Don't write me any more such letters...'

'If you say so, Uncle! I won't write you any more such letters! Rest assured!' said David Turkeltaub in a conciliatory voice, as if his uncle were there to hear it. 'I won't write you any more such letters ...'

'He said what? Don't you write anything to him again! Nothing at all!' exclaimed Betty, his wife, on hearing his muttering. 'After all, what does he think? That we can't live without his dollars? You won't write anything to him ever again! Not a single word, the pig!'

'Betty, Betty!' David gently scolded her. 'Don't lose your temper like that! With or without his dollars, Uncle Sammy is still an uncle, isn't he?'

Samuil Turkeltaub had always been an eccentric, the black sheep of the family. He didn't get on with his brothers and sisters, who had families with numerous children, who kept small grocer's shops or taverns or stores that sold bits and pieces in the villages along the Wischau and Iza valleys. Samuil, or Schmulik, as he was nicknamed, never had the 'Sitzfleisch' to make him put down roots in any one place or any one trade. Which is why he was a jack of all trades. He was a bookkeeper for parcels of forestry land, a clerk in a big clothing shop in Sighet, a planer of planks at a high-class furniture workshop. There was no end of trades that he plied.

Unlike his other brothers, he never married and never settled down in a house of his own. And in the thirties, he boarded *The Hope* and two weeks later disembarked at the docks in New

York. For years after that, nobody had any news of him. Finally, that surly letter arrived: 'I'm alive and well …' A photograph of him was passed around within the family. A man with a round smoothly shaven face and a shock of unruly hair, wearing a light grey suit with very wide lapels and a broad necktie that hung down a very broad chest and which was emblazoned with a horse-riding cowboy shooting his pistol. He looked like a senator from Ohio or an important businessman. It was rumoured that he had become the owner of a cannery or textiles factory. But who could know? In America, every other man is a miniature Henry Ford or a Rockefeller.

After the war, twelve nephews, the children of his brothers and sisters, wrote to him from where they had scattered all over the world: three from Sydney, Australia, two from France, two from Argentina, one from Bolivia, three from right there in the United States of America, and now a twelfth, David Turkeltaub, newly arrived in Israel on a flight from Romania.

And they all received the same wrathful reply: 'You'll not see a cent from me! Don't write me any more such letters! When I first came here, I went around faint from hunger, like a stray dog, and I slept on the street and under bridges …'

Every year, David Turkeltaub sent his Uncle Sammy Turkeltaub of Cleveland, Ohio, a New Year's greetings card. To which he never received a reply.

'Why do you keep sending him them?' his wife Betty chided him.

'What do you want me to do, wife? He's my uncle.'

When their son Iancu, who in the meantime had become an engineer, got married, David Turkeltaub sent Uncle Sammy an invitation to the wedding. He received no reply.

When their daughter Sarah got married, he sent him an invitation to the wedding. He received no reply.

‘A greetings card he might send, maybe even with a little cheque inside,’ Betty would say in disgust.

‘Yes, he might, but also he might not! As you can very well see!’ David would answer angrily. ‘I don’t send him invitations to get cheques in return, but because he’s my uncle! He’s my only living uncle, of Father’s ten brothers and sisters! Don’t you understand, Betty?’

Of the twelve nephews, the children of Uncle Sammy’s brothers and sisters, ten grew angry and broke off all contact with him. ‘He’s a curmudgeon, a lout, a man without a soul,’ they said. Only one, David Turkeltaub, serenely continued to send him New Year’s greetings cards and invitations to weddings in Israel, held in the town of Ashdod, where he lived, without ever receiving any reply, and another, Gabriel Turkeltaub, the youngest of the nephews, used to visit him at his house from time to time. This Gabriel lived in Harrisburg, a town in the State of Pennsylvania, about two hundred and fifty miles from Cleveland, and he would drive to his Uncle Sammy’s at weekends.

Out of the blue, David received a letter from him:

‘My name is Gabriel and I’m your cousin, maybe you remember me, I lived with my parents in the village of Poienile Glodului before the war. I found your address at Uncle Sammy’s and I was glad to find out you’re well and that you and your family have settled in Israel, in Ashdod. Uncle Sammy has retired from business (I don’t really know what kind of business, maybe canning, maybe textiles, or maybe both), and now he lives all on his own in his big house on the shore of Lake Eyrie. He doesn’t much want to see anybody. A woman comes from time to time to do the cleaning and cook. Every time I come to visit him, he loses his temper and shouts, “Don’t you think I know why you come? You’ll not see a cent from me!” But I don’t

care, I come to see him because he's all alone, the poor man, and I repair a doorknob here, tighten a faucet there, and even so, I still exchange a word or two with him. I don't care that he yells at me: "I'm not giving you a cent! Not a penny will you get from me!" I shout back at him: "What do you imagine, Uncle, that I need your money? I don't give a crap about your money!" I shout at him because sometimes he drives me out of my mind. I've got a profession, I'm an inhalation therapist—' and here David marvelled at the occupations they had in that America of theirs '—and I work at the hospital in Harrison, where I use a special machine to treat patients with asthma and other respiratory complaints, it lets them inhale all kinds of medicated vapours, depending on what the physician prescribes, and I earn ten dollars an hour, and I don't need anybody to give me anything. "I don't need anything from you, Uncle Sammy!" I yell at him. And my wife works as a typesetter at a big print works and our two children lack for nothing, praise the Lord ...'

'Nor do we lack for anything,' said David, after reading the letter aloud, at which Betty gave him a rather nasty look. They had opened a 'fast food' place in a good spot, opposite the offices of a big cladding factory. Clerks, workers, businessmen came there to eat and drink something 'fast', a cold lemonade, a hot soup, a sausage, some cheese, and above all the 'house special.' 'Stop! Get your hot soup!' was the inscription above the door to the bodega, which served as both a shop sign and a rousing slogan. The truth was that Betty's soup enjoyed great success: a traditional Transylvanian soup with chunks of beef, tomatoes, peppers, kohlrabi, and pickled cabbage, always served piping hot. But Betty had also learned how to make Eastern dishes, and her zhug was no less spicy than that made by the Yemenis themselves. So, clerks, workers, factory customers all came there to eat and drink, and they all liked it there. But three months earlier the factory had closed its gates.

All the newspapers had reported on the massive bankruptcy. And the customers coming to the bodega naturally dwindled ... But there was David, repeating like a parrot, 'we don't lack for anything, we don't lack for anything ...' 'But what do we have that we don't lack for anything? We have nothing!' Betty thought to herself with a furious laugh.

After that curmudgeonly letter, 'don't write me any more such letters ... You'll not see a cent from me as long as I live,' and so on and so forth, not one more letter arrived from Uncle Sammy in Cleveland, Ohio.

Nine years later, however, a letter arrived by registered mail from a certain John Martens Goulding, attorney at law in the town of Cleveland, Ohio, United States of America, who was honoured to announce that on his decease Mr Samuil Turkeltaub had left in his will half of his money and property to 'Mr David Turkeltaub of Moshe Sharet Street, No. 18, Ashdod, Israel, which half of his estate was valued at one million five hundred and fifty-five thousand U.S. dollars.

The other half had been left to 'Mr Gabriel Turkeltaub of Harrison, Pennsylvania, Thomas Alva Edison Street, No. 29.'

'What a pity that Uncle Sammy isn't alive,' said David, full of grief. 'I would have written to him to say what we have done with the money. To say that we have bought a house for each of our children, and where each house is, and what it looks like, and that we have enlarged our restaurant, and that we have deposited a sum of money in the bank, and at which bank, and at what rate of interest. He wouldn't have written back, not a line would he have written, but I know that in his heart of hearts, he would have been pleased ...'

His wife Betty didn't have anything to reply this time.

1985

The Lizard

It was two in the morning. They were both sitting at the round white table from the kitchen, on the white chairs with the carmine cushions, slowly sipping cold sparkling wine.

The little dog, whose square head, big floppy ears, and greyish-white, beige-tinged long, thick, silky fur made it look like something fresh from a toy-shop window, was looking at the stranger with large black slightly phosphorescent eyes. It cautiously approached him. The man stroked its neck and back, felt the warmth of the soft fur. The little dog licked his feet.

'Betsy, what are you doing?' its mistress scolded it with a laugh.

She took a sip of cold wine before addressing the man:

'There's something to be learnt from this Betsy. You see, she can't abide not being stroked. When I'm upset, when I'm in a bad mood, and I shout at her and send her away from me, she sits in the corner, offended, and she won't touch her food. I get the impression that she could live without food or water, but she couldn't live without love …'

The two of them were sitting close to each other, across from the bed.

'I want to tell you that—' she began.

'No, no! Don't say anything,' murmured the man.

'It's so good ...'

The woman fell silent. After a while, she asked:

'Marc, aren't you thirsty?'

'Are you, Miriam?'

'I am, yes.'

'I am too.'

She went to the kitchen to fetch something. But he appeared by her side.

The white kitchen clock with the big blue hands showed two o'clock. It was two in the morning and they were sitting at the white table from the kitchen, on the white chairs with the carmine cushions, sipping cold sparkling wine from tall, slender glasses.

Marc knew everything about her and yet knew nothing. She didn't hide anything from him. She had had a husband whom she had divorced and a husband who had died of a serious illness. What illness? She had told him, but Marc had forgotten. And what did it matter? Miriam had remained single. She had children somewhere far away, in a foreign country, good children, who sent her postcards and who from time to time phoned her. Marc had children too, two daughters and a son, who lived far away and sent postcards and occasionally phoned him: 'How are you, Dad?' 'Dad, how are you feeling?' Very good children.

Marc looked at her. Her tousled blond hair. Her face, from which she had taken off her make-up, was pale, almost unlined, the eyelashes had grown white, and light grey-green eyes were clear and calm. Everything was in keeping with that white, calm night.

What would tomorrow bring? Who knows?

What had yesterday brought? Marc was sitting on a bench in the park. On the bench to his left, three old men were having a heated discussion about the government's mistaken policies, about the price of fruit, about young people today. 'No, no!' Marc said to himself, 'I've still got a way to go before that!' Politics, prices, young people today, and 'back in our day.' Marc looked at the ground, among the long blades of grass by the bench he espied a yellow-gold lizard, which stood with its legs spread wide, basking voluptuously in the sun. It looked like a delicate, lacy leaf, almost translucent. It was then that she appeared. In a merry company of friends. They introduced her. 'Mrs Miriam Wallen.'

'Marc Nolden,' he introduced himself. And they went out a few times together. They went to three films, a play, four concerts, and two cafés. She had clear, greenish-grey eyes. Tall, slender. They were a perfect match. She was blond, Marc had dark hair with the classic greying temples. Both were single. Both had quarrels with the departed. Questions, answers, reproaches left unspoken in life. Something morbid. But they were aware that it was something morbid. Talking to somebody who is no more. Both still lived in the past. Both were alone in the present. Both peered into the future, looking for something … For some ray of light. For happiness … It made them feel like laughing.

Telephone calls. Engaged tones. Or the angry voice of a man slamming down the receiver: 'wrong number.' Or quite simply, nobody lifting the receiver. They lost touch. She had children somewhere, he had children somewhere. Good children, who sent postcards occasionally.

She didn't answer her telephone.

Marc was sitting on the bench in the park. Nearby, on another bench, three old men were talking about the price of vegetables, about international politics, about 'young people today.' 'Oho, back in our day …' 'No, no!' says Marc to himself, 'there's a way to go before that …' What did she mean, when they were sitting pressed up against each other, across from the bed? It was so good … Marc looked at the ground. The gold lizard was there, among the blades of grass, with its little legs splayed, sprawled voluptuously on its belly. It looked like an autumn leaf, delicate, lacy. Marc pressed down on the lizard's tail with the toe of his shoe. It struggled for a time, and then, abruptly freed, it fled, leaving its little tail under the sole of Marc's shoe. A lizard can live without its tail, Marc consoled himself. In time, the tail grows back, albeit not as long as before. Maybe one day it will recover, thought Marc. Maybe even tomorrow. Or the day after.

1985

Sunday Love

He lay comfortably on the couch and felt the rage slowly welling up inside him. Now he had to get up, just when he felt like lazing on the couch, he had to go and take a hot bath, then a cold shower, to shave, to dress up smartly, lingering for half an hour over the right necktie, and go to hers. Wouldn't it have been better to be able to stretch out his arm at night, any night, while he lay sweetly half-asleep in his big bed, and feel her warm body next to his? And why did they have to meet only on Sundays? Maybe one Sunday he wasn't in the mood and had a hankering for her on a Monday, or a Tuesday, or a Wednesday, Thursday, Friday, Saturday?

Sunday love! Yes, it was becoming clearer and clearer to him: he loved her more on Mondays, Tuesdays, Wednesdays, Thursdays, Fridays, Saturdays ... He'd even started to dislike Sundays. Even to hate them ... He hated the straw-blond boyishly short hair that he loved madly every other day of the week; that bright blond hair, dyed of course, he didn't know what colour it had been previously, he was able to guess only from the reddish-chestnut colour of her hair in other, hidden places. And her dark, beautiful eyes, with the rings around them, and her narrow, rather saucily upturned nose: he liked all those things every other day of the week. But they had started to annoy him on Sundays.

They had met seven months previously, on an ocean cruise around the Greek islands. In the distance they had seen an ancient temple with tall columns.

'What temple is that?' she asked, addressing nobody in particular.

'I have no idea!' he said, quickly striking up a conversation. 'But I think it might be the temple of Aphrodite. Who can deny pampered goddesses like her?'

And they both laughed. She worked in the laboratory at a fruit syrup factory and dealt with sweet syrups all day long. It was as if her whole skin was imbued with syrup. He was a geologist and worked for an enterprise that bored for oil without finding it. He had long since accustomed himself to the hope that someday, somewhere oil would gush up. He was forty years old and a sworn bachelor … She too, the lab worker at the sweet syrup factory, was very nearly the same age. At some point in the past, for a year and three months, she had been married to a district physician, who lived with his mother, always taking her side. Which annoyed her no end, until one fine day they both decided to separate. It was easy for them to separate, since they had nothing to divide up between them. They didn't have children, each had their own job and wage, they hadn't managed to buy anything much jointly, they hadn't had time to save up money in a joint account.

During the fourteen-day cruise, Paula and Daniel saw a great many Greek islands with white marble temples and fishing villages; they saw a great many sunrises and sunsets over the sea, and before disembarking at the end of the cruise, they agreed to meet the following Sunday. It had been seven months since then, and they saw each other every Sunday.

Daniel lay sprawled on his couch and wrathfully asked himself: why does it have to be Sunday? Maybe because both of them felt it was the most suitable day? But who knows? Maybe she had someone else on Mondays, or Tuesdays, or Wednesdays, Thursdays, Fridays, Saturdays? Maybe the director of the fruit syrups factory, an obese man, naturally, who had a nagging wife and three noisy children at home, went to hers on Tuesdays to quell his nerves, since he had to spend his weekends at home and on his best behaviour? Or maybe it was a colleague from the factory, a syrup engineer or sub-engineer, who went to hers on Thursdays? Or maybe the lanky bachelor with tortoise-shell glasses who worked at the town hall and lived in the mansard of her building, went downstairs to hers once a week, on Mondays or Wednesdays or Fridays?

'Hey, hey! Stop!' Daniel mentally yelled at himself. 'You've a right to be jealous on Sundays! But not on any other day of the week. Granted, if she phoned and said: "Daniel, don't come this Sunday!" you'd have every right to be jealous. But she's never phoned to say anything of the sort. Or maybe you want to conquer the other days for yourself? In which case, tell her! How about this very day you stand in front of her, adopting a dignified pose, look deeply into her eyes and tell her: I want you for the whole week ... Every week ... Maybe that's what she's waiting for. But you don't dare to say it, do you? Because ultimately, it suits you to have everything remain the way it is ...'

Daniel looked at his watch and leapt off the couch. He took a hot bath, followed by a cold shower. He carefully shaved, put on his smart light blue suit, selected a white-and-blue striped silk tie, and went out to meet her.

1985

Swerve

On the beach, tensely lying on a lounger, Eugenia abruptly turned her face away him, holding her snub nose high, as if sniffing the salty sea air.

'What's the matter?' asked Paul. 'Why won't you look at me?'

'I'm looking at the sea!'

'I'm not as good to look at as that murky yellow water?' said Paul, attempting a quip.

'Don't be ridiculous!' replied Eugenia, still not looking at him.

Her tone could not have been more serious. Paul felt that tone like a stone flung violently at his chest.

What had happened? What had been the turning point, he wondered. For there had been a turning point, a sudden, violent swerve, of ninety degrees at least. Just a few weeks ago, they were together; each drank in the other with their gaze, they felt each other with their every pore, each thrilled to the briefest meeting of their eyes. Then she began to change inexplicably and he was left to look at her without her looking back at him. They saw each other just as often, they went to the same places, they visited the same friends, as if nothing had happened, but they were no longer together. She was next to him, the same as before, but he felt she was far away, so much so that sometimes it seemed that he couldn't even see her very well ... What had happened? When had it happened?

They were together at a meal with the Morgenthalers. Jack Morgenthaler was the director of a bank, a tall, fat, jovial man with a few strands of red hair combed across his gleaming bald pate. He was saying that he honestly didn't like the painting. His wife, Renata, was a cheerful, slender, rheumatic woman. She had taught gymnastics, but when she started to suffer from rheumatism, she took a course and retrained as a teacher at a school for children with disabilities. She was a great art lover and had filled the walls with modern paintings, which her husband did not so much as look at. They often quarrelled about it. Renata had befriended Eugenia Barton, who taught at the same school: Eugenia was a geography teacher, Renata a P.E. teacher. The Bartons and the Morgenthalers had used to visit each other before, they would meet at picnics with mutual friends, but after Eugenia's husband, a chemist, died unexpectedly, of a heart attack, Renata began telephoning her more often, she would invite her to lunch or dinner, or to go shopping together, so that Eugenia wouldn't feel so alone. But one Saturday, when Renata invited her to a meal, Eugenia told her that she wasn't alone any more. She had met a gentleman by the name of Paul Ingelhart, a construction engineer, and asked whether she could bring him. Renata was left surprised by this, but also glad at the same time. She asked for details and Eugenia told her that Paul had been divorced for a long time, his ex-wife lived far away, over the ocean, he had no contact with her; that Paul was a tall man with a blond moustache and a scar on his chin, which lent him a manly, swashbuckling air. It looked as if it were a duelling scar. But Paul had openly confessed that he had suffered the cut when he was seven years old, playing with a knife in the kitchen. Eugenia and Renata laughed copiously at this bathetic story. Yes, the age of the swashbucklers had long since passed! They spoke on the telephone for about half an hour.

When Eugenia told Paul, 'We've been invited to a meal at the Morgenthaler's place,' he was very pleasantly surprised. He liked to stay at home with Eugenia and he liked to go out with her, to the cinema, to concerts, to restaurants. He felt well in the company of this tall, beautiful woman, who had streaks of grey in her chestnut hair, which she didn't try to hide. They were made for each other, those two who had met by chance, through friends in common: he not wanting to remember what he once was, she wanting to forget what she once was ... And now she had decided not to conceal their connection, to show it to the world.

They also spent a weekend together, at the seaside villa of Kalkenstein the lawyer, and his wife. They went to the Schurmans' together: a dance party that began at eleven at night and ended at dawn. Eugenia was very much in demand. Almost all the men asked her to dance and to Paul it seemed that some of them held her hips too tightly and kept their cheeks too closely to hers as they danced, while she didn't draw back her own cheek. At dawn, in the car on the way home, he told her this, as if in passing:

'You were very much in demand last night! All the men were eating you up with their eyes ...'

It sounded like a reproach.

'But none of them has seen me naked!' came Eugenia's cutting reply.

A pleasant warmth flooded Paul's cheeks. He thought of her warm, vibrant skin, round breasts with delicate pink nipples, the chestnut brown triangle of coarse hair between the round thighs, the long, beautiful legs. Paul suddenly stopped the car in the middle of the road. He leaned across to her and pressed his burning lips to hers.

'You're mad, Paul!' she said, laughing. 'To stop the car like this in the middle of the road ...'

And now, on the beach, she demonstratively turned her head away, held her snub nose upturned in the breeze, gazed obdurately at the sea.

'Aren't I as interesting and handsome as that dirty yellow seawater?'

'You're being ridiculous,' replied Eugenia, angrily.

What had happened? Where had that sharp, unexpected swerve intervened?

'The businessman from Salt Lake City, Utah' were the words that flashed through Paul's mind. How could he not have thought of it before? He had thought the episode to be in the past. But it seemed it had left traces, somewhere ...

One morning, Paul Ingelhart was at home when the telephone rang.

'Who is it? Harry? Harry Berkey? I'm sorry, Mr Berkey, but you must have the wrong number. I don't know anybody by that name ... What? Hershey? Hershey Berkovitch? Now I understand! Why didn't you say so?'

Yes, it was none other than Hersh Berkovitch, with whom he had shared a desk in lycée, until the seventh form, when Hershey dropped out of school, not being studiously inclined, and left for America. They had grown up together in a quite well-off village in a valley of the Carpathian Mountains, Underhill Glade, as the little town's name would translate. They hadn't seen each other for thirty years. And now here he was, a 'businessman,' a 'businessman from Salt Lake City,' no less.

They met that evening at the Cosmos Hotel, where the visitor was staying. Yes, it was Hershey in the flesh, almost unchanged: still the same red hair, now with a few grey strands, the same small, lively, badger-like eyes, the same long, oval face, the same large nose, like a pink potato, which looked like someone had stuck it in the middle of his face for a joke. The same ridiculous, merry Hershey as in their youth.

They sat lolling in deep armchairs in the hotel lobby, reminiscing about that provincial small town and their time in lycée. About how they played truant from maths and chemistry lessons and tumbled with girls in the woods. About how Armand Hancea, the history teacher, a lanky man, as thin as a plank, always used to tell Toma Albeni, a chubby boy with skin as white as a girl's, 'You have a sense for history, Albeni! Come to my house so that I can explain the lesson to you,' scratching himself on the back. It was rumoured that the teacher liked boys with delicate white skin, although over the course of the years, there was nothing tangible to bear out the gossip. They also recalled Tandra Magnes, the French teacher, a plump, ripe young lady, who would enter the classroom trotting on high heels, and on whose football-like breasts the eyes of every boy remained fixed for as long as the lesson lasted.

The two friends chatted away, conjuring up memories of the past as they lolled in the deep armchairs of the Hotel Cosmos lobby. Three times the 'businessman' inquired whether Paul would like a drink, and each time Paul politely declined, but when finally he agreed to an orange juice, Harry Berkey, which is to say, Hershi Berkovitch, forgot to order it for him.

When the subject of his profession and career arose and Ingelhart told him he was an engineer at a construction firm, Berkovitch-Berkey regaled him with the fact that he owned no fewer than five wine and liquor stores in various districts of Salt Lake City, Utah. From that village, Underhill Glade, in the back of beyond, a God-forsaken place, as they say, he had ended up in Salt Lake City, Utah … Thirty years previously, he had arrived in America with five dollars in his pocket and now, praise be to God … Yet another American success story. A miniature Henry Ford … Five stores selling alcoholic beverages, open until midnight. Twenty-five armed robberies, stick-ups, as they're called, to date. Once, the robbers didn't just tell him to stick his hands in the air, but tied him up and shoved him inside the small storeroom outside, next to the empty crates and bottles. A lucky thing they hadn't put a slug in his head. But anyway, five stores into whose tills the dollars day after day, from morning until midnight ...

As the two friends chatted in the lobby of the Cosmos Hotel, Paul began to feel very thirsty and Harry Berkey-Berkovitch had still forgotten to order him an orange juice. And then finally he came to the reason for his coming. He had been a widower for three years. He felt very alone. He had a twenty-five-year-old daughter, who didn't want to live in his house, he'd rented a small apartment in New York for her, and she worked as a secretary there, for some law firm ... Kids today ... And he had received proposals. He was here to meet a woman who had been divorced for three years or so, who designed dresses for a fashion house, if he understood rightly. The date had been set for the following evening, at the White Rose restaurant.

'Could you come along too?' Harry Berkey suddenly asked him.

'Me? Why would you want me to be there?'

'It's all a bit much for me and I'd like you to tell me what your opinion of her is. After all, we're childhood friends.'

And here Paul made his big mistake. A stupid mistake, which led to that sudden and inexplicable swerve ... It would be pointless him going alone, he thought to himself. He would go with Eugenia. Why did he do it? Perhaps out of vanity? Perhaps somewhere deep down he wanted to show off, to show that 'businessman from Salt Lake City, Utah,' the proprietor of five shops that sold alcoholic beverages, what a superb woman he was going out with. It never entered his head, nor could it have ever entered his head, that a woman such as Eugenia

Barton, a respectable geography teacher, could be receptive to a 'businessman from Salt Lake City, Utah.'

Indeed, when he invited her to the restaurant, Eugenia was interested to know who this friend of his was. What does he do in America? What is his profession? Is he rich? The last of these questions rather took Paul aback. What did it matter whether he was rich or poor? What did it matter *to her*?

Rather stung by this, Paul replied:

'From the way he talks, it sounds like he's rich, but how can one know for sure? I for one haven't counted his money, I haven't seen his bank statements.'

That evening at the White Rose restaurant, Eugenia was elegantly attired, cheerful, and the whole evening she spoke almost only to that 'American success story' named Mr Harry Berkey. The woman he had come there to meet managed to get a few words in, but otherwise failed to enjoy any attention whatever. She was not plain-looking, that dress designer, but when she laughed she showed a set of very small teeth and prominent gums, and she laughed not infrequently, rather than keeping her mouth shut. Apart from that, she was an intelligent woman, but very awkward, not knowing how to comport herself in such a situation.

After dinner, they parted in front of the restaurant and Harry Berkey-Berkovitch walked the fashion designer home.

'He's going to sleep with her!' remarked Eugenia suddenly.

'I doubt it. She's not so enticing ...'

'But if the man has an itch ...'

'What's the matter with you, Eugenia?'

Paul was intrigued. The rest of the evening, Eugenia was angry, irritable. Not a trace of her volubility and verve during dinner.

What could have so stirred this beautiful, intelligent woman on seeing a short, red-haired man with badger-like eyes and a large pink potato of a nose that looked like someone had stuck it on his oval face, this businessman-from-Salt-Lake-City-Utah, this success story? Yes, that very evening, Paul ought to have told Eugenia Barton: 'Thanks! Thanks for everything!' and left.

Maybe he ought to have kissed her hand politely and left. Once and for all. Irrevocably. It would have been elegant, dignified. But he didn't have the strength. Why not?

After he departed, the topic of 'Businessman' Berkey-Berkovitch never came up, and the two of them remained together.

And life went on as before, as if nothing had happened. They went out for meals, to the Morgenthalers', to dances at the Schurmans' that went on until dawn, to the Kalkensteins' villa on the seashore, and so on. The same as before. Or rather, not quite the same as before.

'Why won't you look at me, Eugenia?'

'I'm looking at the sea!'

'Aren't I as good-looking at that dirty yellow seawater?' said Paul, attempting a quip.

'You're being ridiculous!' retorted Eugenia, brusquely, without looking at him.

'Why not leave now? Why don't I get up right now, without a word, and leave?' Paul asked himself.

1985

The Murmur of Water

That morning it had rained on and off, in the afternoon the sun had come out, and now, as evening fell, grey clouds were gathering once more. Professor Maximilian Brandwein put on his 'onomatopoeic' raincoat and left the house. That's what he called it: 'onomatopoeic', the dark blue raincoat which, in the fifties, when it was fashionable, everybody had nicknamed 'swish-swish.' And rightly so, as when it was dry, the raincoat swished at every step.

In his wardrobe, Professor Brandwein had another three raincoats, almost new, handsome, modern ones, barely worn, but he liked this 'onomatopoeic' raincoat, which swished for him as he walked, making him feel as if he weren't alone.

He had a ten-minute walk to reach the number seven bus stop. He would get off the bus at the corner of Golan Street and Roses Street, where the Aroma Café was. A clean, quiet little place, the lady had said over the phone, where they served excellent coffee and very tasty cheese pies. 'How would they recognise each other?' he enquired. 'What does the gentleman look like?' the lady wished to know. Tall, grey, naturally, given his age, wearing a navy-blue coat and a light grey tie, although that wasn't much to go by. He would also be wearing slightly tinted spectacles, but nor was that very much to go by. Lots of people wear them ... But anyway, not many people would be there at five o'clock in the afternoon on a work day, and as for her, he would recognise her straight away—here the lady's voice through the receiver sounded slightly sardonic—because she was blond, beautiful, and as would become plain, intelligent and even modest ... Apart from that, she would be wearing a pink jacket and pink trousers.

A woman of sixty, give or take, and dressed in pink, marvelled the professor. She really must be something special. But what could you know? What kind of pink? There were so many shades of pink. And what kind of lady was she?

For five years, ever since his wife left him to go to her eternal rest, having suffered from a heart complaint, his friends and relatives had been looking after him. They proposed all kinds of spinsters, widows and divorcées to him, they gave him telephone numbers, the addresses of very nice ladies, very distinguished ladies, highly cultivated ladies, society ladies, and above all else, very lonely ladies. What have you got to lose if you give her a ring? What if you met her? And he always ended up concluding that his taste couldn't be more different than theirs.

Or maybe he was looking for something else entirely? Always something other than what was on offer.

Maximilian Brandwein was a pensioner, a retired university literature professor, and his book on onomatopoeia had once caused a stir, long ago, at the beginning of his career.

He married Ina Markins, who had left him some five years earlier: a heart attack just after giving a chemistry lesson at the girls' school where she taught. She collapsed at the door of the staffroom, they took her to hospital, but it was too late. Ever since, Maximilian Brandwein had been looking for a woman like her. Actually, he wasn't looking for a woman, but in every new woman he met, he looked for her, without ever saying it, without even saying it to himself. It would have been simply ridiculous. No two women are alike, just as no two fingerprints are alike.

He used to say to her, 'Ina, maybe it would be good if we went to the cinema.'

She never contradicted him, she would say, 'Yes, that would be good.'

And she wouldn't budge from the kitchen. And both of them would stay at home.

Or when he used to say to her, 'There's going to be an interesting concert today. Maybe, we ought to go,' she would answer, 'Yes, maybe we ought to.' And she wouldn't look up from her embroidery. And they would stay at home in their dressing gowns and slippers.

She was a very good chemistry teacher, but fundamentally, she was a housewife, a housewife by vocation.

Was he unconsciously looking for a woman like her, to be busy in the kitchen, to look after the house, and at night to fill the twin bed next to his with her warm soft body? For a quiet woman, a quiet, grey life, mostly spent in a soft dressing gown and slippers? Or maybe he wasn't? Maybe this time he might like and might need a tempestuous woman to make him jump out of his slippers, to drag him with her to the theatre, the cinema, concerts, exhibitions, trips abroad, to Scandinavia, Mexico, the Far East ... Something different, something different than before. Once a man is left a widower, there are two reasons he doesn't remarry: either because he had a happy marriage or because he had an unhappy one. What kind of marriage had he had? Maximilian Brandwein couldn't really tell. A quiet one, obviously, almost a sleepy one, but was it a happy one? Who knows? And what was it he wanted now? A rather cynical former colleague of his, also retired, who had taught medicine at the university, a widower for more than ten years, and therefore with long experience of the subject at hand, told him just the other day: 'Unfortunately, there are very many willing and available single women … But at our age, we in fact have to choose between two categories: either a woman who is past it and whom nobody wants any more or a young woman, whom far too many other men want. Whichever way you choose, it won't turn out well.'

What was he looking for, what was it he really wanted? And if he did want it, was wanting it enough? Professor Brandwein allowed himself a sardonic smile. It's possible to spur yourself on, to make a physical and mental effort, to change your lot in life, but you might find yourself having an apoplectic fit or an attack of the nerves … Life keeps flowing on its natural course, like a river, and it would be ridiculous for that river to try to flow faster or slower than it was naturally inclined, or to flow in a different direction than its bed demanded …

The Aroma Café was a small, pleasant place with carved tables and chairs made of stained wood. There was something antique about it, something settled and reassuring. Only three tables were taken: an elderly couple drinking tea; a blond lad and a chestnut-haired girl with steaming cups of coffee and a plate of cheese pies in front of them, who were giggling together in the corner at the back; and a man with greying temples, absorbed in reading a newspaper.

It was five o'clock. He had arrived on the dot. He sat down at a table with a view of the front door. He asked for a cup of milky coffee and a cheese pie.

She would be ten minutes late, of course, Brandwein said to himself. He had a few years' experience of such rendezvous: she would be late, lest she arrive first, God forbid. And so as to make as much of an entrance as possible … But he hoped she wouldn't mistake him for the greying man absorbed in the newspaper. That would be comical. And embarrassing ... Out of the question! He was wearing a light-grey coat and his spectacles had thick, clear lenses, not tinted ones.

He sipped his coffee. It really was as good as they said. 'Well done, Aroma!' he said to himself, praising the café in his mind. 'You warrant your name.' A few minutes later, he thought: 'What am I doing here? Why am I not sitting quietly at home in my dressing gown and slippers? I have a woman who comes three times a week to cook for me and do the cleaning. Why couldn't I have minded my own onomatopoeia?'

He was working on a book titled *Comparative Onomatopoeia*. It was a study of the natural sounds that can be found in numerous European, Asian, and African languages, sounds which have passed from one language to another or been taken from nature in forms that are similar in different languages. And the differences between them. Why, for example, is the sound of rippling water *susurrus* in Latin, *susurrer* in French, but *murmeln* in German and *murmur* in English?

A bright pinkness suddenly impinged on the tinted lenses of his spectacles. Mrs Malvina Wegweiler had appeared in the doorway. A huge pink outline. Pink jacket, pink trousers so tight that they displayed the rolls of fat on her hips and lower body. And hanging down from her shoulders, like a stage backdrop, a black impermeable cape. Brandwein politely rose to his feet and invited her to take a seat at his table. She wore pink powder on her cheeks, pink lipstick. And her nails were painted with clots of the same colour. 'Good God, the pains she takes to look young, to fool people,' thought Brandwein. But in his mind, he then immediately jumped to her defence: 'As if I myself didn't take similar pains! Don't I treat my dry, lifeless hair with a tonic to make it look healthier and lend it a hint of blond? Don't I massage my forehead with a cream to make it look suppler?

Don't I wear tinted glasses to hide the winkles around my eyes? What did I expect of her?'

Still on his feet, Professor Brandwein waited for her to take her seat at the table opposite him. Once she was seated, he enquired:

'What would you like, Mrs Wegweiler?'

'Turkish coffee.'

'Anything else? The cheese pies here are really excellent!'

'Oh, no, thank you, I'm on a diet.'

'Perfectly understandable,' said Brandwein to himself, and then aloud:

'Perhaps you could postpone the diet until after our meeting?'

'You're quite right,' she laughed.

The waiter, a dapper man with a broad smile on his face, solemnly repeated their order as if it made his happiness complete: 'Turkish coffee and a cheese pie!'

Whereupon he vanished into the kitchen.

For a few moments, an embarrassed silence reigned between them.

'Did you get caught in the rain on your way here?' Mrs Wegweiler finally asked.

'No. Perhaps the rain had also decided to postpone itself until after our meeting.'

Both laughed reservedly. The ice was beginning to break.

'I was ten minutes late,' said the lady. 'Please forgive me.'

'Think nothing of it.'

'You know, in any house there's always something to tidy up, to put in its right place. I like everything to be in the right place.'

'Naturally!' approved Professor Brandwein. 'At my house, nothing seems to me to be in the right place. Three weeks ago, the matte globe of the living-room chandelier broke. I sat down at the table and, all of a sudden, I heard a pop and a piece of glass fell from the chandelier. I keep meaning to buy a new globe, but the more time passes, the more I realise that it's fine the way it is. From the practical point of view, maybe even better than it was: I get more light now, straight from the naked bulb. Likewise, one of my rugs has torn, it's almost in tatters, and I ought to get a new one. I also think the curtains need replacing, as they're a bit frayed. But with each passing day, I realise it's perfectly all right the way it is. If we proceed from the idea, and it's one that strikes me as increasingly just, the idea that man can find contentment anywhere at all, if not even happiness, which is a very big word, one without much foundation or sense, then I think that I could live quite contentedly even in a cave. I would arrange my books in a crevice, the kitchen in an alcove in the rock, I would sleep on a bearskin, and so on . . .'

Mrs Malvina Wegweiler laughed:

'Very nice, but then what is the difference between simply living and living well? Or living better? Having nice rugs, crystal chandeliers, silverware, gold and diamond jewellery, silk sheets rather than a bearskin, and . . . and somebody at your side . . . to hear from the bathroom the murmur of water from the shower, running down his body, to hear the hiss of the razorblade over his cheeks as he shaves, his agitated pacing around the house while his breakfast is being prepared in the kitchen, to hear him praising you and criticising you, for him to teach you and scold you and love you. Yes, for him to love you, why not? As for me, I have crystal chandeliers and rugs and vases and jewels . . .'

She abruptly fell silent, in embarrassment, her eyes fixed on the Turkish coffee in her cup. She must have been beautiful once, this 'lady in pink,' thought Brandwein, with her oval face, which hadn't sagged, which wasn't lined, with her grey-green eyes and her innocent, childlike smile.

Both remained silent for a long moment, slowly sipping their coffee.

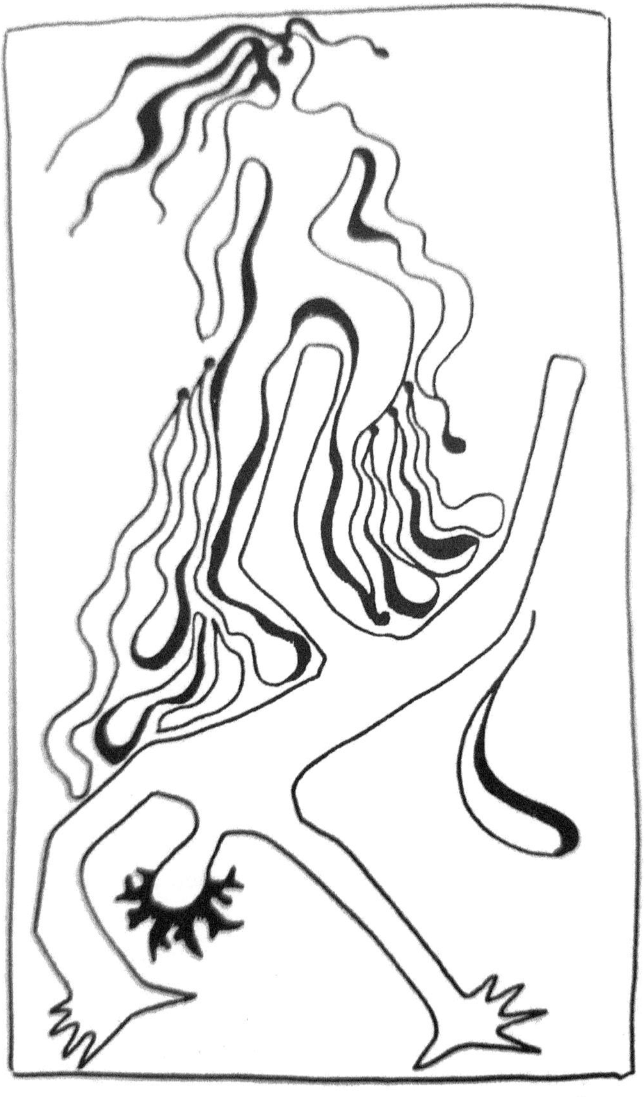

The topic then changed to the past. And each revealed a few details of their lives. She had grown up in the house of a textiles trader, her mother was a housewife, a dedicated housewife, she had gone to the girls' school in her little town in eastern Europe, she had read novels, you know the kind of thing: Scarlet O'Hara and *Gone with the Wind*, *The Citadel* and *The Enchanted Heart*, *The Mysteries of Paris* and *The Lord Handed Me A Lamp*. She'd taken piano lessons, she played the *Polonaise* and *Für Elise* very well … She still tinkled the ivories, you know, from memory … what about the gentleman? He had once played the violin. His mother was a very exacting housewife, everything had to be in the proper place around the house, and here Professor Brandwein smiled at the memory, she had used to arrange the books and school things in his room, she had sent him to the best private violin teacher in Bucharest, she wanted to make a violinist of him, not just any violinist, but a famous one, a Jascha Heifetz at the very least … His father was dead set on his only son taking over his liqueur factory. Brandwein Liqueurs: there was a real brand name! But he had become a university professor. And a literature professor at that … His field was onomatopoeia.

'Oh, oh!' exclaimed Mrs Wegweiler. 'Onomatopoeia, that must be something very interesting … And what about your late wife, may she rest in peace?'

'She was a chemistry teacher and a housewife, a very good housewife, everything around the house used to be in its proper place, until five years ago, a heart attack …'

'Children?'

'We didn't have any.'

'Neither did we.'

The professor would have liked to add something philosophical at this point: 'It was not to be' or 'Fate did not will it.' But he said nothing. After another long moment, he asked:

'And what about your late husband?'

'He was an engineer. Hydraulic ...' Mrs Malvina Wegweiler smiled in slight embarrassment. 'My mother, may she rest in peace, was stubbornly determined that I marry a man only from one of the following three professions, and in the following order of preference: in first place, a doctor, naturally, either a surgeon, or an ear, nose and throat man, or a gynaecologist, but an orthopaedist not so much, and certainly not a venereal specialist, God forbid! And if a doctor couldn't be found for me, a lawyer would also be good, and if a suitable lawyer wasn't available, then maybe an engineer would do. Well, fate found me an engineer, Arthur Wegweiler, an expert in irrigation. We travelled all over the world together, to Mexico, Central and South America, South Africa, the Far East. He worked on irrigation projects, fish farms, pearl farms, and even large projects such as hydroelectric dams. I lived an interesting, busy life, with constant changes of scene, always new places, and theatres, concerts, cinemas, museums, socialising, parties, receptions. For twenty-eight years.'

Mrs Wegweiler fell silent, sipped a little coffee from her cup. Professor Brandwein timidly broke the silence:

'Was he ill before ... before he left you for the eternal life?'

The words sounded rather pretentious to his own ears, but he spoke them nonetheless.

'It was I who left him first,' she stated abruptly. 'People know me for a widow, but I'm actually a divorcée!'

Brandwein looked at her in wide-eyed, honest surprise. She went on:

'Arthur was a healthy man, a sturdy man, extremely hardworking and tenacious. Whenever he began a project, he didn't let up until he had finished it. Once, he came home from the office where he worked on his designs and told me about a new idea of his. Something to do with a correlation between the sound of water and hydraulic force … I didn't understand any of it. I never understood his projects, not one wit, but still he felt the need to share them with me. And I would listen to him patiently. From time to time he would turn on the tap in the kitchen or the bathroom and listen to the murmur of the water … At intervals he would write something down in the blue notebook that he kept in the inside pocket of his jacket, fastened with a button. One day—it was a Tuesday, I remember it like yesterday—I came home from the hairdresser's, because that evening we were going to a concert, and I found the living room flooded with water. One or two inches of water submerging the Persian rug. I dashed to the bathroom and found him in his evening wear sitting on a stool with all the taps running, listening to the sound of the flowing water …

'"Arthur, what's the matter with you? Can't you see the whole house is inundated?"

'"I didn't notice," he stammered, as if waking from a dream.

'"Why did you do such a thing?" I asked, almost in tears.

'He looked around him suspiciously and confidentially told me:

'"I was listening to the murmur of the water. Yes, yes, there is a correlation between sound and force that can be expressed mathematically."

'His eyes brimmed with a secret happiness. I couldn't really understand it, but I realised he was looking for something, tenaciously, with that diabolical stubbornness of his. It was probably a case of insanity. Or else a stroke of genius … At work they gave him extended leave, to allow him to rest. At home, he couldn't be left alone for a single second. He would turn on the taps in the bathroom, in the kitchen, in the toilet, and he would listen, absorbed, he would fall into a trance, in which the world around him ceased to exist. He had to be committed to a "mental illnesses institute," as the hospital was called. The chief physician, an excellent psychiatrist, gave him a separate room with a bathroom so that he could carry on his "research". And when the tub filled up, an orderly would come and turn off the taps until all the water drained away. And then he would wake as if from sleep. He was a gentle madman, beloved by all.'

She paused for a moment to take another sip of Turkish coffee.

'I used to visit him twice a week, on Tuesdays and Saturdays. He would take me aside and say: "My dear Malvina, don't tell anybody anything. I'm being followed. They want to steal my idea."

'"Who does?"

'"They do!" and he would make a vague gesture directed at the world outside.

'"Don't worry, Artie," I would say. "I won't tell anybody anything."

'Sometimes, he would take the blue notebook from the inside pocket of his jacket and, in the utmost secrecy, show me scribbled numbers and letters and strange symbols. "The Sound/Force formula," he would whisper, cautiously looking all around him. "Malvina, please don't breathe a word to anybody!"

'I would visit him twice a week. After which, I started visiting him once a week, on Saturdays. I was exhausted, my nerves were frayed. I couldn't bear to see him like that any more. A year passed, then another, then a third. How long would the ordeal continue? Maybe for the rest of his life … Alone at home, in horror I would count down the days to the next visiting day … It was unbearable! And a thought gradually took root in my mind, boring its way ever deeper, until it became an obsession: Why? My friends, whom I don't see much any more, used to ask me the same thing: Why? Why bury yourself alive? You're still young. You have grounds for a divorce. How much longer can it go on like this? With a tranquil case of insanity like that, he could live decades yet, he may even outlive you … When I told him, he looked at me with those clear eyes of his. And he didn't say a word. When the document was placed in front of him, he looked at it in silence and wouldn't sign. The court decreed the divorce. I tried not to visit him any more. I would find things to do on Saturdays, I would visit relatives who lived far away or go on excursions. It was hard for me, maybe as hard as it was for … A month later he passed away. Later, the chief physician told me that he had curtailed his "experiments", that he hadn't turned on a single tap, that he hadn't listened to the murmur of water any more …'

She fell silent, drank the last drops of the bitter Turkish coffee. For a long time, she gazed fixedly at the bottom of the empty cup. The young couple sitting at the table in the corner at the back left the café giggling.

Mrs Wegweiler went on:

'As for me, I'm "still young," looking for a man to be with me. I've been looking for ten years. I want to hear the water from the shower in the bathroom running down his body and not to be gripped with fear, to hear the hiss of the razor over his cheeks, to hear him pacing impatiently around the house while I make his breakfast … for him to criticise me and praise me, to scold me and make up with me, and for him to love me. Am I asking too much?'

Professor Brandwein was embarrassed. He didn't know what to say. He mumbled:

'Maybe … we all ask for too much … But I don't understand … why … what for …'

'Why am I telling you this story?' she said, helping him finish the thought. 'I don't know. Maybe because I can't not tell the story … After all, I'm silent so much when I'm by myself, all alone, at home … I've had it up to here with being silent. And I feel like saying everything, telling everybody …'

By the time they left the Aroma Café, it was already dark. Heavy clouds hung in the sky. A few yellow lights struggled to pierce the damp evening air.

They parted in front of the café. Professor Brandwein murmured something to the following effect: 'We'll talk … we'll talk on the phone …'

'Yes, certainly …' replied Mrs Malvina Wegweiler, dressed all in pink, with a black impermeable cape over her shoulders. 'Yes,' she replied, without conviction, and walked off down the pavement to the right.

Professor Brandwein headed to the left, in the direction of the number seven bus stop. The air had grown cool. His onomatopoeic raincoat swished at every step: 'swish-swish, swish-swish.' Utterly meaninglessly.

All of a sudden, a heavy grey rain began to fall. The water ran down the raincoat.

The wetted raincoat made not another swish.

1986

The Steps

He had left some books at her house, and a pair of cufflinks, the silver ones with the lion's heads. What was she supposed to do with them? Wouldn't it be a shame to throw them away? Maybe he could find the time one afternoon to come and get them? And they could have a chat over a glass of tea and some biscuits. After all, they were friends, weren't they?

Which books had he left at her house, wondered Lazăr Bogen? And what had made her phone him? After all, they were friends. Maybe. Why not? As a matter of fact, Bogen didn't know what they were: friends, not friends, or neither of the two. What had made her phone him after a whole year? Loneliness, presumably. Or maybe she just happened to be rummaging in the drawer of his bedside table, which is to say, his bedside table of a year ago, and had found the cufflinks. And she had found his books gathering dust on a shelf and now she wanted nothing more than to return them to him. Nothing more than that … For no other reason than that … Which books had he left at her house? He couldn't for the life of him remember. And if he couldn't remember, it meant he didn't need them.

The cufflinks, on the other hand, he would be happy to have them again. They were beautiful, made of old patinaed silver, each embossed with the round-maned head of a lion whose face displayed a lively savageness.

He would go to get his cufflinks. And the books. Why not? She lived on Albala, a swanky street whose broad pavements were flanked by silent palm trees and along which white-haired ladies walked their little dogs on a leash. There was a broad flight of grey concrete steps that led in a half-spiral above the pharmacy to the aluminium front door of the building. On each of the two frosted windows of the door to the Sanitas Pharmacy was painted a green snake coiled around a golden goblet, and in the shop window, in front of which he had often paused, hesitant, before climbing the broad grey concrete steps, in that window, among the stacks of coloured pills and tablets, there were three cardboard advertisements: Benson and Benson's Baby Powder, depicting a pink baby smiling with its two little front teeth, whose chubby little bottom a happy-looking blond mother was powdering; another, larger card, whose pointy letters read: 'Con-Don-Juan—The Knight Who Defends Your Health,' illustrated by a knight in chainmail, holding a sword and a round shield made of thin gum; and a smaller card in the righthand corner of the window display: 'Make Light of Your Troubles with Calmol. Calmol Calms Your Nerves.'

You climb the half-spiral of grey cement steps above the pharmacy to the aluminium front door with its matte panes of glass. You ring, you speak your name into the intercom, you take the lift to the eighth floor. You ring again, the blond-haired, blue-eyed Mrs Arlette Rollberg—almost every woman with blond hair has blue eyes—smiles at you in the doorway. Or else she does not smile at you. Around the dining room table sit the guests, five couples. Always the same five couples. Friends of the house. 'A marvel it is, this salad!' exclaims Mrs Hellsberg, and her husband nods, and the others all ceremoniously repeat her words: 'A marvel! Only at Arlette's can you taste such a salad.' And Mrs Arlette Rollberg makes acknowledgement to left and right. She has a diploma of higher gastronomic studies from the Santa Barbara Girls' School in Huxville and used to be an important official in the diplomatic ceremonies department of the Foreign Ministry.

There are *thés dansants* on the eighth floor of the building with the concrete steps above the Sanitas Pharmacy. Judge Gottesgabe, a short, weedy man, dances with his pointed nose nestling between Mrs Arlette's breasts. Another two couples glide over the parquet floor of the salon. Elsberg the banker dances with Mrs Hellsberg, the wife of the dealer in ginseng and marine plants. Mr Hellsberg sits in a deep armchair with his legs comfortably outstretched and explains to Mrs Gottesgabe, the judge's wife: 'I'm no intellectual, I didn't go to no university, but these here hands are worth fifty million, Madam … I made my millions with these here hands and this uneducated head of mine …'

Mrs Gottesgabe, a mignon brunette with small, dark, lively eyes, nods in admiration, casting furtive, sidelong glances at her husband's eager dancing with Mrs Rollberg.

And after the guests leave, saying goodnight with loud smacks of the lips, Arlette and Lazăr Bogen find themselves on the wide bed, each on his and her own side, more bored than tired.

They had met some three months earlier, at another five-o'-clock tea, at Dr Brockfeld's, the plastic surgeon. Lazăr drove her home in his car, she invited him to a tea dance for couples the next day, and they parted at the bottom of the flight of grey concrete steps. He climbed back in his car. He didn't start the engine or turn on the headlights, but watched as the blond woman in a flimsy white coat climbed the steps that rose in a half-spiral above the pharmacy. In the brightly lit shop window, the posters screeched in every colour: 'Calmol Calms

Your Nerves' and 'Con-Don-Juan. The Knight Who Defends Your Health' and 'Benson and Benson's Baby Powder.' Arlette vanished into the tall building above. A few moments later, a light appeared on the eighth floor.

After the third tea party at her house, they both found themselves naked, adrift on the wide bed.

The first tea party at Arlette's house they had each drunk sitting demurely at opposite ends of the low table in the salon.

At the second tea party, she had sat down next to him on the sofa and shown him some photographs. There she was in Venice. Lagoons, gondolas. There she was with her husband in front of the Colosseum in Rome. The husband, who passed away more than a year before, was a doctor of something or other, she had told him what, but Bogen couldn't remember. Photographs, photographs. Her husband receiving the Pankin Grand Prize for a paper on something or other, she told him what, but he had forgotten. There she was behind him, elegantly attired, smiling broadly, happy for him. There she was on the beach, in front of the Foreign Ministry, at a dinner for foreign dignitaries in smoking jackets and bowties.

After the third tea party at Arlette's he had bidden her goodnight in the doorway. Suddenly, they embraced, they frantically kissed, pressed each other close, and then they found themselves in the bedroom, shedding their clothes. One of the buttons on his underpants—they were the rather outdated kind, with two front buttons—refused to come undone. He thought to glimpse a smile on her lips. In bed, amid their writhing, they both realised that they were not really so ravenous. Their desire had been inflated by ambition and by the fear of not appearing to be past it, or of not actually being past it ... They wanted to appear young, much younger than they were, and all they did came more from memories than from any present urge.

Arlette in particular, having reached the age of almost sixty, or perhaps older, was obsessed, she wanted to live, to live how she remembered living in her youth. She was in a constant state of overexcitement, she felt that she was wasting precious moments ... And she didn't realise that she couldn't keep it up, ultimately that she didn't even need to any more, but she was gripped by the obsession, by the fear that she might be wasting ... In the house of her father, lawyer and notary public August Nudelmann, she had learned, like every other decent young lady, to tinkle the ivories, and now she wanted to play melodies that she had never played before, to play by ear, rather than from the score provided by Life's composer, in which every note, every accent, every rest came in its allotted place, according to a plan familiar to none ...

Nor did Lazăr Bogen wish to be outdone. He wanted to look stronger and more virile than he was. And he made a conscious effort to this end. Self-suggestion, vitamin pills. What was to be done? Animals eat only when they are hungry, they drink only when they are thirsty, they sleep only when they are tired, and they mate at the allotted moment. But humankind has reached such a condition of refinement or madness that people eat without being hungry, they drink without being thirsty, they sleep whey they aren't tired, and they pursue all kinds of pleasures ... Excitation of the senses and conscious awareness of the instincts are perhaps the most unfortunate, the most insane, discoveries of humankind ... Or maybe they are not so insane and so unfortunate after all? Maybe this is what lends meaning to humankind? When you speak of what is human, maybe you also include this? Who can know which are the natural human urges and which aren't?

Arlette and Lazăr met quite regularly, two or three times a week. They would go to the theatre, the cinema, concerts. And on Saturday mornings, they would loll in the wide bed. They would read. From time to time, he would bring books from home. He mostly read plays and short stories, he didn't have the patience for *romans-fleuves*, and his reading was quite eclectic: Chekhov and Kafka, Tolstoy, Camus, and William Saroyan—he especially liked Saroyan—but besides the literature, Bogen also used to bring technical books. As an engineer, a researcher in the field of materials' strength, his whole life he had studied the ways in which metals tire, and now, as an occasional consultant at the Standards Institute and various factories, he had to keep up with the latest specialist publications.

They would lie in bed and read, while classical music played on the radio.

'Schubert's unfinished symphony!' exclaimed Lazăr, all of a sudden.

'You don't say! Do I give you the impression of not knowing which symphony this is?' asked Arlette, irked.

'Not at all! But I awfully like this music ... If I said, "What a wonderful sunset!" would it mean that you gave me the impression of not knowing what a sunset was?' Lazăr rejoindered, irritated in his turn.

She fell into a sulky silence. They often got on each other's nerves for the flimsiest of reasons. Outside, on the street, at the theatre, at the cinema, at concerts, Arlette was blithe, carefree, even exuberant. Even if the play was a tragedy, she would be sad at it against the backdrop of an irrepressible gaiety. In restaurants, she would sit at the table ramrod straight, majestic, her face radiant; she liked choice dishes, the clink of cutlery, the murmur of conversation from the nearby tables, the ceremonious bowing of the waiters. But at home, when she wasn't holding a *thé dansant*, when there weren't guests for dinner, she would sit in front of the television and study her nails in boredom. She would sadly watch a delightful comedy, or irritably listen to a favourite classical record.

'How sad,' Lazăr would hear her say as she heaved a deep sigh.

'What's so sad, Arlette?'

He couldn't understand her. He felt very happy to be at home.

Arlette would make no reply, instead casting him a sidelong glance, as if he were some narrow-minded man with no understanding of life.

'What's so sad?' Lazăr would repeat, genuinely incapable of understanding. He liked to stay at home of an evening, to sit in an armchair wearing slippers and a dressing gown, lolling in the classic pose, to watch television, more often than not without seeing what was on but letting his thoughts wander at will. He felt relaxed and free, the same as in childhood when he used to run through the endless field of wheat at the end of the village where he grew up.

'Did you say something, Arlette?' Lazăr asked her one evening.

'Are you deaf?'

'No, I'm not, but I wasn't paying attention.'

After a while, he went on:

'Yes, maybe I am deaf. I've gone deaf in this house.'

Outside, he heard the voices very well. On the street, he had begun to notice, to listen eagerly to the snatches of speech and sound. Yes, he had grown deaf in the house of Arlette Rollberg. And blind.

'Don't you see that glass on the sideboard?'

He didn't see it! When he heard that voice of hers, he felt gripped by panic. He didn't hear well, he didn't see well, he couldn't distinguish colours and shapes. And it was as if the air had thickened, it had become unbreathable. And his skin felt puckered, because of his nerves.

He could hear her voice clearly over the phone, her warm, enticing voice: 'Come over, I'll be expecting you,' but at her house, the voice was transformed into an indistinct, sarcastic murmur, into an incomprehensible wheeze.

'Come over ... I've found some books of yours and your cufflinks. The silver ones, with the lion's heads ... Maybe you'll find the time one afternoon to come over and get them.' Arlette's voice sounded warm, enticing.

Which books had he left at her house? Lazăr couldn't remember. Not for the life of him. The cufflinks, yes, he would be happy to get them back ... And lolling in an armchair at home, in his mind Lazăr arrived in Albala, the elegant street flanked with silent palm trees where distinguished, immaculately coiffed ladies walked their little dogs on a leash. Here was the flight of broad grey concrete steps, which rose in a half-spiral above the Sanitas Pharmacy. The adverts in the shop window: 'Con-Don-Juan', with the knight in chainmail, wielding a sword in one hand and a shield of thin gum in the other; and the happy mother powdering the round little bottom of her dimpled smiling baby with just the two front teeth; and 'Make Light of Your Troubles with Calmol. Calmol Calms Your Nerves.'

There was a light in the window up on the eighth floor.

No, he wouldn't climb those steps. Lazăr knew he would never climb those steps ever again. And in his mind, he carried on down Albala Street before quickly turning onto another road.

1987

An Amended Will

Attorney Borenstein was about to lock up his office and go home when at the door there appeared Nitsana, a neighbour from his building, a very nice woman, whom he often asked to babysit his children when he and his wife went to the theatre or to visit friends.

The lawyer was rather taken aback to see Nitsana, with her brown silk headscarf covering her white hair and her large brown shawl over her shoulders. Nitsana never came to his office.

'Is anything wrong, Nitsana?' he asked, noticing the grave look on her face.

'No, mister arttorney!' That's what she used to call him: arttorney, and for the life of him he couldn't get her to pronounce the word otherwise. 'I've come to see you so you can do me that bit of writing about who I leave things to when I won't be here any more.'

'Your will?' asked Borenstein in amazement.

'Yes, that's it!' replied Nitsana.

Borenstein hesitated for a few moments, then sat down at a table. He invited Nitsana to take a seat across the table from him.

'What do you want to write in your will, Nitsana?'

‘That I, Nitsana Haselich, once I leave this world—’ she began to dictate.

‘You mean, “after my decease,”’ said Borenstein, translating her words into the correct legalese.

‘The big painting in the dining room will go to my eldest daughter Margareta.’

‘I leave my daughter the painting,’ murmured Borenstein as he wrote. ‘What does the painting depict?’

‘A child who’s crying and a mother who’s wiping away his tears. My daughter really likes that painting.’

Borenstein wrote it down. Nitsana went on:

‘And the two silver candlesticks, I leave them to my younger daughter Veronica.’

Borenstein wrote it down on the headed legal paper and waited.

‘And further?’

‘There is no further,’ Nitsana replied. ‘I don’t have anything else. I rent the place where I live, and my clothes, who would need them? They’ll be given to the poor, obviously.’

‘Very well,’ said Borenstein and after rereading the few lines of the will, he said: ‘And now, please sign here, Nitsana.’

She signed. The attorney then put his signature to the document, certifying it, and pressed down on the paper with his big round rubber stamp, which read: ‘Dr Herbert Borenstein. Attorney and Notary Public.’

Borenstein handed Nitsana the document.

‘You hold on to it, mister arttorney. What would I do with it? As long as I’m alive, I don’t need it, and once I’ve gone off to the other world, what can I do with it?’

Borenstein smiled. Nitsana was perfectly right.

‘So, you have made me executor of your will,’ he said. ‘In which case, we shall open this file and place the document inside it and … I wish you long years!’

Nitsana went to open her small black handbag.

'Don't insult me, Nitsana! After all, we've been good neighbours for a long time, haven't we?'

Nitsana left in great satisfaction.

A few weeks later, Nitsana once again turned up at the office of Dr Herbert Borenstein, attorney and notary public. Her white hair poked from beneath her brown silk headscarf in disarray.

'What's wrong, Nitsana?' asked Borenstein in fright.

'Forgive me, mister arttorney, but I want to alter something in that will. I'm not giving that painting from the dining room to my eldest daughter Margareta any more! Her and her husband, who owns a fish cannery, moved to a new house, a villa in the north of town. They invited lots of fancy folk over to celebrate the move. The girl came to me and she said: "Mama, give me the painting now! What do you need it for? I have a nice place for it in a niche in the hall. The child and the mother wiping away his tears in a niche ..." You understand, mister arttorney? I thought she came to invite me to the new house. But what business would I have there, me, a tailor's wife, who's spent her whole life between the kitchen and the workshop, where I used to help my late husband, so that we could raise our two girls and send them to school, what business would I have among all those fancy ladies and gents? I was supposed to go the next day and eat the leftovers ... what did I need the painting for? You understand? Please, mister arttorney, take it out of the will!'

Borenstein took the document from the folder and added a few lines to it, murmuring, 'I hereby annul ... I do not leave my daughter Margareta the painting in the living room ... The weeping child and the mother wiping away his tears ...' and so on and so forth.

'But to whom are you going to leave the painting, Nitsana?'

'Who am I leaving it to? Who am I leaving it to?'

She sat in silent amazement for a few moments, before saying with determination:

'But what? Don't I have another daughter, thank the Lord! Yes, when I won't be here any more, it'll be Veronica's, the painting...'

Borenstein wrote it all down and made Nitsana sign the amended will. He then appended the certification and applied his big round rubber stamp.

A few weeks later, Nitsana Haselich again appeared at the door of attorney and notary public Dr Borenstein. Her face was red with fury, her white hair was awry, rebelliously poking from beneath her headscarf.

'What's wrong this time?' asked Borenstein.

'Please forgive me, mister arttorney, but I want to change that will. I'm not leaving the silver candlesticks to my younger daughter Veronica. Last night she came to my house and said, "What do you need them for, Mama? Why not give me them now?" Her husband's a clerk at the Ministry of the Post Office and Telephones and she says some fancy clerks from the ministry are coming to visit them and those old candlesticks, they're very fashionable now...'

'But to whom do you wish to leave them?' asked Borenstein.

'Who? Who?' said Nitsana in confusion. 'Don't I have somebody I can leave them to? Don't I have another daughter, thank the Lord? I'll leave the two silver candlesticks to my daughter Margareta!'

The attorney looked at her wide-eyed in astonishment:

'But Nitsana, that means that each daughter will inherit that which has been bequeathed to the other.'

Sitting perfectly still the old woman looked at him. She hadn't thought of that.

‘Oh well,’ Borenstein assured her, ‘when the time comes, they will come to an agreement and swap the things between themselves.’

‘Come to an agreement? They haven’t spoken to each other for five years. Not since the silver watch left by their father.’

Borenstein said nothing more. He added a few lines to the will, amending it. He made Nitsana sign it, and then he certified the signature and applied his big notary public’s rubber stamp.

Just three days later this time, Nitsana once again visited ‘arttorney’ Borenstein. Her face was weary, pale, as if she hadn’t slept for three nights.

‘Please forgive me, mister arttorney, but I’ve been thinking that I’m their mother after all, and they’re my daughters, so why cause them grief? I want to leave the painting to my eldest daughter Margareta and the silver candlesticks to my youngest, Veronica.’

Attorney Borenstein smiled. He wrote it down, murmuring the words. Nitsana Haselich, the mother of Margareta and Veronica, signed it. Dr Borenstein, the attorney and notary public, certified the signature placed before him, and pressed down hard with his big round rubber stamp.

1987

Afterword

LUDOVIC BRUCKSTEIN

Me: An Unabridged Autobiographical Novel

The time has definitely come for me to write my autobiography. To write down all the interesting things in my life. No matter how many hefty tomes it will fill. The world, posterity need to know everything . . .

Well, let me begin with the fact that I was born. Of good parents. A good father and a good mother. Not better than other parents, although for a long time I believed they were. That's because I have never been the child of other parents. But even so, the more deeply I think about it, the more certain I am that they were good parents. I remember that when my aunts used to tease me and ask, "Which do you love the most, your mother or your father," I always unhesitatingly answered, "I love both the same."

In time I grew up, with the result that on every birthday I became a year older. I went to primary, secondary and upper schools, and sometimes I did well, sometimes poorly. I had good teachers and mediocre teachers. I learned a large number of things, both useful and useless.

I was unlucky with women. Because they didn't want to be the way I imagined they should be. I also was fairly lucky with women. I had ideals and illusions; I had disappointments and was dealt slaps in the face both stinging and soft. I even came a step away from suicide, but I didn't take that step.

I travelled the world, to a moderate extent. I saw museums, temples, ruins, hotels, and beautiful air stewardesses.

I have been through a major, global war and two minor, regional wars, seven concentration and forced labour camps, a flood, two minor earthquakes, three childhood diseases, a number of spiritual crises, and I am still alive. Why? I don't know.

I have earned my daily bread doing various kinds of work and in various jobs. I am married. I have a son who lives his own life.

I never rode Rosinante, because I have never had a horse. Not that I know how to ride. Nor did I ever tilt at windmills, because no windmill has ever barred my way. Nor am I skilled in the ways of war.

And ... what else might I add? Nothing.

1985

Ludovic Bruckstein and his young wife,
Choppy, in Sighet, Romania, in 1948.

THE AUTHOR

The writer Ludovic (Joseph-Leib, Arye) Bruckstein was born on the 27th of July 1920, in Munkacs, then in Czechoslovakia, now in Ukraine. He grew up in Sighet, a small town in the district of Maramureș, in the Northern region of Transylvania, a town well known for its flourishing pre-war Jewish community and Hassidic tradition. He wrote a number of successful plays including *The Night Shift* (*Nakht-Shikht*, 1947), based on the Sonder-kommando revolt in Auschwitz. His other works include *The Confession* (a novel, 1973), *The Fate of Yaakov Maggid* (seven short stories, 1975), *Three Histories* (three short historical stories, 1977) – which have been amalgamated in this edition along with stories from *As in Heaven, so on Earth* (1981) – *The Tinfoil Halo* (short stories, 1979), *Maybe Even Happiness* (short stories, 1985), *The Murmur of Water* (short stories, 1987). *The Trap* (two novellas) appeared posthumously in 1989.

THE TRANSLATOR

Alistair Ian Blyth is one of the most active translators working from Romanian into English today. A native of Sunderland, England, Blyth has resided for many years in Bucharest. His many translations from Romanian include: *The Bulgarian Truck* (Dalkey Archive Press, 2016), *The Book of Whispers* (Yale University Press, 2017), and *Life Begins on Friday* by Ioana Pârvulescu (Istros Books, 2016). He is the author of the novel *Card Catalogue* (Dalkey Archive Press, 2020).

www.ingramcontent.com/pod-product-compliance
Ingram Content Group UK Ltd.
Pitfield, Milton Keynes, MK11 3LW, UK
UKHW020427190226
468187UK00002B/33

9 781912 545551